RAMA M

inside the aveli

PENGUIN BOOKS

PENGUIN BOOKS
Published by the Penguin Group
Penguin Books India Pvt. Ltd, 11 Community Centre, Panchsheel Park, New Delhi 110 017, India
Penguin Group (USA) Inc., 375 Hudson Street, New York, New York 10014, USA
Penguin Group (Canada), 90 Eglinton Avenue East, Suite 700, Toronto, Ontario, M4P 2Y3, Canada (a division of Pearson Penguin Canada Inc.)
Penguin Books Ltd, 80 Strand, London WC2R 0RL, England
Penguin Ireland, 25 St Stephen's Green, Dublin 2, Ireland (a division of Penguin Books Ltd)
Penguin Group (Australia), 250 Camberwell Road, Camberwell, Victoria 3124, Australia (a division of Pearson Australia Group Pty Ltd)
Penguin Group (NZ), 67 Apollo Drive, Rosedale, North Shore 0632, New Zealand (a division of Pearson New Zealand Ltd)
Penguin Group (South Africa) (Pty) Ltd, 24 Sturdee Avenue, Rosebank, Johannesburg 2196, South Africa

Penguin Books Ltd, Registered Offices: 80 Strand, London WC2R 0RL, England

First published in India by Gulab Vazirani 1977
Published in the UK by the Woman's Press 1994
Published by Penguin Books India 1996

22 21 20 19 18

ISBN 9780140261202

Printed at DeUnique Printers, New Delhi

To Mohan Kaka and Bhabhi,
who gave me of their affections
and made for me a home in Udaipur

PENGUIN BOOKS
INSIDE THE HAVELI

Rama Mehta was born in Nainital, India, in 1923.

She became a top sociologist, lecturer and novelist, and her non-fiction writings include *The Western Educated Hindu Woman, The Hindu Divorced Woman*, and 'From Purdah to Modernity'.

One of the first women to be appointed to India's foreign service, Rama Mehta was forced to resign her position upon marriage. Rama Mehta died in 1978.

SECTION I

Chapter I

UDAIPUR WAS ONCE the capital of the State of Mewar; now it is only a town like many other towns in Rajasthan. But the change in its status hasn't diminished its beauty, nor the air of mystery that hangs over what is now known as the 'Old City'. It is surrounded by a bastioned wall, which after four hundred years is crumbling; in fact there are now big gaps, but the wall still divides Udaipur into two halves. The new township is beyond the old wall and the city within it.

The west side of the city is bounded by Lake Pichola. Men bathe in it; washermen unload their donkeys and beat the clothes clean on slabs of granite on its shores. Women on the river banks go to ring the temple bells before they return to light the household fire. The waters of the lake that touch the city are not clean; they even give off an offensive odour at times but that's only when the rains have not replenished it.

To the north of the city is the hill of Sajjangarh. It is steep and at one time it was covered by a dense forest in which the royalty hunted tigers and leopards. The poor climbed up to the slopes and collected twigs and branches for their daily fuel. But today the trees stand stark and exposed; there is no thick foliage that made the paths into the forest invisible. Everything in Udaipur depends on the rains and when they fail then the lakes dry up and the trees wither.

In the city wall there are four gateways to the city. These gates are huge with metal spikes on each panel. In the days when the kings of Udaipur were ever ready to meet the invading armies of the Mughal rulers they were shut during the night. Now there is no danger, so they are never shut. All traffic flows through them in and out of the city.

There is only one main street and that leads to the palace. But there are many little gullies that branch off from it and reach deep into the city; some are wide enough for a car if none other is coming in the opposite direction. There are others in which only a cyclist can pedal; broad or narrow little shops are on either side of the gullies. Through the network of gullies every house is connected and the children can run from one house to another carrying messages of a birth, a marriage, a death. On both sides of the main street are the big shops; they are always crowded. The pink, orange and green silks and satins hang from the ceiling to attract the passer-by.

The white granite palace in which the Ranas held court for four hundred years stands on the crest of a ridge that overlooks Lake Pichola. The palace with all its splendour was near the humble huts and houses of the people. They looked at the lights and heard the grunts of the elephants and were content. Their king the Rana was there to take care of them. It was only twenty-five years ago that the palace lights were dimmed and the flag of Mewar came down. The people were sad, for the Rana had lost his power and his ministers were no longer in charge of the treasury and could no longer give away land. Everything had changed in the State of Mewar and in its capital. But the people in the old city remember the days when everything was bright and gay, when the Rana sat on his throne and received his people, rich and poor alike. No one in the city can forget those days when Udaipur belonged to the people.

They know a new township has developed outside the old city wall. They have seen the rows of neat houses on either side of the broad tarmac road. The houses have neat gardens in which roses grow and the grass is green. The air is clean and in it there is no cow dung smoke but there is no soul in the new township. Its people have no memories of what Udaipur was like, they are newcomers, they don't have common ancestors, they don't know what they did, who they worshipped, what sorrow and joy they felt. They don't belong to the soil of Mewar; they have come to the town because of work; they love the lakes and the low-lying hills that keep them cool in the hot summer months. In the new town the rich and poor are separated by the rose gardens; they don't know each other; they live separate lives. The only thing common between them seems the tarmac road, on which the poor too have the right to walk.

The people in the new town explore the old city, again and again. They cannot understand why the people don't move out of the congestion, the smells, the little gullies, and come and join them where the air is clean, where there is land to build on. More than anything they are puzzled by the wall-enclosed havelis, some in marble, others in stone; they wonder how much gold lies buried in the vaults. There is no way they can look into the courtyards; the windows are so high that no one can look through them. The town people leave the old city, without having fathomed what goes on inside men's and women's apartments of the haveli.

Sangram Singhji's haveli like so many others of the nobility was in a gully. Its first courtyard was built three hundred years ago and there were only three rooms around it. But, like a banyan tree, once it had taken root it spread. Today the haveli has many courtyards with many rooms. Its roots have sunk deep into the soil and nothing shakes the foundations although the hot winds of summer dismantle the wooden shelters of the poor and the monsoon rains melt the mud walls of the poorer in the same gully.

Sangram Singhji's haveli is the biggest in the gully although it is not the biggest in the old city. The haveli has no real shape to it; the marble and stone seemed to have been hastily piled on top of one another. It expanded through the years but without any plan, it recedes in places leaving empty land, and yet it pushes out in other directions, making the gully even more narrow where it bends around the mansion which has three storeys.

The haveli may have no shape from the outside, but inside there is a definite plan. The courtyards divide the haveli into various sections. The separation of self-contained units was necessary because the women of Udaipur kept purdah. Their activities were conducted within their apartments. The courtyards connected their section with that of the men. The etiquette established through years permitted only close male relatives to enter the women's apartment. Even so no man entered the courtyard without being properly announced.

The servants in the haveli once slept wherever they found room to spread their mats but now they, too, have a courtyard of their own. Their quarters are not on the same elevation as the haveli, but a few steps below. In their courtyard there is no dividing wall, the maids are free to talk to their husbands; they don't have to wait till the darkness of night settles over the haveli to share their thoughts with them.

There are no secrets; there could be none in the haveli. It is one household, all the courtyards are connected.

Chapter II

SITA WAS BORN just after midnight one stormy night in the servants' quarters of Sangram Singhji's marble haveli. After her birth, Sarju, the midwife, sat beside Lakshmi who lay on her mat on the floor quietly, too exhausted to speak. Sita sucked her fingers beside her mother wrapped up in a piece of cloth.

Sarju waited for a while hoping that the rain would stop. But when she heard the thunder and saw streaks of lightning flash past the door, she stretched her legs and rested her head on a bundle of clothes.

'It is a girl,' sighed Lakshmi's husband Gangaram when he heard the child's cry. He and Khyali the cook sat on the verandah of the haveli waiting to hear the news of the birth. Gangaram was right; had it been a boy, Sarju would have come out in the rain and thunder shouting, in her shrill voice, 'It is a boy; it is a boy. Give me money.' Gangaram took a long puff of his bidi and then threw it away in disgust.

'Why worry? God takes care of all those He sends into

the world. Girls are a burden, I admit,' said Khyali with sympathy, 'but what can one do once they are born? So far I have been lucky. But who can tell of the future?' The cook yawned, stretched his hands and then added in a sleepy voice, 'I wonder what the young mistress will have. The lady doctor went up three hours ago. Whatever she has, I hope it is soon; half the night is already over; the fortunate forget that the servants too need rest.'

'Of course, she will get a boy. The rich always get what they want; it is the poor who have all the bad luck,' said Gangaram with bitterness. Then as he opened his mouth to speak again there was the sound of footsteps and the courtyard door creaked open.

'The servants of this haveli are nowhere to be seen when there is work. Who could say that there are fifteen servants in this house? You would think there is only one old woman,' said Pari in a thin, scornful voice, staring accusingly at the two men. 'I have been on my feet for the last twelve hours. And why not? After all the first great grandchild of my master, Sangram Singhji, has been born,' she announced rather grandly. Then she took a deep breath and said with a sigh, 'So what if it is only a girl? That does not mean that servants vanish. Is this the time to be sitting and smoking? Where is Ganga?'

The two men did not wait to answer the maid. They slipped through the open door and went inside the courtyard door.

'Ganga, oh Ganga, where are you?' shouted Pari. 'Are you dead that you do not hear me?'

'Jiji,' Ganga said, running up the stairs to the verandah. 'Jiji, I went down just this minute to see Lakshmi. She has had a girl.'

'So has your mistress; go upstairs and don't waste time talking. Looking at you one would think that Lakshmi is rejoicing the birth of a girl. The poor girl must already be worrying about the dowry which will have to be given, especially if the child looks like the father.' Having got the servants on their feet, Pari sat down on the floor and took her snuff box from her blouse. She took a little pinch, placed it delicately under each nostril and sniffed deeply.

Pari was only a maid servant in the haveli like the other eight, but with her tact, hard work and devoted service for forty-five years, she had established a special place for herself in the family. She had come to the haveli as a child of eight. The year her father had brought her to the mansion there was a terrible famine in Rajasthan. Pari's parents had lost three of their seven children. Pari was her father's favourite child. He did not want to see her suffer from hunger and then slowly wither away like the other three. So he decided to give her away. In this he was following a common practice of feudal Rajasthan where villagers in desperate circumstances gave their sons and daughters to the care of aristocratic families.

Once accepted, these children became the responsibility of the family. When Pari entered the gates of Jeewan Niwas, Ram Singhji, the father of Sangram Singhji, was the head of the family. Even as a child, she was helpful to the mistress and soon became her favourite child maid. Two years later she was married. But after fifty years she could recollect neither the day she was married nor the day she became a widow. But she remembered the many mistresses she had served in the haveli, and how they had singled her out for little extra favours. She had already known four generations of the family, shared in the joys of births and of marriages, in the sorrow of deaths and misfortunes of the haveli. She knew the traditions and rituals to be followed and gifts to be exchanged on every occasion. The new daughters-in-law looked to her for guidance and followed her instructions when they came to the haveli as brides. They knew that she had to be given the same respect as one paid to a relative. She was a maid only in name and she never tried to be anything more. But the other servants knew her position and treated her with deference. They took her orders as if they were those of the mistress.

As Pari stretched her thin legs out and watched the rain coming down in torrents, she plunged into thought. 'So what if it is a girl?' she said to herself. 'After all it is the first time in sixty years that there are four generations together under the roof of the haveli. This birth must be celebrated as if a boy had been born to the family. That is certain. But there is no time for dreaming now. I must get back.' Her mind made up, the blood raced through her veins. She was already thinking of the details of the festivities to come. She got up agitated, put her snuff box in her blouse and hurriedly went inside.

As soon as Pari entered the young mistress Geeta's room, the lady doctor took hold of her shoulder and pleaded, 'Parijiji, tell these women to talk somewhere else. I am tired of telling them to be quiet; no one listens to me. I managed to send two out and two more came in. Your Binniji and the baby must sleep.' The doctor having made her final bid to get quiet in the room picked up her bag and left.

'These doctors think having a baby is like having an operation. "Be quiet, do not talk, wash this, boil that." What a fuss for nothing. Sarju has delivered ten babies in this very room, but I have never seen this kind of fuss before,' said Pari looking at Ganga and the other maids who nodded their heads in agreement and giggled.

Geeta dropped off to sleep in spite of the chatter in the room. The rain had stopped. The sky was again calm. The gentle sound of the drizzle seemed to lull the two baby girls to sleep, one born to the mistress, the other to the maid, of the haveli.

Chapter III

LAKSHMI, LIKE PARI, came to the haveli as a young girl of ten. The other servants teased her saying that her parents had given her away because she was dark and ugly and that her dowry would have been heavy. But Lakshmi did not care what anyone said. She was happy when playing in the backyard of the haveli, but grumpy when she had to work. Sangram Singhji's wife, who was a shrewd judge of character, had arranged Lakshmi's marriage when she was fourteen to Gangaram, who was a servant in the haveli. Gangaram was gentle, soft spoken and kind to everyone. The servants' children loved him. He did not scold them when they laughed at him as his legs wobbled under the weight of the firewood that he carried every day to the kitchen. He did not mind the children making fun of his crooked nose on a pock-marked face. He went about his work quietly, never complaining, never grumbling. But Lakshmi found everything wrong with him. She complained about his temper and about his tattered clothes. She even blamed the mistress for marrying her to a poor man, and that too with a crooked nose.

Pari would comfort her. 'Look at me,' she would start, 'though I have been a widow almost all my life, I am still not free of my in-laws. You have no one to worry about, no mother-in-law, no brothers-in-law; you can enjoy your pay and do what you like with it. I never have a penny left after the demands of my in-laws. And what do I get from them? Nothing. Not even a blouse. But I don't complain. We all have to accept fate. There is no escape from that.'

Lakshmi would listen but nothing would convince her that cleaning and sweeping was wonderful or that she was fortunate in having Gangaram as a husband.

Lakshmi paid equally little attention to Dhapu, another maid, who kept reminding her that she was no longer a child but a married woman. 'Look at you with your head uncovered. Were it any other man he would beat you, but Gangaram is a saint. I warn you, Lakshmi, that if you sit pouting the whole time, even Gangaram will turn one day. Which man can put up with a wife who does not make him comfortable?'

But Lakshmi went her own way, doing work when told to, otherwise sitting around day-dreaming. Her favourite pastime was to wash and polish the silver anklets and bracelets given to her by the mistress. After all, she was only a little over fifteen.

Lakshmi lay on the floor of her small, dark, damp room content with life. 'I will have a child every year. This is the only way to get rest and comfort,' she said the next day, smiling to herself. 'Twenty-one days of rest from sweeping and washing. If only women were considered unclean for longer what fun it would be,' she thought. Having found an easy way to escape the haveli drudgery, Lakshmi picked up Sita who nestled beside her and nursed her.

The door of the room creaked open and Ganga slid in as if she were a thief and said excitedly in a loud whisper, 'Lakshmi, do you know that the birth of Vijay Bai Saheb is going to be celebrated as if she were a boy? Don't glare at me like that. Don't you realize what this means, you silly girl?'

'I knew something was on that old woman Pari's mind when she came to see me in the morning. She hardly spoke. Just sat scratching her head. She must have been going over the list of the saris to be distributed on the great occasion.'

'You are really impossible to please. Lakshmi, everyone is excited but you. We will get sweets and new clothes. There will be dancing and singing, what more do you want?'

'Do not be so sure, I can already hear Pari saying "Do not give Ganga this, she is lazy, don't give Champa that, she will be spoiled." In the end I know we will all be handed out threadbare saris, dyed in bright colours to make them look like new. Remember, I didn't come to the haveli yesterday.'

'Sh! sh! sh! you talk too much,' chuckled Ganga. 'You will get me into trouble too.'

As if she had suddenly remembered something, Lakshmi sat up erect, her eyebrows knitted together and nodding her head she said: 'Now I know where Sarju is, with the mistress of course, trying to flatter her so that she gets what she wants. Just let her come. Who does she think she is? After all, I am also paying her for my delivery. She is not doing it for nothing. But that woman is so greedy that for a few more rupees she would gladly see anyone die.'

'You are a fool, Lakshmi! How many times have I told you that walls have ears but you go on babbling as if this haveli belongs to you.' Ganga drew the sari over her face, opened the door and went out.

Sarju walked in the open door grinning. 'Lakshmi, you better get up soon or you will miss all the fun,' said the midwife tucking the end of her sari into her skirt, all ready to start massaging the baby.

'I hope you have made sure that you will get gold bangles on this occasion, then at least my lying here in pain would have served a purpose,' said Lakshmi, sitting up, her eyes shining with anger, and voice full of sarcasm.

'Who do you think you are that you dare talk to me like this?' said Sarju, putting her hands on her hips, 'I am not your servant. Keep your ten rupees and get another midwife. I am not about to starve that you can talk to me in this fashion. Did you think for types like you I would neglect Binniji, especially with her first child? Don't forget I have eaten the salt of this haveli for twice as long as your years. Now lie down and don't waste my time, I am in a hurry, there are still two houses I have to visit.'

For once Lakshmi lay down like a little child who had been given a proper scolding and put in her place.

Sarju cleared her throat, took a little oil in the palm of her hands and started rubbing Lakshmi's stomach. The even sure strokes of the midwife soothed the girl, her furrowed brows straightened out and her anger subsided.

Sarju also forgot the exchange of harsh words and said in a voice full of warmth: 'I told the young mistress to be really generous and not to forget that she had given birth to the first great grandchild.' Then lowering her voice she added: 'I have been here long enough to know how things work in the haveli; that is why I went before Pari could get a word in.' Lakshmi opened her eyes and smiled.

'Now go to sleep, I promise not to be late tomorrow,' said Sarju, rubbing her oily hands on her arms and straightening her sari before she went out.

Chapter IV

IT WAS THE eleventh day after Vijay had been born. Geeta lay in the huge four-poster teak bed with thick puffy pillows on either side. The pale green mosquito net was loosely draped around the stained brass poles. There was no one in the room; Geeta felt relieved. Outside the window near her bed she could see dark monsoon clouds floating, ready to break their silence any moment. The threat of rain had kept even the vendors off the streets. Geeta closed her eyes and let her mind wander.

Two years ago when she left her parents' home in Bombay, she did not know that she was leaving behind a way of life in which there was a free mingling of men and women. Geeta had met her future husband Ajay in the company of her brothers' friends. She was not quite sure which of the young men had come to see her. When her parents asked if she liked the man in the grey suit, she had said, 'Yes'. Her parents seemed sure that she would. Her mother had told her that Ajay came from an old aristocratic family of Udaipur but he, unlike many in such families, was highly educated. He was a science professor. He was not interested in entering a more prestigious service much to the disappointment of his parents. Geeta's parents' only doubt seemed to concern Ajay's family. The women of the upper class in Udaipur, among them his mother, remained in purdah. Geeta had been differently brought up. She had gone to college and studied with boys. How would such a girl learn to live in the constricted atmosphere of a world of women, to give her elders the traditional deference? But, they reassured themselves, since Ajay was of the new generation, he couldn't possibly believe in the old customs. Her parents' anxiety was not really so much about Geeta's adjustment, but about whether a girl like her would be approved by Ajay's parents. The more orthodox relatives might be afraid of an educated girl and caution them against her, particularly one who was not from Udaipur. Geeta knew that her mother had worried that she would spoil everything by talking too much on the day Ajay came to see her.

There was a week of suspense before the reply came from Udaipur. Geeta had been approved.

In between getting the trousseau ready, Geeta remembered her mother's advice and smiled. 'Keep your head covered; never argue with your elders; respect your mother-in-law and do as she tells you. Don't talk too much.' She didn't think it necessary to tell her about purdah. Geeta wondered whether she knew anything about it.

Geeta's eyes had filled with tears as the train lost speed and was getting ready to halt at its last stop. Her light pink bridal sari was stained as she wiped the tears off her cheeks before Ajay could see them. Bombay seemed so far away; her mother was not within call; and she was alone in the compartment with a man she hardly knew. But her tears had dried up and the thoughts of her mother had vanished the minute she had put her foot on the platform. She was immediately encircled by women singing but their faces were covered. One of them came forward, pulled her sari over her face and exclaimed in horror, 'Where do you come from that you show your face to the world?' Geeta, bewildered, frightened, managed to get into the car without talking to the women who followed her, singing as loud as they could. It was when the car started she realized that her husband was not going to join her. She had lost him while the women had crowded around her. Two young girls of about sixteen who were his cousins-in-law along with four women had all squeezed into a four-seater Fiat car. Geeta felt suffocated but dared not lower the glass. The maids had chattered away excitedly as the car gained speed.

When the car slowed down to enter the city gates, Pari had said, 'Binniji, this is Surajipole gate. That building on the right belongs to your elder uncle-in-law, Pratap Singhji.'

Geeta had lifted her face and pulled the sari back to see. 'No, no, you cannot do that,' Pari had snapped, pulling back the sari over her face. 'In Udaipur we keep purdah. Strange eyes must not see your beautiful face.' Then as the car came to a halt, to let a cow cross the street, Pari had pointed her finger. 'That house on the extreme left belongs to Gopal Singhji, your mother-in-law's brother. At the corner of that gate is Nandu Bua Sa, your aunt-in-law's haveli, and next to it is Kanta Bai Sa's house.' Nothing had made sense to Geeta who had listened to the maid with her head bent.

'That pink house belongs to Manji Bua Sa, your widowed aunt-in-law,' Ganga had said lifting Geeta's head a little but pulling the sari lower over her face. As the car turned into an even more narrow street where cyclists got down to let the car pass, Ganga had stretched her hand out and said , 'That, Binnijii, is your mother-in-law's parents' haveli.'

To Geeta it had seemed that the whole city belonged to her in-laws. Every gate they passed, the maids sat up erect and with pride pointed to a house that belonged to the family.

'Do not look so confused. Soon you will know everyone. It is in these families that you will have to make your reputation as a good devoted daughter-in-law. Don't ever forget that your head must always remain covered,' Pari said solemnly and with authority.

Then, before Geeta had recovered from Pari's last remark, the car came to a halt. Geeta could only vaguely remember the events of that day when she first stepped into her husband's haveli, Jeewan Niwas. All that she could recollect was that strange women crowded round her till she nearly fainted, each one trying to lift a little of her sari to see her face. She blushed as she remembered one of them saying disappointedly: 'She has good strong features but she is dark. Let us see how she adjusts. After all she is educated and on top of that she is not from Udaipur. What a risk to get an outsider, especially when there is only one son.'

As Geeta awkwardly bent down to touch the feet of what seemed to her a hundred women, they said, 'Look at her, she does not even know how to touch the feet properly.' The elder women shook their heads in disapproval but welcomed her with, 'May you have eight sons.' Geeta had followed their instructions automatically, her gaze fixed on the ground, terrified all the time lest she should trip over someone's feet. For the first time she noticed that all the women, young and old, had their faces covered even when no men were in sight. The only women who moved around freely with faces uncovered, she later discovered, were daughters of the family. At that time she was wholly confused by the mass of covered faces. As she remembered that first day, her lips parted in a smile.

Geeta turned on her side and opened her eyes to look around and make sure that a maid had not slipped into her room. The rain was now coming down in torrents; it was like a thick curtain blotting out the outside world.

Geeta dug her face into the soft pillows and said to herself: Oh, the lovely luxury of being alone and to feel secure that no one will burst in to share a bit of gossip. She turned on her back and thought of her life in the haveli. Even after two years her father-in-law and his father were strangers to her. She had never spoken a word to them. The men, including her husband, seemed to disappear as soon as it was daylight. The whole day they were away in their offices or busy in their section of the house. They came into the interior courtyards only at meal times. Though to her they were only names, their presence was felt everywhere in the haveli. Nothing was done without consulting them. It was around their desires that the whole routine of the house revolved.

A little shiver went through her body as Geeta thought of the day when she had trespassed into the men's apartments. She already knew all the nooks and corners of the zenana. But she had never been into the other side of the haveli. It intrigued her and she longed to know how the men lived; where her husband relaxed when he came back from the university, where her father-in-law received his many visitors. She knew this section was out of bounds for women, but one day when her mother-in-law was out visiting a sick relative and her grandmother-in-law was asleep—even the maids had disappeared—Geeta thought it was safe to cross the courtyard that led into the men's apartments.

The room she entered was large like an audience hall with

high ceilings from which hung pale green chandeliers. The floor was paved in intricate mosaic tiles. The walls were painted with murals depicting various hunting scenes. There was no furniture except for a few low stools and a large mattress on which a white sheet was spread with big velvet bolsters to rest on. Two big richly embossed silver spittoons stood on two sides of the mattress.

Geeta stood for a while in the richly decorated but austere room, before she looked up to see the walls from which hung gilt-framed portraits of her husband's forefathers in their court dresses.

The finely chiselled faces framed in neatly groomed beards seemed to be looking down as guardians of the haveli and observing how succeeding generations were living up to the traditions bequeathed to them. Their hands with long tapering fingers wore rings, the wrists, bracelets; from the neck fell heavy enamelled necklaces studded with precious stones. Looking at the strong determined faces, Geeta had thought with pride these must have been the kind of men who had fought and won battles against the Moghuls. Just as she took a step backward to get a better view of the handsome faces, a cold hand touched her shoulder.

'What are you doing here all alone, Binniji? I know you are an outsider but it is time you learned our ways. In this section of the haveli women come only when properly escorted.' Pari's tone was severe. 'What would your father-in-law think if he saw you with your face uncovered? Binniji, daughters-in-law of this haveli do not behave like this.'

At first Geeta was embarrassed but later she was filled with anger. She wanted to say accusingly, 'I am here because you left me alone to go down to the servants' quarter for a little gossip.' But luckily her anger choked her.

In the first few months of her marriage she had found the

separation of men and women romantic, full of mystery. In her parents' home men and women talked quite freely, her mother respected her father but didn't hide behind a screen when his friends were present. But in the haveli men were regarded with awe as if they were gods. They were the masters and their slightest wish was a command; women kept in their shadow and followed their instructions with meticulous care. And yet, her mother-in-law was a force that could not be ignored. The huge haveli was managed by her, she kept the servants going from morning to night and saw to it that the men were free from household worries.

When Geeta first came to her new home, she had no one she could trust. Everyone was waiting to find fault with her. Yet, if she was to do things right she needed advice. Her husband was the only one who could have helped her but she only saw him in the night. The whole day she spent with relatives who only talked of other relatives and that kept her constantly in fear of making mistakes. Besides, she yearned to talk with someone who could tell her what was happening in the world. Ajay realized her need and occasionally came upstairs on some excuse or the other but these visits were short and hurried; Geeta was embarrassed by them. The maids laughed as if they understood why he came so often to the women's apartment.

After his marriage Ajay too had found the segregated way of life in the haveli oppressive. Geeta was a companion to him, with whom he could talk and discuss things that were not related to Udaipur. But he had to wait till the evening to talk to her. Though men could come to the women's apartment when they wished it was not considered dignified to do so during the day except when women had to be consulted on some family matter. Like everyone else in the haveli there was a form that men maintained too. It was in deference to this form that Ajay left the suite of rooms he shared with his wife after he had bathed and dressed. It was in his section of the haveli that he worked and received friends. Even though Ajay did not agree with this kind of formality, at the same time he was not prepared to do anything to challenge his father's authority, whom he admired and respected.

In those first few months her maid, Dhapu, was her only friend and guide. Dhapu told her the etiquette which was expected of daughters-in-law. She never made Geeta feel embarrassed not even when she instructed her that a daughter-in-law talks only when talked to by her elders. Without Dhapu, Geeta would have insisted on going back to her parents. She couldn't have taken the taunts about her upbringing with the proper meekness. The period of loneliness and uncertainty was brief. Geeta soon discovered that she had little time to brood over her difficulties. If she was not sitting, head bent, with relatives, then she was in the kitchen, helping to prepare refreshments for them. In spite of the many maids and a cook, her mother-in-law was in and out of her kitchen, seeing that there was no waste. After the morning meal when she went up to her room, the maids gathered round her and chatted. She was hardly ever alone; she had not read a book in six months. The day passed quickly and by the time evening came she was exhausted and ready to drop off to sleep.

Though only relatives came and only relatives were visited, even after two years Geeta had not got the various aunts and uncles in their right relationship to her husband. This did not bother her; everyone she met was either a Kaki Sa, Mami Sa, Bua Sa or a Bai Sa. Some were close relations, others were three or four generations removed, but everyone was related. Gratefully remembering Dhapu's warning she seldom spoke. All she had to do was to shake or nod her head demurely; the questions to her were answered by her mother-in-law. She came to love the veil that hid her face, this allowed her to think while the others talked. To her delight she had discovered that through her thin muslin sari, she could see everyone and yet not be seen by them.

She heard the rain slashing down as if it were making up for not having quenched the earth the year before. Geeta picked up the book she had started to read a month ago. Just as she found the page, Pari appeared at the door with the baby in her arms, looked around and then exclaimed: 'What! Are you alone, Binniji? Is there no maid here, has no one brought you juice, what has happened to these girls, every day they get more lax in their work!'

'I have had my juice,' said Geeta, feeling guilty for not having called someone. Pari put the sleeping baby in the crib and sat down beside the bed. After peering at the baby she wiped her nose with the end of her sari and then sighed. 'Binniji, do you know when Bapu Sa, your husband, was born, I did not leave your mother-in-law for a minute. But the times have changed. These days maids have ideas of their own.' Then she stretched out her wrinkled hands and stroked Geeta's head as if to apologize for not having been more attentive herself.

'You see,' she continued, her thin lips parting in a smile and her tiny watery eyes lighting up, 'I was a child when I came to the haveli and your great grandmother-in-law trained me. She was strict. I had to be up winter or summer at four in the morning and she kept me busy the whole day. Then once I became a widow, she would not let me put on coloured saris or bangles like the other girls. I don't know what colours a widow can put on in your part of India, but in Udaipur we can only wear grey or black.'

Pari paused a little and continued. '"To be young is dangerous," your great grandmother-in-law used to say. She was right.' The maid took a deep breath as if re-living the past was like lifting a heavy bucket of water.

'Parijiji, you must have been very unhappy,' said Geeta gently, in a voice full of sympathy.

'Unhappy, did you say?' asked Pari surprised. 'I was too busy to think of things like happiness. By the evening I was so tired that I slept like a child. It took two maids to wake me up. Besides, I do not even know what the word means. When I had a minute to myself I stitched my clothes; and that was not often. After I had washed the utensils, and there were at least fifty pots and pans, and swept the courtyard, the morning was over. In the afternoon I pressed your great grandmother-in-law's feet till she fell asleep. But before her afternoon rest she always gave me a sack full of grain to clean. You forget that in those days there were twenty-four family members to feed and that's not counting the servants. The mistress was shrewd. She knew if I had time on my hands I would get into mischief. After all I was young and loved talking with the servants. I was not allowed to play like other girls of my age. It was not considered proper for a widow to be gay and carefree. I was too young to understand this and thought the mistress was unfair. But Binniji, in those days there was always noise and laughter in the courtyard. Those were great days when your great-grandfather-in-law and his three brothers, their wives and all the children lived in this haveli.' She looked at Geeta, with a mischievous look in her eyes, and said in a teasing voice, 'You remember, do you not, the portraits of Ram Singhji, Akhe Singhji and Jeewan Singhji Ba Saheb; well then you know of whom I am talking.'

Geeta looked away in embarrassment.

'Then when Sangram Singhji's wife Bhabha Sa, your grandmother-in-law, became the first lady of the haveli, life was more difficult for me. Some day your mother-in-law will tell you what it was like to be a daughter-in-law of Bhabha Sa. Now your grandmother-in-law is too old to keep you in check. But in her time she ruled the haveli with an iron hand. No one ever dared raise their voice in front of her. Her word was law. The young maids were not allowed out of the courtyard till they were married. There was no question of disobeying her; she kept a stick near her and we knew she would use it, too. Bhatianiji and I were her personal maids. We accompanied her wherever she went, even to the palace.' The word 'palace' evoked a nostalgic sigh in Pari. Then she continued, 'What a pity you never saw the palace when Udaipur was the capital of the State of Mewar. In those days even the havelis had more glitter. Now it is all so different, everyone thinks he is equal; how is that possible?

'Our Maharana was like God to us; so generous, so kind, he knew every child in the city; he worried about the poor. And the Maharani Sa—she loved dance and music, she was fond of entertaining. This kept us maids also busy. The women of the nobility were called to the palace to celebrate the most minor festival. It took me two days of hard work to get the clothes and jewellery ready for my mistress. The Maharani Sa was particular not only how the ladies of the court dressed, but also their maids. She herself was always resplendent in her jewels. Oh! those days were wonderful, even though I could never wear any jewellery and my sari as now was always grey. But my eyes have seen such splendour that I feel you have been cheated.'

Geeta was again about to say a word of sympathy when Pari got up. 'Look at me talking to you when I should be with Bhabha Sa. These days she feels neglected if she is left alone even for a second. Bhatianiji is as old as she and as frail; she cannot sit and talk to her for long. I must go. Another day I will tell you more about those old times.' Pari straightened the sari over her head, dusted her skirt and walked slowly to the door; her thoughts were still of the past.

'Bhabha Sa has been calling you, Jiji; Bhatianiji is sleeping,' said Dhapu coming in with a tray of food.

'I knew I had stayed too long, but once I get talking of those days, I can't stop,' said Pari quickly going out of the door.

'See how clever I was,' said Dhapu winking, after Pari left. 'I did not give Parijiji time to scold me. She thinks that we are all like her without families. She can't understand why we go down to our quarters, poor thing. She has never known what it is like to have a husband and children. Her whole life has been devoted to the haveli. But she is the type that would neglect even her own child for the sake of the mistress. There is no one like her, certainly not me.' Dhapu put the tray of food down and bent over the crib to see Vijay who slept.

'You really are a cunning old thing,' said Geeta sitting up, relieved to be with Dhapu. Pari always made her feel inadequate. There was a kind of authority and self-confidence in her that made Geeta uncomfortable, but with Dhapu who was in her early thirties, she felt at ease.

'If one were not cunning in this household, Binniji, one would be lost. I am simple compared to the others. That's why I do more than my share of work.' She made a face and grinned.

'You call yourself simple, do you?' said Geeta tauntingly.

'Never mind what I am; eat your food and just remember that you will not even get maids like me these days; so you had better learn to cook. Reading and writing will not keep the rats from nibbling at the sacks of wheat,' said Dhapu teasingly. She was small-built and pretty. Her pug nose went well with her button mouth. Her husband lived in the village taking care of the land that Sangram Singhji had given him. He visited her from time to time. She was the mother of three girls and all of them were married. But only one was old enough to live with her husband; the other two still lived with her in the haveli. They played in the courtyard or did errands for the mistress.

'Bai, oh Bai,' Champa, Geeta's junior maid, said coming into the room panting. 'The accountant of the haveli is just this minute discussing the details of the celebrations with the master. I overheard the most important thing. The whole community is to be fed; the celebrations will be for three full days. They will be exactly as if a son had been born and not a girl.'

'Don't tell me that you came running up here just to tell me this,' said Dhapu disdainfully. 'Once Parijiji had made up her mind, I knew she would persuade even the master. The thing now to do is put in our demands before Parijiji has time to think about us.'

'Three days of ceremonies and feasting,' said Geeta, her eyes wide open full of surprise and fear.

'What are you afraid of, Binniji? We will dance and sing, wear our best clothes, and eat as many ladoos as we can. You have just to sit in a corner and see that your sari falls well over your face. I will not be there to keep pulling it down for you,' said Dhapu frivolously.

'But Bai,' Geeta started to say something.

'Now don't you discourage the mistress. As it is, Bhabha Sa has started mumbling about the expenses. If not on this occasion, then when will the servants get gold and silver?' said Dhapu in a crisp voice.

'Binniji, don't forget I want a red sari with a matching skirt,' said Champa before Geeta turned and pulled a pillow over her ears.

'It's my turn to get something more than just a sari,'

added Dhapu. 'On this occasion I will demand gold. It's my right. After all, I was the first to hold Vijay Bai Sa in my hands.'

Geeta paid no attention to Dhapu. She thought of the courtyard full of women looking her over and criticizing her as they had the day she arrived, and felt depressed. She, like Lakshmi, looked forward to the twenty days' seclusion of her room; she had enjoyed the peace and quiet of the last two weeks. But now the period was more than half over. The thought of three days of feasting and merry-making made her feel positively ill. Geeta tried to take comfort in the hope that her stay in Udaipur was temporary. Her husband was not quite satisfied with the university. They had often discussed the idea of going to Delhi. Geeta felt better as she dwelt on the prospect of leaving the haveli.

Chapter V

GEETA TOSSED AND turned in her bed. A cold sweat erupted all over her body as she thought of the day ahead of her. The noise from the kitchen below her room woke Geeta up well before dawn. It was twenty-one days after Vijay had been born. Even after two years in the haveli she felt nervous when relatives gathered; she was still not comfortable moving around with her face covered.

The women of the haveli, rich and poor, young and old, knew exactly what to do; they were never awkward. No matter what they were doing they carried themselves with effortless grace. Geeta got no confidence from her college education. Nor did the admiration and constant reassurance from her husband make her feel more at ease. The remarks the women had made on her first day in the haveli came back: 'She will never adjust. She is not one of us.'

As the clamour of voices and the clanging of utensils grew louder, Geeta decided it was time to get out of bed. Any minute the maids would be there to prepare her for the festivities. She went into the adjoining bathroom to bathe and had returned to the bedroom to put on her sari when her mother-in-law came almost noiselessly into the room.

'Binniji, Dhapu will bring your clothes. I have brought the jewellery. See if you like the pearl set, if not, I will take out the enamel one,' said the mistress of the haveli, sitting down on the floor. She seemed preoccupied as she carefully separated the bangles from the bracelets, the anklets from the armlets, the necklaces and the earrings.

Bhagwat Singhji's wife was called Kanwarani Sa by the servants. She was a tiny person with small bones delicately fitted which made her look frail and fragile. Her complexion was smooth though sallow from lack of exposure to the sun. Her movements were birdlike but she held herself erect. Her mouth was firm; there was rigidity in her thin lips when pursed together. She walked with indescribable self-confidence and exuded strength and dignity as if she were naturally born to command.

'Binniji,' she said gently but firmly, 'keep your face covered; by now you should be able to move around without uncovering your face.' Then, after a brief pause, as if to give emphasis to her words, she said, 'Do not talk too much to your young cousins-in-law, it's not becoming. You know, the women are critical because you are still clumsy. I want to show them that even an educated girl can be moulded. That I was not wrong in selecting you as the wife of my only son. Besides, I am getting old now and soon you will have to take over,' she said, and carefully fastened the bracelet on Geeta's wrist.

Then as an afterthought she added, 'Give Parijiji all the money you receive for Vijay; the accountant will note it down so we know what to give on a similar occasion in another haveli.'

'Yes, Hukkum,' said Geeta, using the politest form of address to cover her humiliation. She knew all her fears were justified. No one thought her worthy of the family. Everyone was afraid she would embarrass them by an indiscreet word or a faulty move.

'Binniji,' said Bhagwat Singhji's wife, getting up, 'I know you don't eat properly when there is confusion around you. As soon as the women sit down to eat, you come upstairs. I will have your thali sent up. Wait till Dhapu comes to put on the rest of the jewellery,' she said lightly shutting the door behind her.

This was the kind of concern and affection that made Bhagwat Singhji's wife so difficult to fathom. Though she was strict she was not uncompromising. In many small ways she showed an understanding of Geeta's nature and tried to adjust to her needs. But on essentials she did not compromise.

From the day Geeta came into the family she had to abide by the form and the etiquette of the haveli. Her mother-in-law's personality was such that it was difficult to contradict her or even express a different point of view. She had her own way of prevailing over others, a blend of craft and tenacity. She never lost her temper, she was always seemingly considerate and gentle. She never raised her voice; she was patient and prepared to listen. It was due to her tact and her gentle persuasion that Geeta had been gradually drawn into the life of the haveli without even wanting to resist it. There was something in this way of life that frightened and fascinated her at the same time.

Dhapu came into the room smiling with the bundle of clothes balanced on her head. Since Geeta was pensive she said, 'Binniji, has something upset you that you sit staring at the floor?' as she put the bundle of clothes down. 'Today I have no time to hear your complaints about the haveli. I have a thousand things still to do.' Dhapu started to unfold the red brocade sari with quick strokes of the hand. 'Oh, I nearly forgot, Kanwarani Sa told me to warn you not to lift the baby or show any concern for her in front of others, not the way you lifted Vijay Bai Sa and kissed her the other day in the presence of your aunt-in-law.'

'Stop lecturing me, I am fed up with all the pretence that goes on here,' said Geeta in a high-pitched voice, at last releasing the irritation she felt. 'I hate all this meaningless fuss! Don't tell me what I should do with my own child!'

Dhapu cringed a little, she wasn't prepared for this outburst. 'Binniji, don't be angry with me. Today is a very special day for us servants. We have waited for it for twenty-seven long years,' she said in a voice full of emotion, and silently continued to drape the sari round Geeta's slim waist, then with deft fingers closed the clasps of the bracelets and anklets. It was when Dhapu pulled the sari over her face that Geeta knew she was ready.

As she came out from her room, her head was bent more than usual, as much by the heavy jewellery she wore as with anxiety at the relatives gathered in the courtyard.

When at nineteen Geeta had come as a bride to Jeewan Niwas, she was lively and spontaneous. She had not been taught to stint in giving affection; nor was she taught to keep her feelings concealed. Her parents had encouraged her to speak her mind. There was a child-like enthusiasm in everything she did or said. She knew marriage meant going into unfamiliar surroundings, but she was not afraid. In her youthful confidence she believed that with love she could win over anyone, anywhere. But after two years she was not so sure of herself. In the haveli no one really expressed their feelings. They covered their emotions in an elaborate exchange of formal gestures and words. Even her husband talked to his parents as if they were dignitaries with whom he could take no liberties. The form and courtesy which the young maintained before the old lacked spontaneity. In the two years Geeta had never heard any really unpleasant exchange of words between different members of the family. She was aware that certain relatives were not liked and others were definitely disliked; but each time they came to the haveli, her mother-in-law met them as if she was overjoyed to see them. Everyone moved cautiously; every word was weighed before it was spoken. Even with the servants no one lost their tempers; they were reprimanded with polite but cutting words which was almost worse than if they had been openly abused.

In the two years Geeta had lost much of her exuberance but still she was unable fully to control either her words or her feelings. She was still capable of talking frankly with her younger in-laws. Because of this, her mother-in-law kept reminding her of the importance of reticence.

The courtyard was already full of chattering women in bright red, green and orange saris and a host of unruly children in their tinsel embroidered frocks. The widows, some of them young girls, were in black, the contrast of their saris with those of the married women like a blot in a spectrum of bright colours. Everyone was talking as if they hadn't seen each other for years. As more guests arrived they joined in; there was no need for introductions: everyone knew each other. The children played hide-and-seek behind their mothers' skirts, shrieking with delight, but nothing disturbed the women; they kept on talking.

Pari steered Geeta through the crowd to her grandmother-in-law. Bhabha Sa sat on her bed in the covered verandah of the courtyard. Vijay lay next to her. Her maids, Bhatianiji and Gopi Bai, fanned the flies off the baby's face.

Geeta bent down and touched her grandmother-in-law's feet. 'May you have many many sons, my child, and may you always wear red,' said Sangram Singhji's wife, fondly stroking Geeta's covered head.

In the centre of the courtyard the priests sat under a canopy, chanting prayers. Then, at the exact time set by the astrologers, Bhagwat Singhji and his son entered the courtyard. There was an immediate lowering of voices. They walked slowly with great dignity to the canopy as if what they were about to do was of great significance. As the priests lit the pile of sandalwood fire, Pari escorted Geeta to the specially erected platform and seated her next to her husband on one side of the fire. Bhagwat Singhji and his wife sat on the opposite side. The chants grew louder as the priests poured melted butter on the fire, and instructed Bhagwat Singhji and his son to follow suit. The incantations of the Vedas were drowned in the screams of the children who continued to run around the courtyard. But as if noise were a natural accompaniment to prayers, the priests went on undisturbed.

The worship over, Bhagwat Singhji and his son quietly went out of the courtyard. As soon as the men left, the women relaxed; their voices rose again; they started where they had left off. Pari helped Geeta off the stool, adjusted her sari and then pushed her way to the senior-most relative for the ritual of touching the feet. Geeta could hardly see through the gold embroidered sari; the tinsel tickled her nose and she wanted to sneeze. She had never felt so nervous before. She walked cautiously lest she trip over someone's feet in the congested courtyard. As she bent down to touch the feet she vaguely heard, 'May you have eight sons; may the gods bless you. May this haveli flourish forever.' The words barely registered in her mind; all she was aware of was the next pair of feet she must touch without losing her balance. The heavy sari, the full pleated skirt, the gold, all combined to make her feel as if she was a heavy log of wood that had no mobility. When Pari led her back to sit down next to Bhabha's bed again, Geeta could hardly believe that the ordeal was over.

The noise and confusion were getting worse; the air was stifling around Bhabha's bed, as one woman after another came to her offering their congratulations and placing money in the tiny clenched fists of Vijay. The amount they gave was according to the status of each haveli and its relationship to Sangram Singhji. The family accountant with his steel rimmed glasses sat with his head bent, noting down the name of the haveli and the amount, as it was called out by Pari.

It was nearly twelve o'clock by the time the last woman had greeted Bhabha Sa and blessed her little great-granddaughter. The priests had left with gifts of fruit, grain and cloth. The maids had spread thick white strips of cloth along the verandah surrounding the courtyard and on the edge of the cloth they placed large green banana leaves for plates and cups made of dry leaves pinned together with thin twigs. Steaming rice, dal, vegetables and different kinds of curries were in buckets, ready to be served. The sweets were in large thalis. The aroma of spices, mixed with incense, made the air heavy.

Once everything was ready, Bhagwat Singhji's wife, with great formality, invited the women to sit down to eat, as if they were guests who had come to the house for the first time. Tantalized by the smell of food, the children were getting restless. They jostled and scrambled to get what places remained or squeezed themselves next to their mothers or grandmothers. The chatter of voices was soon replaced by the smacking of lips. The close relatives served the guests. As soon as the serving buckets were empty, full ones were brought.

Bhagwat Singhji's wife with her elder relatives went around coaxing the guests, 'Have some more rice', 'One more puree', 'At least a ladoo'. There were protests, but finally they were persuaded to take something more. Having eaten with relish they belched with satisfaction and got up, washed their hands and crossed into the adjoining courtyard where there was room for them to stretch their legs and relax.

The first group of women having finished, the maids quickly picked up the leaves and cups and threw them outside the courtyard wall. The stray dogs and cows were ready to lick them. The maids moved rapidly; through years of experience they had become experts at feeding a large number of people without getting flustered. The relay of feeding and clearing went on till all the guests had been served. Bhagwat Singhji's wife was on her feet till the last row of women had been served.

In between the eating sessions Geeta was given the sign that she could go up to her room. When after two hours she came down she felt a little more composed. There was less noise, the maids were busy cleaning up the puddles of dal and curry, sweeping the grains of rice and savoury crumbs off the floor. The ladies were quiet; the heavy spicy food seemed to have dulled their spirits for a while. Bhabha Sa seemed happy. The elder women sat around her bed talking. She would doze off for a few minutes and again sit up. She did not want to miss anything. The younger women had formed a group of their own at the other end of the verandah so that they could talk freely. But still their saris fell over their faces lest some elder relative see them. Geeta came quietly and sat down among them.

Late in the afternoon the household seemed to be astir again. The professional singing group had arrived and started to serenade the ancient house of Sangram Singhji. The families of these women had served the havelis for several generations, singing and dancing on festive occasions. As the singing gathered momentum, an elderly lady got up and came to where the young married girls sat huddled together and said, shaking one of them by the shoulders: 'You have had enough time to digest your food. Get up and dance. This is an auspicious day, you have also talked enough.'

The girls coyly demurred and dipped their hands deeper into their laps. 'Come on! Don't act as if you have fresh henna on your feet, as if you are a bride,' said Kanta, the widowed niece of Bhagwat Singhji. 'In my days I didn't wait to be persuaded; in fact I had to be forcibly taken off the floor. Ask Parijiji if you do not believe me.'

One of the girls reluctantly got up, pulled her sari well over her face and shyly went to the centre of the courtyard. At first she made graceful gestures with her hands but her body refused to tilt or bend to the beat of the drum. She tried for a while and then fled in embarrassment. The singers did not conceal their disappointment.

After nudging and nagging a tall slim girl got up and went hurriedly to the centre. At first she too faltered and hesitated, but then her limbs became supple. Her body turned and twisted with grace, her skirt swirled and her hands were cupped in the shape of a lotus and the arms turned into floating fishes. The singers raised the pitch of their voice and the drummers quickened the beat. The courtyard echoed with rhythm and song. The girl paused for a moment to pull the sari over her face and then she started again.

'She is graceful, she is talented,' the women said with admiration as they came up with their rupee notes, carefully taken out from inside the blouse. Solemnly they encircled the girl's head with the money and then threw it into the lap of the singers. Thus the evil spirit was bribed from casting its envious eyes on the youthful dancer.

'Come on, you are next,' said Kanta to a plump girl who sat bundled up, her head between her knees. She shook her head vehemently but Kanta took her by the hand and led her to the middle of the courtyard.

The girl stood awkwardly for a second and giggled and then she looked through her sari at the drummers. They took the hint that they had to go a little slow; the singers cleared their throats and struck the tune that was romantic but languid.

'Oh! She can dance,' said the women surprised as the girl swirled effortlessly around the courtyard.

'Who could have said that with a heavy body like that she could be so graceful?'

'She was slim once; it is after her fourth child that she became fat,' put in another woman.

The girl's tight face relaxed and she smiled, then her lips parted and she began to sing with the women. Her body contours kept the romantic mood and her gestures portrayed the sentiments of love.

'One more dance. No you cannot now sit down,' the women shouted as the girl stopped to wipe the perspiration from her face. Geeta was relieved when the girl did not leave the courtyard. She was terrified lest anyone asked her to perform. She did not know that there was no danger of her being asked as she was not considered strong enough after child-birth.

The senior women got up as before, encircled the rupee notes over the head of the dancer and then gave them to the smiling drummers. The singers glanced at the ever growing pile of notes and continued with their singing with renewed force. The ladies of the havelis for once were not going to stint. This was a special occasion. Even the older women shed their reserve and danced to the slow familiar rhythm they had heard a thousand times before.

Amidst the singing and dancing the women didn't notice that the sun had gone down and that the evening light was turning dark; the lights were switched on unnoticed, but the ladies were in no hurry to leave. The singers had cast a spell that kept them longer than usual.

'Binniji, come with me,' whispered Dhapu in Geeta's ear. She got up half in fear. Had she done something wrong? 'I have never seen you sit so quietly for so long; don't tell me you are not longing to see what is going on in the other side of the haveli.' There was a mischievous glint in Dhapu's eyes. 'Follow me; no one will miss you at least for some time.'

Geeta followed Dhapu out of the women's apartment, not quite sure where she was being led, but glad to be away from the noise. 'No, no, not that way,' said Dhapu in a frightened whisper. 'Come up these back stairs from here; we can see better and no one will know we are looking.' She led Geeta through a dark passage up the narrow stairs to the men's apartments. 'Stand on this step,' she said helping her up.

Geeta looked down through the lattice window, shading her eyes with her hands to get a good view. She saw her husband, Ajay Singh, in a white knee-length coat and a red turban, standing beside his father who wore a multi-coloured turban with a white coat. Father and son had the same clear-cut sculptured features; they looked exactly like the portraits on the wall; they had the same aristocratic faces with piercing eyes. The guests looked elegant in formal attire with turbans and coats of silk brocade over tight fitting pants. There was a quiet dignity in this gathering. Even the many servants moved quietly serving sherbet and sweets to the guests. Geeta's eyes rested on her grandfather-in-law Sangram Singhji who sat erect on the mattress; his white flowing beard made him look like a prophet. He was frail with age, but still one could see from his fiery eyes and determined lips that he was a man of strength. His face was gentle but not soft. His eyes had a faraway look, as if he were not interested in those present, but recollecting the past. He remembered the day his grandson Ajay was born twenty-nine years ago. A month after his birth the Maharana of Udaipur himself had graced his haveli to celebrate the birth of a son in his family. Instead of the hundred guests present there were then five hundred. The room was filled with gifts of silver and gold; the Maharana had sat on a red and gold brocade mattress with his courtiers around him, receiving homage from the nobility. A score of women had danced in front of the guests. He could still see the colour of their saris float before him as they whisked round so fast that no face was clear, not even their forms. He closed his eyes for a second; then the vision faded. A smile lit his grave face as the relatives and friends with folded hands bent their heads, congratulated him and moved on. His son and grandson were never far from him, bending down from time to time to get his instructions.

Geeta stared at the scene below as if hypnotized. Even though Udaipur was no longer a feudal state the traditions of Mewar seemed safe in the hands of these stern looking men, all of whom seemed so composed, so determined and so refined. A glow of pride and affection filled Geeta. These were good people, gentle, kind and chivalrous. Looking at the men below she forgot her daily irritations; she felt proud to be the young mistress of the haveli. How could she allow little discomforts to blind her to the great traditions of the family?

As she withdrew her face from the latticed stone slab, Dhapu said, 'Don't be afraid, I know when we must leave. You must hear the famous singer from Jodhpur, I wish she would start. She takes five hundred rupees an evening and only sings for men! She is not like those old women with cracked voices singing inside our courtyard. My eardrums are still hurting.'

Geeta stuck her face again to the lattice window but she could not see the singer. She heard someone clear her throat. Geeta tried various angles to get a glimpse of the woman but failed. Then the voice was raised to the right pitch; it was clear, melodious and sweet.

She started with a song of chivalry which recalled the glory of the Rajput soldier ready to leave for the battlefield. Her voice soared to the ceiling, filling the room and the hearts of the guests. Their faces glowed with pride for the land of their birth.

'Now that you have heard the great song, we must go. The mistress must be fussing around looking for me,' said Dhapu anxiously.

'Just a few minutes more, Bai,' said Geeta, her face still pressed to the lattice grill.

'Never scold me again,' said Dhapu teasingly. 'But for me, you would still be sitting with the women with a splitting headache. Now you have heard the best and seen the real grandeur of this important day. But now we can't stay a minute longer,' the maid said firmly.

Reluctantly and yet filled with joy Geeta withdrew her face from the marble screen, and followed Dhapu down the steps.

The girls were still dancing. The singers' voices were tired and hoarse but the heap of rupee and two rupee notes kept them going. The ladies were getting ready to leave, they had already stayed longer than usual. Bhabha Sa had fallen asleep. No one disturbed her. In her place Bhagwat Singhji's wife with great modesty accepted the lavish praises for the day's celebrations, as the ladies and their maids quietly went out of the courtyard.

It was late before the activity in the courtyard came to an end. The relatives staying the night retired to their rooms. But Bhagwat Singhji's wife, tired as she was, locked up the leftover ladoos and the savouries in the kitchen cupboard. The maids swept the courtyard, washed the utensils, counted the silver plates and cups and stacked them on the shelves. It was only after everything was put away that they relaxed. Though it was late they were too tired to sleep; they sat together singing in the courtyard. They sang softly the songs of gods and goddesses, of Radha and Krishna, of Ram and Seeta, of Shiva and Parvati. Their voices faded only when the jackals howled and the dogs barked. When the silence of night became forbidding, they quietly lay down to sleep.

Chapter VI

GEETA HAD DONE very little to contribute to the festivities, but yet she felt exhausted. She got up later than usual; she knew she should be downstairs with her mother-in-law but she didn't have the energy to get out of bed. Even Dhapu was taking her time as she bathed Vijay in Geeta's bathroom.

'Binniji, Binniji,' said Ganga as she burst into the room, 'I got the red sari and skirt to match I wanted. I don't have the time to put them on now and show you. I must go and help Khyali in the kitchen, he is already screaming.' Ganga left her bundle next to Geeta's bed and bumped into Champa as she left.

'I also got what I asked for,' said Champa entering the room. Her face beamed as if she held the world's choicest brocades in her hands.

Geeta was touched by their genuine pleasure, there was nothing false in their expressions of gratitude. For the first time she felt that the celebrations were worth the trouble.

'So, you went up to Binniji to show your saris,' said

Lakshmi as she stopped sweeping the verandah on which Bhabha slept. Holding a broom in her hand, her voice full of sarcasm and eyes filled with malice, she added, 'Has Parijiji shown you the gold bangles she got and Sarju her gold earrings? Even Dhapu got a gold ring; you wouldn't think so looking at her face, but I know for certain she got a gold ring.'

'And so what if she did? Did you think we all would get gold?' retorted Champa defiantly.

'I am not a fool to think that, but on this great occasion I expected at least a new sari. Mine won't stand two washes,' snapped back Lakshmi in anger.

'Keep quiet! Bhahba Sa may be hard of hearing but she is not deaf,' said Champa putting her hands to her ears as if she didn't want to hear any more.

The maids' voices woke up Bhabha Sa. As if suddenly remembering something, in a sharp shrill voice she shouted: 'If there is no food cooked for me, tell me, so that I can at least sleep in peace. Half the morning is already over and still my thali has not come. No one cares if I die of starvation. I don't know why God keeps me alive. No one has any use for me now.'

Bhatianiji, who was by her bedside, gently stroked her legs and told her that it was not yet time for her food. Then seeing the maids chatting, Bhahba Sa recalled what she really had on her mind. 'I told you, Bhatianiji; it is no good spoiling servants. Look at these shameless girls, flitting in and out of the courtyard, but do you think any one of them has the decency to show me what they got? Why should they? I have nothing to give them. I am no longer the mistress, my days are over. I am on my way out.'

'Don't talk like this. It does not become you. Take God's name when you are angry,' said Bhatianiji soothingly, putting her thin wrinkled hand on her mistress. 'See, here comes your food,' the old woman added as Ganga placed the silver thali on a stool beside the bed. Then she helped the old mistress to get down from the bed and sit on the floor.

Kanwarani Sa and Pari came and sat opposite Sangram Singhji's wife. The old lady first picked up the silver cups one by one and brought them close to her eyes to see what was in them. She made a grimace and put a cup outside the thali.

'Try a little. They are fresh beans from the garden,' said Bhagwat Singhji's wife almost in a whisper, putting the cup back in the thali.

'No, I don't even want to taste it. You know I have never liked beans.'

'Try a little, just a very little,' Pari coaxed.

For fifty years Bhagwat Singhji's wife had sat with her mother-in-law while she ate. Bhagwat Singhji's wife had come to the haveli at the age of twelve or at most thirteen. Bhabha Sa was strict even with the child-bride. The veil had covered the still unformed face from her eyes and even now when she could hardly see, the veil hid her daughter-in-law's face from her.

'No, I cannot eat more than two rotis. You know I cannot digest food any more,' said Sangram Singhji's wife pushing her daughter-in-law's hand away.

'That is a small soft roti. Have just this one,' insisted Bhagwat Singhji's wife as she put one in the thali. As if against her will, Bhabha Sa surrendered.

'So, how much did you spend, Binniji, on these elaborate celebrations?' asked the old mistress in a thin crisp voice, slowly chewing the roti without relish. But before Pari could come to her mistress's defence, she went on: 'Binniji, for fifty years I have tried to teach you the value of money. But I see I have failed. What would you have done today had I been as extravagant as you are? I too could have been lavish, but I thought of you and your children. But I was a fool. And now it is too late to have regrets.' She sighed and then with reinforced vigour said, 'But Binniji, remember, without money no one will look at you. Keep what I have given you and do not throw it away on trying to please servants. This is my advice to you, but you have never listened to me.' Her voice gradually faded. She was tired after her outburst. Pari helped her to get up and then gently lowered her head on the pillow.

'Bhabha Sa, if Kanwar Sa had not fed the community on this occasion, what would the people have said?' said Pari after the old mistress lay down. 'Would you have approved if your son had not kept the traditions you brought him up to respect?'

Sangram Singhji's wife raised herself immediately and retaliated, 'Did I say not to feed the community? They come first, but why give these wretched girls new clothes? You deserve gold bangles, but why give them to Sarju and Dhapu? Why not wait till a son is born? I know the mentality of servants. They will forget they received gold on the birth of a girl. Not one of the maids has shown me their saris. Why should they? The old are forgotten by everyone.' Then changing her tone of voice she continued, 'Of course, my son did the right thing to feed the community, but he can't be expected to see what goes on in our part of the haveli. That's our responsibility. Did you see the children with three and four ladoos in their hands? Sugar is expensive these days. Binniji is to be blamed for the waste.' The old mistress spoke aggressively, looking at her daughter-in-law accusingly.

There was a moment of awkward silence. Then suddenly Pari shouted, 'What are you girls doing hiding behind the pillars? You should be ashamed of yourselves. Today you are what you are because of Bhabha Sa. She arranged for your marriages, fed you, and yet you stand there grinning like so many little monkeys. Go and get your new saris and place them at her feet. Get her blessings.'

'Do not scold them, Pari. They know whom to please in the haveli. They are wise. I have given away every tola of gold to Binniji. I have nothing left to give and they know it,' said the old mistress with bitter resignation in her voice.

For fifty years, Bhagwat Singhji's wife had heard her mother-in-law taunt her, scold her, find fault with her in this manner. She had gotten used to her sarcastic words. She did not mind them any more. In fact, when a kind word escaped the old lady, she was amused. But in spite of everything, Bhagwat Singhji's wife was devoted to her. For fifty years they had shared the joys and sorrows of the family which bound them together. Nothing could break such a bond. Just as the old mistress was about to doze off, the maids came tripping into the yard with their little bundles tucked under their arms and sat down next to the bed. Bhabha Sa sensed their arrival and was wide awake again and looked at the assembled heap of colours.

'Is Lakshmi pleased or not?' asked the old mistress in a feeble voice, as she felt the texture of the sari with care. 'She is the difficult one to satisfy.'

But then suddenly she lost interest, and with the edge of the sari still between her fingers, she closed her eyes. The maids picked up their bundles and left without looking at Pari who stood over them.

The women's courtyard was always quiet once the midday meal was over. The servants collected the food from the haveli kitchen; some ate in the verandah of the kitchen, others took their rotis to their quarters and ate with their husbands. This was the time when the servants relaxed after the morning work. The children of the servants kept the mistress amused telling her stories. She needed only a little sleep to feel fresh again. Neighbours or maids from other havelis dropped in to see the mistress of Jeewan Niwas during the afternoons. They sought her help and advice on a hundred things; they told her the latest gossip in the city and what was happening in the other families. In fact, Bhagwat Singhji's wife was happiest when the verandah was full of women. She hated being alone. Noise did not bother her, but silence she could not bear. While the maids talked they also worked. They put the utensils out to dry in the sun, cleaned the rice and wheat. Bhagwat Singhji's wife had a way of getting work out of anyone.

Lakshmi never came up to the verandah in the afternoon unless she had to. She preferred being in her own little room. After Bhabha Sa fell asleep, Ganga and Champa joined the other maids on the verandah, but Lakshmi took her bundle and went out of the courtyard.

Just as she had put one foot on the steps, from the front verandah of the men's apartment a muffled voice said, 'Take this, I brought it for the child.' It was the voice of the driver, Heeralal. But before Lakshmi could turn her head, the short slim figure disappeared behind the pillar, leaving the packet in her hand.

She ran down the steps, without looking to either side. She nearly dropped Sita in her confusion. Once she had shut the doors behind her, she felt better. She looked at the newspaper package with surprise. Then she tore it open. 'Oh, this is beautiful, really soft and lovely. It's real silk,' she exclaimed. She turned the pink blouse in her trembling hands and caressed it to feel better its soft, smooth texture. Her cheeks became purple with excitement. In spite of the shafts of fear that ran through her body, a soft glowing warmth filled her. She stood still for a second, confused, not knowing what to do: whether to rush out of the room and go straight to the mistress with the pink blouse or to tear it into shreds and throw it out. Then, as if it not quite certain of what she was doing, she went to the corner of the room where she kept her boxes. She lowered the tin box and opened the larger one below it and threw the soft silk blouse among her old clothes and locked the box. Then, hurriedly, she arranged her hair, picked up her sleeping child and went out of the room again.

Chapter VII

FOR WEEKS AFTER the celebrations Sangram Singhji's haveli had been the talk of Udaipur. After all, everyone from the closest relative to the family barber had been invited to the festivities. The shop-keepers said, 'What a noble son of a noble father! Real aristocrats do not change overnight.' The men in the bazaar had reason to praise Bhagwat Singhji's generosity. They were aware that the lands of the nobility had been forfeited and that the days of feudal generosity were over. To have been lavish in the days when the Maharana of Udaipur ruled was nothing extraordinary. He had given generously to those who served the state loyally. But the times had changed. The Maharana could no longer help the nobility. He had lost his revenue; so had the aristocracy. Even so, Sangram Singhji and his son had not forgotten to include distant relations and those who had served him in the past. Who else would have thought of the smallest menial in such difficult times to celebrate the birth of a great grand-child, and that too only a girl?

The monsoons were over, the skies were clear; the nip in

the evening air heralded the approach of winter. The dense blackness of the night had not yet spread over the city. Inside the haveli was quiet. Geeta could hear from her rooms the last calls of the street vendors before they packed up for the night.

Ajay sat at his desk deeply engrossed in reading. The table lamp with an orange shade spread a warm glow in the spacious bedroom. The three-room apartment of Geeta and her husband was on the side of the women's apartments. Geeta had made these rooms comfortable and cheerful. She had hung paintings and hangings on the wall. The sitting room was lined with bookshelves. Geeta had no opportunity to buy books but her husband did. The servants chided her for this extravagance and she knew that they were echoing the sentiments of her mother-in-law. She had turned a deaf ear to their advice, and continued to ask her husband to buy books. In fact, no one approved of her way of spending money. She bought old statues and brass objects; the dealers once they knew of her interests came to the haveli.

Geeta sat on the thick mattress on the floor, her head uncovered, her hands tightly wrapped round her drawn up knees. She breathed heavily as if what she held within was choking her. 'Ajay,' she said with sudden sharpness.

He turned, and seeing the indignant face of his wife, immediately sensed that something was wrong. Ajay shut the book and came and sat down next to Geeta; he realized that she needed to talk to him but her sullen face inhibited him from making casual conversation and so he said, 'I know, it is difficult for you here, but, Geeta, by being depressed, you will not change things.' Ajay's voice was anxious and gentle. He paused and then in a slow, soft voice added, 'I have neglected you and not thought enough of your life in the haveli. This life in purdah is not meant for you.

Help me to try and see what you could do in this atmosphere. You must always have confidence in me that I will support you in whatever you decide to do.'

'But Ajay, you said we would be only be here for a short time. It is nearly three years,' replied Geeta with a certain hopelessness in her voice.

There was silence, neither spoke. Ajay's face darkened, his shoulders drooped, he lowered his head as if to hide his confusion. Then in a heavy, weary voice he said, 'You are not happy in my family.'

'Of course I am,' she said hastily. 'Who said I was not happy? I was only thinking of you. With your academic qualifications you could not be satisfied working in Udaipur.' There was force in her voice even though it lacked conviction. She knew she had upset him and wanted to dispel his doubts regarding her happiness. Ajay Singh broke into a smile. His face lost its austere look. He looked at his wife and smiled. He understood that Geeta was trying to hide her own frustration at living in a constricted atmosphere so as not to hurt him.

'So you are worried about me,' he said tenderly. Then as if the magic of Geeta's concern had lost its power over him, he sat up. His face became taut, and he spoke looking through and beyond her. 'As far as my work goes, I am quite happy at the university. I like my students and I like my subject. No, do not start protesting. Listen to me first,' he said firmly as Geeta opened her mouth to speak.

'I have not given up the idea of going to Delhi University. We will some day, but I do not know when. Just now my father needs me here. I do not want to leave him alone; he is getting old. The problem is not of my happiness but yours.'

'I know the men have no problems in this world of Udaipur; you are all pampered. You lead your lives and think women are mere chattels,' replied Geeta with anger.

'In fact, I don't even see any point in being here. I may as well go and stay with my parents. You won't miss me; there are hundreds of people to take care of you.' Geeta's cheeks burned with emotion and her tone was bitter. She no longer hid her feelings.

'You are right, we men are spoilt, but surely you know how important you are to me. I never thought that you would also make my parents happy. Do you know, Geeta, I could never have been content in Udaipur had you not adjusted to the ways of the haveli. I would then have really run away from here.' Ajay paused and then in a controlled voice said, 'I am really proud of you, but that's little consolation to you.'

Geeta looked vacantly at the floor. There was nothing more to say. But at the same time the dream of leaving Udaipur died in her heart. She realized that her husband was too rooted in the traditions of Udaipur. To leave his parents would be impossible for him at a time when his father needed him. And yet, deep down she felt relieved. At last she was sure that her life was to be in the haveli. She could not afford to regard her stay in Udaipur as temporary. Ajay did not say anything; there was nothing he could say. Both Geeta and he sat silently absorbed in their thoughts when suddenly there was a knock at the door.

'Bapu Sa, Bapu Sa, come down, Bhabha Sa is ill,' said Pari from behind the closed door. Her voice was broken as if she was controlling the sobs from choking her words.

Geeta and her husband were out of the room even before Pari had turned her back.

Bhagwat Singhji stood beside his mother's bed; his wife sat on the floor next to the bed. The doctor was examining the old mistress. After the doctor finished, he stepped aside.

'Doctor, how serious is the heart attack?' asked Bhagwat Singhji in a calm voice.

'Kanwar Sa, your mother is no longer young, but who can tell? The last attack she had was also very severe; yet she recovered.' After writing out the prescription, the doctor left.

As soon as the doctor had gone, Pari lifted the sari from her face. The old mistress opened her eyes and with a slight nod of the head, beckoned her son near her.

'Bapu,' she said in a feeble voice as Bhagwat Singhji bent over her, 'You know the heavy gold bangles I am wearing, I want you to give half of one to Bhatianiji and the other half to Pari. The other bangle, give to Geeta.' Then she paused, took a deep breath and said with difficulty, 'Bapu, do not forget to give my relatives saris, especially my sister's children who are poor. Feed the community, but be careful. Do not let Binniji be too lavish; times have changed.'

'Hukkum, your every wish has always been an order for me. Don't worry about anything. Think of God and repeat His name. You will soon be well,' said Bhagwat Singhji in a grave and respectful voice.

'Bapu, you have been an ideal son. God bless you,' she said, placing her hand on her son's head. Then, turning her eyes, she asked, 'Where is Binniji?'

Bhagwat Singhji's wife put her hand on her arm to indicate that she was near her.

'Come nearer to me, Binniji,' said the old mistress impatiently. 'I know you have had a hard time understanding me, but God bless you. You have been a good daughter-in-law. Look after my son.' The mistress of Jeewan Niwas closed her eyes suddenly, as if it were painful for her to see the faces of those she loved. Her daughter-in-law held a cup of water to her lips. She sipped the water but breathed uneasily.

The news of Sangram Singhji's wife's illness had spread even during the night. Early next morning men and women began coming to Jeewan Niwas. The courtyards of both the men and women were full of people. On one side of the bed sat Sangram Singhji, his son and grandson, and on the other side the ladies. Relatives sat silently along the verandah. The women with their saris well drawn over their faces talked in whispers. The whole day people came and went but close relatives stayed on.

The first lady of the haveli slept uneasily. From time to time she lifted her weary eyelids and gazed around her. She recognized her family, her eyes showed contentment. There was peace on her face as if she had done her earthly duties to her satisfaction; her lips muttered the name of the god, Ram. There was no fear of death, no panic that the end had come. To the very last she was aware of feminine decorum. As long as she was conscious, she insisted the maids cover her face before the doctor.

It was early in the morning on the second day after the heart attack that the end came.

Overnight, the verandah in which Bhabha Sa lay lost its colour and noise; even the children were quiet. The loud, frivolous chatter of women while picking stones from the grain had been replaced by women walking and working quietly. Even the jingle of anklets seemed muffled. There was still a bustle but it was the bustle of the priests, the family accountant and the servants going in and out of the courtyard assisting the maids to prepare for the cremation.

Bhagwat Singhji's wife and her daughter-in-law sat on the floor against the wall of the verandah adjoining the main courtyard with the elder relatives. The women wailed loudly and with abandon, as if they wanted the mistress of Jeewan Niwas to know that her death was being properly mourned. The empty terrace, upstairs the courtyards, almost every crevice in the haveli seemed to echo the sound of death.

As the relatives and women of the community approached the haveli gates, their wailing grew louder. They entered the courtyard, and still crying, they sat down in the verandah. They joined the chief mourners in their grief. When, exhausted from their crying and their throats dry, the relatives moved forward, they touched Bhagwat Singhji's wife and said with feeling, 'Do not cry, you have been an ideal daughter-in-law. There is no one in all the havelis who can even touch the hem of your skirt.'

'You are weak, conserve your energy. You are now in charge of this great haveli that has stood here for three hundred years. You cannot afford to shed tears. You have to start from where Bhabha Sa left off,' said an elderly relative, clasping Bhagwat Singhji's wife's head in her hands.

'Only the truly blessed die still wearing red. Don't cry. Your tears will distress the departed soul,' said another.

Between sobs, Bhagwat Singhji's wife replied, 'She has left me alone. For fifty years she guided me. To whom shall I turn, now that she is no more? I am lost without her; the haveli has lost its light.' Her feelings were genuine, even to the relatives who knew that Bhahba Sa had been a demanding mother-in-law and that Bhagwat Singhji's wife had suffered under her.

The visitors, after they had consoled the ladies, moved to Bhatianiji who everyone knew had been with Bhabha Saheb for sixty years. Some other maids had served her for thirty years, others for forty, but none for sixty. As the ladies came near the maids and Pari, the wailing started again. Bhatianiji was too weak to join in their loud outpouring, but streams of tears rolled down her shrivelled cheeks.

'I have lost a mother. I have lost everything,' sobbed Bhatianiji, hitting her head with her hands. 'Bhabha Sa should have taken me with her. In her lifetime she never went anywhere without me and now she has gone alone leaving me behind. God is not just.'

'Listen,' a woman said, 'no one has control over life and death. You will go when your turn comes and not a day before. If only tears could bring death, there would be no suffering.'

Wiping the tears from Bhatianiji's face with the end of her sari, a woman said, 'You served your mistress as a daughter-in-law and daughter combined. No one will ever be able to match your devotion.'

The younger relatives and the junior maids had meanwhile bathed the body and draped it in a red sari, the colour that brides wear, and put bangles on her hands and rings on her toes, the jewellery that only married women had a right to wear. She lay adorned in death as she had been when she was alive. She had gone before her husband and that was considered the good fortune of those blessed. As soon as the dressed body was placed on the bier, the priests started chanting the vedic hymns.

In the male section of the house a hundred relatives had gathered ready to join the funeral procession. They were barefooted and wore white turbans. They came in light cotton clothes each bringing a towel, indicating that they were going to join the head of the family in the cremation ceremonies on the banks of the river.

As Bhagwat Singhji and his son lifted the bier from the verandah with the help of two other relatives, a crescendo of wailing went up. The ladies touched the feet of Sangram Singhji's wife for the last time.

The chanting of prayers grew louder as the body was brought out to the men's courtyard. Bhagwat Singhji and his son stood aside as Sangram Singhji came out of his room. The elderly man's chiselled face, behind his groomed beard, was calm, but his eyes were misty and there was a faraway look in them.

As the body left the men's courtyard the mourners shouted, 'Ram, Ram, Satya Hai, God is truth.' People stood on either side of the gully and threw flowers on the bier. The family accountant scattered small silver coins before the bier to be picked up by the family sweeper and his children. Sangram Singhji stood there watching the procession till it was out of sight. He was too weak to walk to the cremation grounds.

An eery silence descended on the women's section. The ladies of the house and close relatives prepared for their purification bath. The touch of death had to be washed away before the living could start once again their daily routine. As the ladies went in to bathe, Sarju, the midwife, and her assistants, scrubbed the ladies and helped them change into clean new skirts and saris.

It would be hours before the men came back from the cremation grounds. Meanwhile, it was necessary to make preparations for the thirteen days of mourning. Relatives and friends who were not in Udaipur would also come to condole with the family. They would all be fed and housed in the haveli. Arrangements to feed two hundred guests for the thirteen days had to be made. Even in sorrow, hospitality had to be appropriate. But the immediate problem was to prepare the evening meal for those who had accompanied the body on its last journey.

The maids peeled vegetables in the verandah; relatives kneaded the dough in the courtyard; the cook carried large utensils into the kitchen. Pari weighed the wheat and dal to be ground for the days ahead. But there was no confusion. Silently everyone went about their allotted work.

This was not the first death that the family mourned. In the courtyards for three hundred years, birth, marriage and death ceremonies had been performed. The walls of the haveli had remained firm while they absorbed the echoes of joy and the wails of death. For seventy years Sangram Singhji's wife had walked in the corridors of Jeewan Niwas as the trustee of the family traditions. She had lived always in the shadow of her husband's ancestors. While she carried on her duties, she had at the same time carefully instructed her daughter-in-law in the rituals and customs of the haveli. That was the only way to ensure the continuity of family traditions. Therefore, even though Sangram Singhji's wife was not there to light the wick of the little earthen saucer, its tiny flame flickered as always in front of the family deity.

Bhagwat Singhji was the first to enter the women's courtyard when the mourners returned. His head clean shaven, he stood at the door of the prayer room. His face was grave as he reverently touched the floor with his forehead. He stood for a moment in front of the smiling image of the goddess of fortune and then walked away.

Even before the sun went down the leaf plates pinned together with little twigs were laid in the courtyard. The food was ready to be served. The women sat down without any fuss. It was the custom to eat at the house of the dead. They spoke to one another in subdued tones. There was no joy, no sparkle in their voices.

The two parts of the haveli mourned the death separately. There was no wailing in the men's side of the haveli. The visitors came in quietly; they sat down in the big hall which had been cleared of all the furniture; a white sheet had been spread to cover the floor. At least one member of Sangram Singhji's family was always there to receive the rich and the poor, the great and the humble, who came to express their sympathy. Whatever their status, members of the family would get up to receive and say farewell to the guest.

Sometimes not a word would be said—their visit conveyed the sense of shared grief.

The women's courtyard was never quiet. The wailing women came and went till the evening shadows fell on the courtyard. Then an uncertain quiet spread over the huge sprawling haveli. In spite of all the relatives, an air of emptiness hung over it that nothing seemed to fill.

Chapter VIII

IT WAS THE sixth day after Bhabha Sa's death. Lakshmi had worked hard with her heart in her work. No one had to tell her anything. She was everywhere. But while she worked, she remembered the feel of the soft silk blouse. Each time she thought of it, electric waves seemed to pass through her body, giving it new energy to sweep and clean. It was after the women had eaten their evening meal that Lakshmi went out of the courtyard to rest a while in her room. As she went down the stairs and put her foot on the ground, a familiar voice said almost in a whisper, 'Take this, it is for you.' Heeralal, who was standing near the car, took out a package from inside his coat and threw it in the girl's hands.

Laskhmi could not stop. There were men on the verandah and on the open terrace in front of it. Once safely in her room where Sita was sleeping soundly, she tore open the newspaper, her heart beating faster and faster. But this time her body was covered with perspiration. There was no thrill, no joy as she looked at the light pink sari. The cloth she held in her hand seemed unclean. She threw it on the ground and stamped on it. Then she quickly lowered the trunk and opened the one below. She picked up the sari with the tips of her fingers as if she did not want to soil her hands and threw it in. Lakshmi moved rapidly as if a new force had entered her body. She put the trunk back, picked up the sleeping child and walked out of the room, her shoulders thrown back in indignation.

The courtyard was full; some women talked, others slept. They were tired, for wailing was more exhausting than crying. Lakshmi spread her mat on the verandah floor and lay down next to the other maids.

'What shall I do now?' she thought. 'No one will believe I am innocent. "Why did you hide the blouse? Why didn't you tell us then?" they will ask. "We know you, lazy good-for-nothing; it's all your fault. You are a bad woman. We know how you like the good things of life." If only I had torn that blouse into shreds and then taken the pieces to the mistress, she would have believed me. But now it's too late. No one will believe I did nothing wrong.'

Lakshmi lay awake, thinking. Her throat seemed parched and she felt sick in the stomach. The maids around her snored and she longed for their peace of mind.

'What have I done to deserve this?' she kept repeating to herself while the rest of the haveli slept.

It was the thirteenth day after Bhabha Sa's death. The professional cooks had installed themselves in the backyard, dug a fireplace in the ground for the large utensils to rest on. Tins of oil and drums of wheat and cans of rice stood open before them. The little hired helpers had already cut and peeled the vegetables. This was the last feast in honour of the dead. The whole community, friends of the family and their servants were to be fed on this final day of mourning.

It was late in the afternoon when the last group of women

and children sat down to eat. Lakshmi swept the floors and washed the utensils in the kitchen, as the relays of women poured into the courtyard for the morning meal. She worked faster than any of the other maids. It kept her from feeling giddy.

'Lakshmi, go up to the little terrace,' said Pari tenderly as Lakshmi picked up the broom to sweep the courtyard once again. 'Go and rest a little and nurse your child in peace. You have worked so hard, Bhabha Sa's spirit will bless you.'

Lakshmi picked up Sita who lay sleeping in the verandah, crossed the courtyard and went behind the store-room where the staircase led to the little secluded terrace on the far side of the inner courtyard. The narrow staircase was common to the two sections of the haveli. Once on the landing she walked with quick steps to the side of the terrace that had a high wall. The fresh air soothed her aching head but the dull throbbing pain in her heart continued. Lakshmi sat down, leaning against the parapet wall. She put Sita across her lap to nurse her. Just as she was about to lift her blouse, something fell before her. 'This is special halva, you will like it,' said Heeralal, thrusting his head out of the open door and quickly withdrawing. Lakshmi looked stunned as if she had been struck by a rod on the head. Her eyes dilated with terror. She clutched the child in her lap till it cried out in pain. The cries of the child brought her back to the reality of the packet on the ground. She got up, picked up the packet and threw it behind the old earthenware pots and rushed down as if she were being pursued by a thief.

The women and children had finished eating. They were already taking leave of Bhagwat Singhji's wife. Lakshmi put Sita down on the floor and mechanically gathered up the dirty leaf plates and cups, and stacked them outside the courtyard.

By evening the haveli was quiet. There was little activity

in the courtyard. The last thirteen days had been emotionally and physically exhausting for everyone. As soon as the courtyard was swept, the maids spread their mats on the verandah and lay down. Lakshmi continued polishing the silver thalis.

'Before anyone gets up, I will go up and throw the halva to the dogs. Then I will tell the mistress what a rascal, a thief, she has in the haveli—a man who will take the honour of women—who does he take me to be? A cheap street woman, that he throws presents at me. I will show them the blouse and the sari and I will see that he is dismissed.' Then something blocked her thoughts; a long, hopeless sigh escaped her. 'Who will believe me? No one, just no one, not even the young mistress.'

'Leave all the polishing for tomorrow, Lakshmi,' said Bhagwat Singhji's wife coming out of the kitchen. 'Go and sleep. You have worked hard all these days, very hard. For the next few days take rest; or you won't have enough milk for the child.'

The maids were already asleep in the verandah. Lakshmi lay down with Sita beside them and closed her eyes.

Before it was dawn, Lakshmi crept out of the courtyard and went up the stairs on to the terrace. There was a certain calm within her. But then as she stood before the pots her heart stopped beating. The packet was not there. Instead, an army of ants were busily carrying away bits of crumbs that were left behind. She stood dazed for a second and then, as if she were sleep-walking, she retraced her steps back to the verandah and lay down beside her sleeping child.

The day broke as usual, but the haveli did not seem to come to life. The thirteen days of mourning were over. Now there was no urgency. The maids got up leisurely. The mistress herself was tired. Even she got up later than usual. Instead of going to the kitchen, she sat outside her room while one of the servants' children pressed her back and another massaged her feet.

Ganga and Champa sat lazily in the little dark room along the verandah, in which Pari kept her clothes, where the brooms, the baskets and the stone grinder were also kept.

'Look, Ganga, what I found on the terrace behind the pots last night,' said Champa in a quivering voice, taking out the packet of halva from behind the stone grinder. Then, as if her being on that particular terrace needed to be explained she added quickly: 'I went up to hang Kanwarani Sa's skirt to dry on that terrace. It gets the last rays of the sun. As I stretched out my hands, I stumbled against the pots and what do I see: a neatly tied up packet of this expensive halva. I did not dare tell anyone. Ganga, you had gone to help Manji Bua Sa in her haveli, so I hid it behind the grinder and waited till I was alone with you.'

'How on earth did this get up there?' chuckled Ganga, her eyes narrowing to examine the sweet. 'None of us can afford to buy this halva and then to hide it behind broken pots; this is all very mysterious.'

'I know nothing more. Now don't involve me in all this. I just found it there and took the packet so that no one else would find it,' replied Champa in a dry, hurt voice.

'Did I say you knew how it got up there? Stop pretending. This is a serious matter and you know that. The packet did not walk up to the terrace. That is sure,' said Ganga with a sense of importance. 'Wrap it up before anyone else comes in and put it behind the grinder again.'

But before Champa could do so, another maid burst into the room. 'Ganga, are you going back to sleep?' she asked looking into the room through the half-open door.

'What do you want? Can't you leave me alone?' said Ganga in an irritated voice. 'Once in my life I am allowed to rest and the whole haveli seems to be asking "Where is Ganga? Where is Ganga?"'

The maid came in and quietly shut the door behind her. She was surprised to see Champa there. She looked at both of them and asked with a twinkle in her eyes, 'What were you two girls whispering about? Why are you looking so agitated, Champa? Has your husband run away with someone?' she said jokingly.

'Stop fooling, you, too, would be agitated if you knew what I know. I will tell you later,' said Champa, giving a side glance to Ganga.

'Come out with your secret, Champa. When did you get so secretive? Everyone knows you are the greatest gossip amongst us and can't keep anything in your stomach for long,' laughed the young maid.

'Don't be silly. Look at this and then let me see you giggle,' said Champa, opening her palm with bits of halva stuck to her perspiring hand and thrusting it in front of the girl.

All three were silent for a moment. Then Ganga got up, dusted her skirt, and said in a conspiratorial voice, 'If you want my advice, keep your mouths shut. I know someone is in for trouble. I just hope it is not one of us.'

Lakshmi saw the three maids come out. The way they glanced at her and looked the other way she knew that they had discovered the halva. She lowered her head and continued polishing the cooking utensils with ash to bring out the shine.

'What were you girls whispering about in that room, leaving me alone? Even your children have not come up today,' moaned Pari, sitting scratching her head in the verandah. 'These days Dhapu never comes down from Binniji's room. She is always with the baby. Kanwarani Sa is with the accountant and here I am sitting all alone while you girls gossip inside.'

The maids, with solemn faces, came and sat down with Pari. Bhatianiji, who sat outside her dead mistress's room, came and joined them.

'Everything seems different now,' said Bhatianiji, her tiny eyes filling up. 'There is no one left to shout at me. No one to tell me what happened fifty years ago.'

'Yes, Bai, look at us all. Do you think even I would have dared to sit and talk at this time of the day had Bhabha Sa been still with us?' said Pari with a long sigh.

'I will soon join her. I have nothing left to do,' said Bhatianiji, with a tinge of self-pity.

Bhagwat Singhji's wife, the new mistress of the house, came out of her room and joined the maids. She, too, was lost without Bhahba Sa. There was no one now to make impossible demands on her. She found her freedom irksome.

As they talked, they seemed to have forgotten the day's routine of getting the vegetables cut, the rice and ghee taken out of the storeroom. The sun was already streaming into the verandahs. But no one was in a hurry to start. It was only when Khyali, the cook, came in with a tray of uncut vegetables they suddenly realized that the log in the kitchen fire had been burning without anything on its flame to cook. Bhagwat Singhji's wife gave hurried orders to the cook and selected the vegetables to be cleaned and cut.

Just as the maids started to peel the potatoes, they heard the screams of Gangaram and their hands froze with fear.

'Where is that rotten woman? Let me catch her! I will kill her! I will wring her neck till she chokes to death.'

The maids got up petrified. Bhagwat Singhji's wife stood up as if someone had struck her. Gangaram stood breathing heavily, looking around wildly. Then as he saw Lakshmi, he ran across the yard and caught her by the neck. She was quick and wriggled out of his grip and ran towards the mistress.

'Do not let her touch you, Hukkum. She is dirty,' said Gangaram as he spun around and faced the women. 'Ask her, who gave her this and this. Ask her! She is worse than a street woman,' he said, flinging the blouse and the sari on the ground. His red eyes like fire balls bulged over his long crooked nose. He raised his hand high, but before he could touch Lakshmi, the quiet but commanding voice of the mistress came.

'Leave my maid alone. Get out of here. Who are you to talk to her in this fashion in front of me? I have brought her up. How dare you raise your hand in my presence? Did I marry her to you that you treat her like this? Remember, she is your wife.'

Gangaram's hand fell limp to his side as if someone had hit him on the head, but his body trembled with anger.

'Keep her, Hukkum. I will never see her face again. The children are running around gathering the crumbs of the halva that your trusted maid threw away. Ask her who gave her the halva, the blouse, the sari.' Gangaram's voice was thick, but before he could continue the mistress said with authority: 'Not one more word from you. Leave my presence.'

The cook came from the kitchen and dragged Gangaram out of the courtyard.

Lakshmi had been pushed inside the tiny store-room and Pari stood guard outside. Once there was quiet, the mistress opened the door. Lakshmi sat with her head buried in her knees, sobbing, speechless and helpless.

'Get up and wash your face. Do not leave the haveli for a single second,' said the mistress, lifting Lakshmi gently.

The rest of the day passed. There was an oppressive gloom in the courtyard. The maids worked silently; no one spoke.

Everyone felt relieved when the dark night covered the haveli courtyard.

Bhagwat Singhji's wife took Pari aside and said in confidence: 'Tomorrow, Pariji, you talk to the girl. Someone has been taking liberties with her, poor thing. After all, she is still only a child. It is natural for her to get tempted. It is not her fault. Men are men. They take advantage of the innocent. No wonder Bhabha Sa disapproved of bright clothes and jewellery for young girls. It is my fault. I have neglected Lakshmi. From now on I will be more vigilant,' said the mistress.

'Do not worry, Hukkum. Tomorrow I will sort everything out. Who could have dared to do this when I am here keeping my eyes and ears open twenty-four hours a day?'

It was a dark still night. The jackals howled and the dogs barked. Lakshmi lay awake on the verandah. She heard her husband's accusing voice, 'You are a cheap street woman. I never want to see your face again. You are a street woman.' Her lips tightened and her body burned with rage. The barking of the dogs sounded like thunder in her ears. She thought they would never stop. Then as the night grew more black, the dogs became silent. She knew it was the dead of night and even Gokul, the master's servant, would be asleep. She smiled defiantly and with steady hands she took off her anklets, tied her skirt tighter round her waist and got up. As she tiptoed out of the courtyard, the snores of the sleeping women faded out of her hearing.

Chapter IX

IN THE MORNING Ganga discovered Sita lying all alone where her mother had slept. The baby sucked her fingers and kicked her tiny legs. Before the child cried from hunger, Ganga picked her up thinking that Lakshmi had gone down to wash before Sita woke up. Ganga knocked at Lakshmi's quarter and getting no response, went behind the servants' quarter to the wash-room of the servants. She was not there and no one had seen her in the morning. Sita began crying from hunger; Ganga decided the first thing to do was to feed her. She had no difficulty in finding a woman who could nurse the child.

Ganga left Sita with the woman and went upstairs. The maids were up. Dhapu slept upstairs in Vijay's room. The morning routine of getting bathed and ready had kept everyone busy. Lakshmi was not missed, she like the others was assumed to be changing. Ganga went up to Geeta's apartment. She had a vague fear about Lakshmi. She did not want to alarm the younger maids about not finding Lakshmi in the servants' quarters.

Dhapu sat with Vijay in her lap massaging her body before her bath.

'Bai,' Ganga said sitting down beside her, 'Lakshmi is not in her room, nor in the wash-room.' Her face was serious and her voice had lost its usual playfulness.

'Where is Sita?' asked Dhapu putting Vijay in her crib.

'I left her to be nursed with Gokulji's daughter.'

Dhapu picked up Vijay and left her with Geeta saying she would be back soon. The two maids came downstairs without saying a word. As soon as they came into the courtyard, they realized that Lakshmi's absence was a serious matter of concern for Pari and the others.

'Where could she have gone on such a dark night?' asked Dhapu breaking the ominous silence. 'She must be hiding from Gangaram.'

Pari sat with her head in her hands and in a tearful voice said, 'No, Lakshmi has gone. She is not hiding, Dhapu, it is all my fault. The way she worked from morning to night, I should have known that something weighed heavily on her heart. I should have talked to her and drawn the poison out of her; instead I admired her and thought being a mother had made her mature.'

'But why did she leave?' Dhapu insisted. 'Bhabha Sa always said bad temper was a person's worst enemy and she was right.'

The other maids stood behind the pillars, sniffing and wiping their noses with the ends of their saris. They all felt guilty in some way.

'What is all this crying for? One would think Lakshmi was dead. Parijiji, even you, with all your experience, are sitting there shedding tears. Is this the time to do that?' said the mistress, trying to keep her voice steady.

'Kanwarani Sa, in times of trouble it is men that count. Women are good only at shedding tears,' said the cook coming out of the kitchen, shaking his forefinger reprovingly at Pari.

'You are right, Khyali,' said the mistress gratefully.

'Kanwarani Sa, I will go to Arjun, the fortune teller. He is the one who found the thief when Dhapu's gold bangle disappeared.'

'I forgot all about Arjun, the fortune teller. Of course, he is the man who will know where Lakshmi is. But Khyali, go first to my brother's haveli. There is an aunt of hers who lives in the little gully that runs parallel to his house. In the night, where else could the poor girl have gone but there?'

'Hukkum,' replied the cook unconvinced that this was a good idea.

'Parijiji, you go with Khyali. It will help. Tell the girl I am waiting for her, that she has nothing to fear and that her child is crying. Tell her what you like but bring her back.'

'Hukkum.'

Pari got up, the cook washed his hands under the kitchen tap. He left instructions about the dal on the fire. Then both of them went out through the back door.

They walked silently. The streets were still quiet; even the vegetable sellers and vendors had not started their morning rounds. The two walked fast. They didn't want to meet people. This was not the time for Pari to be out except on urgent business. But, nevertheless, there were people on the streets.

A man shouted from the sidewalk, 'Khyali, what brings you out so early? I hope all is well in the haveli.'

'With God's grace, everything is well in the haveli,' replied the cook coolly and walked on.

'Parijiji,' said a woman known to the haveli with a water pitcher on her head, 'what are you doing in Surajipole at this time?'

'I am taking medicine to Kanwarani Sa's brother who,

you know, is ill,' replied Pari without a moment's hesitation.

The woman nodded and went on her way.

The cook and Pari began walking faster. They turned into a little gully with a row of thatched mud houses.

'This is the house,' said Pari, pointing to a broken-down wall. Then she adjusted her sari. She stopped and cleared her throat before shouting, 'Kaluji's wife, are you there?' Pari lifted the sari from her face as she stood in front of the hut.

There was a bustle inside. A woman hurriedly came out of the door and said, 'Jiji, how fortunate I am to see your face first thing in the morning. Come in, Jiji. The house needs repairs but my husband is away in the village. What can a woman do alone?' she said nervously to cover up her surprise at seeing Pari. Khyali sat down on a stone slab out of view of the two women.

'You are right. A woman cannot do anything alone,' said Pari in a flat voice.

'Jiji, let me make you a cup of tea.'

'No, no,' said Pari impatiently, fumbling with her sari. After a brief pause during which she mastered her agitation, she asked politely, 'Kaluji's wife, did Lakshmi come here by any chance?'

'Yes, Jiji, she came in the dead of night. I was fast asleep. She said her great aunt was ill in the village and she had to catch the first bus. But now that I think of it, there is no bus that goes from here. I got up specially early to make a cup of tea for her but she had left.'

She moved nearer to Pari. 'Jiji, is there some trouble?' asked Kaluji's wife.

'No, of course not. Lakshmi wanted to see you before going to the village. Poor girl, she must have forgotten that buses do not run from here. I must be on my way,' said Pari abruptly and started to walk on. Khyali got up, seeing Pari leave, and joined her.

'I told you, only Arjun will know,' said Khyali with a proud grin. He turned back and took the road to Hathipole, the southern gate of the city, and entered a gully on either side of which were little brick houses with cows and buffaloes tied in the yard close by. The street was slushy and smelly. For Pari the stench of decaying hay was overpowering. She had forgotten what it was like to live in dirty, damp surroundings.

'There is Arjun the bhopa's hut,' said Khyali in a low voice. 'Follow me, do not say a word, just sit and listen.'

Arjun's oily hair was parted and fell in unstudied strands on the sides. His eyes were large and looked as if they might warm up with the right persuasion. He sat on his haunches on the ground outside the hut smoking a hukka. Cows and three calves were tied in front of his half-mud half-brick hut. Khyali jumped over the puddles of cow dung and urine and stood with folded hands in front of him.

'Come and sit down. I can tell something is wrong in the haveli,' pronounced Arjun gravely as he saw Khyali approach him. Pari sat down in a corner and pulled her sari even lower over her face.

Khyali, hands still folded, replied respectfully, 'Last night one of the maids left the haveli, Bhopaji.'

'Yes, I know,' he said prophetically and continued to draw on his hukka in silence; his dark eyes had an opaque look.

Khyali took out a five rupee note and put it at the feet of the bhopa. As if there was magic in the paper note, Arjun put his hukka down, crossed one thin leg over the other and closed his eyes. His face was strained as if he were trying to pour all his energy of mind and body to see better what was happening in this world. After a few seconds his body became stiff as if it had been cast in stone. Then, as if a top had burst inside, he began quivering and moaning. His body contracted into weird shapes. Then just as suddenly as he had started to shake, he became calm. He panted heavily, his eyes became dilated and his lips started moving but no sound came. He was in a trance—in another world, as if he were trying to gauge what lay in the future. That was the moment to ask questions.

'Bhopaji, where is Lakshmi?' asked the cook reverently.

'She is in the city.'

'With whom is she staying? In which gully?'

'Yes, I can see her smile; she is in a room with no windows. The house leaks; it is dark inside. Now I can see her better.' The bhopa blinked and groaned. 'Yes, she is all right. No harm has come to her.' Then the bhopa was silent.

The bhopa began grunting and whining alternately as if the clarity he had achieved did not satisfy him. Then suddenly as if to wake up the spirit within him he began beating himself, first his chest, then his bare thighs. Then again he was calm and in an unnaturally thin voice said, 'She is in the third or fourth house next to the Jagdish temple in the row where the cobblers live. The planet Saturn has cast its spell on her, but she will return to the haveli; yes I can see her temper is already subsiding.'

The cook and Pari touched the ground with their foreheads before sitting up. They shook their folded hands several times in front of the bhopa, who sat stiff like a statue, and left.

'Next to the Jagdish temple, in the gully where the cobblers live,' repeated the cook, impressed by the powers of Arjun and satisfied with the information.

Pari, engrossed in thought, walked briskly behind the

cook. They took the short cut to the temple. The cobblers lived in a row of houses behind the temple.

'You stand here, Parijiji. I will go and see which house it is,' said the cook wiping the perspiration off his forehead.

He had walked on only a few yards when Pari saw a man stop him. 'Khyali, how are you? It is a long time since I saw you,' said the man tapping Khyali on the shoulders.

'You know, Jeewan Niwas has been in mourning,' replied the cook sternly.

'I am sorry, I forgot. Are you looking for someone? Can I help?'

'Yes,' replied the cook in a tight cold voice.

'Are you by chance looking for Lakshmi? I saw her this morning; you know I open my shop early.'

The cook smiled, he lost his aggressive manner and this encouraged the man to continue talking.

'I saw her going into that house with a broken wall,' he said pointing to the left. 'It belongs to Hari, the betelnut seller,' said the man and grinned, as if he wanted to crack a joke. But seeing Khyali's face he restrained himself.

'Yes, of course, she went to return some money she had borrowed from the rascal,' the cook said casually. The man walked away, and Khyali beckoned to Pari to follow him.

'She is in Hari the panwala's house, not in the cobblers' gully,' said the cook in a loud whisper, and turned into one of the side alleys behind the temple. As soon as he came to the brick house, he straightened himself, cleared his throat and then shouted loudly, 'Is anyone in?'

A thin man wrapped in a loincloth came out. His brows were tightly knit together. As soon as he saw the cook, he threw back his shoulders and looked defiantly into Khyali's eyes.

'You are Hari, the panwala?' asked Khyali accusingly.

'Yes, I am. What do you want?'

'Where is Lakshmi?'

'How do I know! A woman came this morning and rented a room from me. That is all I know. I am not a man who asks questions; everyone in the gully knows I have two extra rooms to rent. How else do you think I feed a wife and eight children?'

Khyali took a step forward as if he were going to strike the man for being insolent, but he stopped as he saw a woman coming to the door. It was Lakshmi. She stood before them, her hands on her hips, and her face uncovered.

'What do you want?' asked Lakshmi defiantly. Her eyes were red and swollen.

'Come home, Kanwarani Sa is waiting for you. The whole haveli is weeping,' said Pari in a tearful voice, rushing to the door.

'Jiji, go away, I will not come back. Never! I will starve but never return to the haveli. Do you think I am an orphan that has no home? Well, you will see that I am not. I will show my husband that I am no street woman either. Go back to the mistress and tell her Heeralal is a thief, a rascal, a scoundrel. Just go and tell her that and leave me alone.' Then, as Lakshmi paused to take breath, Pari took advantage of the pause.

'Lakshmi, Gangaramji was wrong in calling you names, you know he has a bad temper, but you cannot leave your home and your child,' Pari pleaded.

'I don't want any advice. I know you all. For the rest of my life you will poke your fingers at me and say, "That bad charactered woman. She enticed Heeralal to give her gifts. She would do anything for a sari". I know your sweet words now don't mean anything. Have you all not acccused me before for being frivolous and untrustworthy? No, I will never, never return to the haveli to be taunted and jeered at by all the servants and their children for the rest of my life.

No, never.' Lakshmi's voice was sharp and contemptuous. 'Go away, Jiji. You and Khyaliji both of you go away or I will shut the door right in your face,' Lakshmi screamed, and moved threateningly towards the door.

'Listen to me, Lakshmi. I have brought you up, even slapped you, when you were naughty, but you didn't run away. Every husband has a right to scold his wife, even beat her if necessary, but it does not mean a woman runs away from her husband. Listen to me, Lakshmi,' Pari pleaded almost beggingly.

'I have told you I don't want your advice. I know what it's worth. Now go or I will shut the door. I warn you, Jiji, leave me alone.' Lakshmi's voice wavered. Even as she shouted, her eyes were filling up with tears.

'Your child is crying for milk. Have you thought of her? She will die without a mother,' said Pari, sobbing.

'Let the child starve to death. That will teach her father to control his long, poisonous tongue,' shouted back Lakshmi, brushing aside the tears defiantly from her cheeks. And then she banged the door in Pari's face.

'What a woman,' said Pari obviously shaken. She stared at the door, but moved away finally, a little unsteady on her feet.

In the haveli the maids sat with the mistress in her room trying to while away the time till the cook and Pari returned. They got up the minute the outside door rattled.

Pari walked in, her head drooping. The cook who followed her had lost his confident smile.

'Forget that girl, Hukkum. The devil has taken possession of her,' Pari said bitterly.

'You saw her? You talked to her?' the mistress asked eagerly.

'The bhopa was wrong. Lakshmi will never return. She is

staying with Hari, the panwala. She has taken a room there,' said Pari. 'I never liked his wife. She is good for nothing, a bad influence,' Pari added thoughtfully.

'What did Lakshmi say?' the mistress asked dismissing Pari's remarks on the panwala's wife.

'She said, "Let my child starve, let her die, but I will not return to the haveli".' Pari sat on the floor and putting her head between her knees she sobbed loudly.

The maids scattered in various directions, gagging their sobs with their saris. The mistress went into the kitchen. Nothing more was said about Lakshmi.

SECTION II

Chapter I

FIVE MORE WINTERS had been added to the three hundred years of Jeewan Niwas. The whitewashed walls were a little more yellow; the mildew a little more widespread over the lime plaster, the iron gate had begun to corrode with moisture. But the haveli stood firm as if good for another hundred years. Inside the haveli life had changed. In these years Sangram Singhji had died; Bhatianiji had been carried to the cremation ground a few months after the death of her mistress. Pari complained a little more of pains and aches, but her voice was firm as ever and her authority remained unchallenged. Dhapu had transferred her attention to Vikram, the baby who was born three months after the death of his great grandfather. There were no celebrations this time. The family goddess had been quietly worshipped.

Bhagwat Singhji's wife had not forgotten Lakshmi. In the beginning, she did all she could to kill the gossip that women shared with her under the pretext of being concerned. First she hid the truth by telling everyone that Lakshmi had unexpectedly been called by her brother who needed her help because his wife was seriously ill. But she was not able to convince anyone. The news had quickly spread through the bazaar that Lakshmi had run away from the haveli. Some said she had fled because the mistress had beaten her for stealing a silver cup. But no one outside the haveli knew the real reason. The servants of Jeewan Niwas refused to talk. This aggravated the inquisitive women who tried every means to penetrate the secret. When Lakshmi was not seen around in the gullies, it was rumoured that she had committed suicide by jumping into a well. There were others who said that she had run away with the peddler of old clothes who every three months went to the haveli to buy old newspapers and whatever else he could get.

But even after five years Bhagwat Singhji's wife never tired of hoping that one day Lakshmi would come back to the haveli. Every two months she would send Pari or Khyali to get news of her whereabouts. After a time Khyali resented this futile effort on the part of the mistress and even hinted to her that Lakshmi was leading a life that was not honourable. But Bhagwat Singhji's wife never believed him. She had heard that Lakshmi had gone away to her village but, not being able to face the anger of her relatives, had come back to the city. Lakshmi's brother had refused to keep his sister fearing that it would annoy the elders of his family. No one in his family understood Lakshmi's behaviour. To them it was natural that a husband scold his wife. In fact, they were sure that once she knew that no one was on her side, she would return to the haveli. But they were proved wrong. Once Lakshmi knew she was not welcome in her brother's home she had returned to Udaipur. She had moved from Hari, the panwala's house, to work as a servant in the house of a tailor in the city. When she was recognized by someone known to the haveli in the bazaar she would turn her back and refuse to talk to them. But Bhagwat Singhji's wife was satisfied to hear that she was in Udaipur and seen from time to time. She secretly hoped that Lakshmi would regret the day she foolishly left the haveli and that she would come back to her, if not to her husband.

Five years had passed since Lakshmi had left the haveli. Geeta felt more at ease. She could now admire the graceful movements of the women without feeling clumsy herself. But she had made no friends. The daughters and daughters-in-law of her age in the other havelis were no companions to her. With all their bashful glances and their timid ways she found them shrewd and calculating. They never expressed an opinion and never revealed their feelings. They seemed like little canaries in a cage who sang and twittered but seemed to know no passion. Their large eyes full of yearning and longing looked dreamily on the world beyond from behind their veils. Though young, some unknown fear seemed to have eaten away their natural exuberance. They followed the traditions of their families at the bidding of their elders, but they lacked the same faith or commitment to it. It seemed to Geeta that they were waiting for the day when they would be freed from their confinement. But on the surface they showed no dissatisfaction. In fact, Geeta longed to feel their placid acceptance of life.

Bhagwat Singhji's wife complained that she no longer had the energy to manage the household but she continued to supervise every detail. She was still the first to be up in the morning and the last to go to bed. It was she who coaxed Vijay and her brother Vikram to eat, and it was she who received women from the havelis.

In spite of herself, Geeta, too, had changed. She had lost much of her girlish impetuousity; her temper was more subdued. She had gradually forgotten her own carefree girlhood, in which there had been uninhibited laughter and freedom. Though she still kept a little apart, Geeta had become more and more involved in the routine of the household; she accepted the discipline of the haveli without protest. But there were many times when she felt the crushing weight of the walls that shut off the outside world. The chatter of the maids, the gossip that floated into the courtyard, were amusing distractions, but not sufficient to be really satisfying.

The house was unusually quiet. The mistress of the house had gone to spend a few days with her brother's family and Bhagwat Singhji and his son were on business out of town. The courtyard was bathed in the soft yellow light of a wintry moon. The maids huddled in the courtyard verandah around a twig fire lit in a broken earthenware pot.

Geeta sat on a mat, a shawl wrapped round her shoulders; her hands were spread over the crackling twigs. She stared at the little flames that erupted each time a twig was added to the fire. The flames lit her face but her eyes were remote as if she was somewhere else, and there was a weariness in her expression.

'Binniji, it will not be long before it is midnight,' said Pari concealing a yawn. 'If Kanwarani Sa were here, then you could have gone to bed. But on the night of the full moon Lakshmi the goddess of wealth, the giver of all, must be worshipped,' said Pari in a low earnest voice.

Geeta nodded her head and pulled the slipping shawl around her shoulders.

'It is not the same without Kanwarani Sa,' said Dhapu gloomily. 'If she were here, do you think we would be all gazing at the flames? We would have been talking and laughing; not even a child would have slept.'

'Binniji is different,' said Pari. 'She is educated; she has other things to occupy her. Gossip is for those like us who cannot read or write.' There was a slight trace of sarcasm in her voice.

'Dhapu is right, Parijiji,' said Geeta ignoring her remarks. 'Without Bhabhi the haveli seems quite empty. How much longer will she be away?'

'The midwife came in the afternoon and said your uncle-in-law was not well. Kanwarani Sa will have to stay at least two or three days more,' replied Pari and took out her snuff box.

It wasn't until the barking of the dogs had died and even the jackals were silent, that Ganga got up and woke the women who had fallen asleep in the verandah. The time had come for lighting the wick that illuminated the face of the smiling goddess.

The sleepy eyed women walked drowsily to the little prayer room where the image of the goddess of wealth stood buried in flowers, fruits and nuts. The incense sticks on the stand were ready to be lighted.

'Binniji, first put kumkum on the forehead of the goddess,' whispered Dhapu.

'Now put the coconut,' she said after Geeta had followed her directions, 'then the fruits and the sweets at her feet.'

After a pause Dhapu added: 'Now light the sacred lamp.'

Geeta did as she was told. As soon as the silver lamp was lit, the women joined the palms of their hands and sang the hymn of the goddess. The sweet smell of incense filled the tiny room. The worship over, Geeta distributed the consecrated fruits and nuts to the women.

'May you always wear red and live to see your great grandsons,' said Pari in a caressing voice as Geeta bent down to touch her feet before going up to her room.

The two children slept soundly in their room. Sita as usual had curled up near Vijay's bed.

Dhapu who had accompanied Geeta waited till she was in bed, then lay down on the carpet next to the bed.

'Binniji, do you know why Kanwarani Sa is with her brother?' said Dhapu sitting up in a voice full of mystery.

'No, tell me why, that will put me to sleep,' said Geeta with a smile from under the soft silk quilt.

'Well, if you want to know the truth, I will tell you.' Her eager voice showed that she was yearning to talk. 'Gopal Singhji, Kanwarani Sa's brother, is ill but not so seriously that your mother-in-law has to stay with him,' Dhapu started. Her lips smacked as if she were relishing the taste of some hot and spicy food, and then she added: 'You know he is very rich with lands and lots of gold. The wealth has not yet been divided and even the rich have to die, whether they like it or not.' Dhapu paused and took a long breath as if to get renewed strength to continue talking.

Geeta lifted her head, her curiosity aroused.

'He has children, then what has to be worried about?' she asked puzzled.

'Of course, his sons will get the property. Did you think he would divide it among the servants? But it is not all that simple,' replied Dhapu edging up to Geeta's bed. 'You have forgotten that Gopal Singhji has one son from his first wife and two from his second.'

'And two daughters,' added Geeta.

'Daughters do not get property. They were given their share of the gold when they got married. They are no problem,' said Dhapu, dismissing the interruption. 'Now let me go on, or we will never sleep. When Gopal Singhji's first wife fell ill, his wife's sister came to nurse her. She was really wonderful. For a whole month she stayed up nights looking after her ailing sister. I saw her with my own eyes getting thinner and thinner every day.'

'Go on, come to the point. How you love embroidering everything,' said Geeta.

'Don't be impatient.' Then, in a loud whisper, as if what

she was about to reveal was highly confidential, she said, 'You remember how Bhabha Sa never parted with her small tin box, poor thing she didn't have much in it; till the last she had it under her pillow. Well, Gopal Singhji's wife also had a small box in which she, too, kept pieces of jewellery and money. Even when her body was burning with fever, her hands would go under the mattress and feel the box. Well, the night she died; the whole family was at her bedside but when they looked for the box it was not there. It had vanished.'

'Don't tell me that. I have lived here long enough to know that not even a piece of halva can go undetected. And you want me to believe a box full of gold just disappeared. Didn't everyone run to Arjun, the fortune teller?' said Geeta with biting sarcasm.

'There you go again attacking the havelis. Whether you like us or not, it is here that you have to live and the sooner you understand us the better,' said Dhapu with a little giggle. Then as if to calm Geeta she put her hands on the silk quilt, clearing her throat in preparation to reveal the great secret known only to her.

'All right, if you must know, I will tell you,' she said seriously. 'They say that Gopal Singhji's wife's sister stole the box. I am sure she is keeping the ornaments for her sister's only son; how wise of her!'

'Who says she stole the box?' asked Geeta indignantly.

'No one really, but everyone hints that it is the sister. How can one accuse her directly? There is no proof but I have seen the sly looks women give whenever she wears a new piece of jewellery.'

'What a bunch of ungrateful hypocrites you are. Talking always of family love and unity and yet you don't hesitate to call a poor innocent woman a thief. Anyway, what is Bhabhi doing in her brother's haveli?'

'She is not talking any chances this time. She is there to see that everything is divided equally among the three boys, especially the remaining gold of the family. After all, you cannot expect a step-mother to be fair. Kanwarani Sa knows human nature. Her brother is old and she wants everything partitioned while he is still living. Is that hypocrisy, too?' said Dhapu mockingly.

'No, she is quite right. When it comes to gold no one can be trusted,' said Geeta acidly and turned her back to Dhapu.

Chapter II

THE NEXT MORNING Geeta got up earlier than usual. With her mother-in-law away, the responsibility of taking out the daily rations fell on her. As she combed her hair, she heard Champa's loud voice from Vijay's room.

'Get up, Sita, you spoiled child. Who do you think you are? The future mistress of Jeewan Niwas, or what, that you sleep even when Vijay Bai Saheb is up and ready.'

'It is so cold, Bai,' Sita pleaded, snatching the quilt from the maid's hands. 'Just a few minutes more.'

'Get up immediately or I will really give you a slap. What has come over you? Day by day you are getting worse. Soon you will be asking to eat from a silver thali. You are no longer a child. Remember that! Learn to clean and sweep or even the mistress will have no use for you. Just because Vijay Bai Saheb plays with you, don't imagine you are her equal.'

Sita got up, rubbing her eyes, rolled up her bedding, pushed it under Vijay's bed and ran down the stairs. Champa followed her.

Geeta finished dressing and followed them a few minutes

later, to the kitchen. She found that Pari had already taken out the day's rations, sorted the vegetables, measured the oil and the ghee in little cups. When the old maid asked her if what she had taken out was not too much, Geeta's face flushed with embarrassment. Her mother-in-law did not have confidence in her judgement as far as the running of the kitchen was concerned, and this undermined Geeta's confidence. Besides the maids had been in the haveli for much longer than she. Therefore, in the role of the young mistress of the haveli she felt awkward. She was afraid to instruct or dispute with the maids, especially Pari, who knew more about managing the kitchen than she did. Though she had noticed the cook lavishly spreading ghee on the servants' rotis, she did not have the courage to tell him that.

Just as Geeta had finished looking over all the provisions before her on the floor of the kitchen verandah, Vijay came down tightly holding on to Dhapu's hand. She looked neat and tidy in her starched blue and white school uniform. She stood before her mother as if to get her approval.

'Sit down there and drink your milk, or you will again be late for school,' said Dhapu trying to release her hand from Vijay's tight grip.

'I will not sit here. I will drink my milk in the other verandah,' said Vijay defiantly and looked across the courtyard, to where Sita sat huddled trying to keep herself warm.

'Sit down at once and don't make a fuss,' said Geeta firmly.

Vijay was taken aback, no one really spoke to her harshly. She looked up at Dhapu with her large moist eyes.

'If children get on your nerves, leave them to me,' said Dhapu. She picked up Vijay and walked swiftly away from the kitchen. 'Imagine scolding a little child of five for nothing,' the maid muttered as she left.

A thin smile hovered round Geeta's mouth as she sorted out the vegetables. The only chance for Geeta to discipline Vijay was when her mother-in-law was away. But even then the maid pounced on her if she said anything and immediately accused her of being a heartless mother. But in spite of all the indulgence the servants showed to her, Vijay knew the limits to which she could go with her tantrums.

'See what a good girl Bai Saheb is. She has drunk the last drop of milk,' announced Dhapu a few minutes later proudly putting the empty glass in front of the young mistress.

'Stop grinning and go or the car will never reach the station in time for Kanwar Saheb,' said Geeta.

Dhapu quickly gathered her skirt in her hands and rushed to get Vijay. She had forgotten that Bhagwat Singhji was arriving by the morning train from Chittor.

Vijay grabbed Sita's hands and pulled her from behind the pillar where she stood shivering.

'Come to school with me, Sita. It would be such fun if you too went to school, at least come with me to the car,' said Vijay dragging the girl behind her.

'Leave the girl alone, Bai Sa. She already gets into enough trouble because of you,' said Dhapu sharply.

'If I can go to school, why can't Sita?' Vijay insisted petulantly, holding on to Sita's cold hands.

Dhapu took Vijay's hand with force and released Sita from her hold.

Sita went back quietly to her place behind the pillar and sat down with her head buried between her knees.

'Now what are you sulking for? Get up and wash your face. If you go around with matted hair and a running nose,

Vijay Bai Sa won't play with you,' said Champa shaking the girl. But Sita kept on sitting and did not move.

The maids scolded Sita, even slapped her at times, but they loved and cared for her. They hid her in their skirts when Vijay was in a bad temper, to protect her. It was only when Sita was difficult, that they reminded her that she was motherless and ugly and they were not paid to do her work. In spite of seeming harshness they indulged her. They had brought her up since the day Lakshmi had walked out of the haveli and kept a strict eye on her as they did on their own children, never allowing her to play in the streets.

Vijay found Sita a willing slave. She bullied her, pulled her hair, but if ever Sita got into a bad mood, Vijay bribed her with toffees and toys. She preferred her to all the other children of the havelis.

Pari locked the storeroom, then came and sat down in the kitchen. It was nice and warm inside.

'Parijiji, just look at Sita. How stubborn she has become. In spite of my telling her to get up she sits there sulking,' said Champa, trying to pull Sita up by the hand.

'Bai, leave me alone. I do not want to wash my face,' whined the girl and freed her hand from the maid's clasp.

'Do you think I care if you are covered with sores?' Champa snapped back. 'But when lice crawl in your hair and your face itches, don't come crying to me. I am fed up with you.'

'Stop nagging her, Champa. Let the sun grow a little warmer. Then she will get up. Don't you see she is cold?' said Geeta, in a stern voice. She was distracted; her mind was on what Vijay had said as she left for school.

Pari got up to warm her hands over the kitchen fire. Then when she saw Champa leave in a huff and Sita continued to sit where she was, she said, 'Binniji, I know you love Sita but she must not be spoiled. After all, she is only a servant's child and without a mother to care for her. If she gets used to a soft life, she will suffer later on. Besides she must learn to obey us, the maids.'

'I suppose you are right, Parijiji,' said Geeta apologetically.

The sight of the huddled girl seemed to put Pari in a reminiscent mood. With a faraway look in her eyes she said: 'Binniji, I will never forget that day five years ago, I can still hear Kanwar Saheb's deep voice saying, "Get out of my sight, you rascal, Heeralal, you good for nothing", while Heeralal stood trembling before him. "You have betrayed my trust. Heeralal, do you hear me? Get out of this haveli and never again show your face. Did I bring you up from a child that you dared to take the honour of an innocent woman?" Binniji, you would have seen Kanwar Saheb's gentle face swept with anger. He could hardly speak, he was so angry. But Heeralal flung himself at his feet and held them sobbing. "Forgive me, Andata, Giver of Bread", he pleaded. "I meant no harm; you can kill me; you can do what you like with me, but I will never leave the haveli. It is better you throw me to the vultures than dismiss me from your service."'

Pari could say no more. She burst out crying.

Geeta's eyes were also heavy with the unshed tears. She gulped down the lump in her throat.

'What is the good of crying, Jiji?' said Khyali. 'It is all over now. Heeralal is not the same man since that day. He never lifts his eyes when a woman is anywhere near him. He goes about his work quietly; even with us men he keeps a distance,' he said reflectively, stirring the lentils on the fire.

'Yes, Khyali, Heeralal has got his punishment, but what about poor Lakshmi?' sobbed Pari.

'In which world do you women live?' Khyali asked with a

sneer. 'Lakshmi is flourishing. I told you I saw her in Hathipole the other day. I could not recognize her at first. She has grown so fat. When I tried to speak to her, she proudly turned her head away. You should have seen her eyes, seething with hate as she looked at me, but Kanwarani Sa continues not to believe me when I tell her that she will never enter the haveli gates again.'

Geeta only half listened to the servants. Her face was serious and her lips were tightly pressed together. She looked across the courtyard, her eyes resting a while on the curled up bundle of flesh on the verandah. Then she sat up erect as if she no longer could contain her thoughts and said with quiet authority, 'Parijiji, Sita must go to school.'

Pari stared open mouthed at the young mistress as if someone had struck the maid on the head. The cook quickly went inside the kitchen and stirred the dal on the fire.

After the initial shock, Pari pulled herself together and said decisively, 'Binnijiji, Sita is a child of a servant. She cannot go to school.'

Geeta looked at the maid defiantly. Her voice quivered with anger as she said, 'Vijay goes to school and you do not object. Why shouldn't Sita?'

'Vijay Bai Sa, God bless her, is the daughter of this haveli. How dare anyone point a finger at her? She has the protection of wealth and family. What does Sita have? She must be protected from the outside world. Binniji, you do not yet know Udaipur and its customs. Sita has to marry. Leave her to us, the servants. We know what is best for her.' Pari spoke with unusual bluntness.

Geeta felt outraged at the maid's accusation. Her eyes flashed in challenge, but she controlled her natural impulse to answer back.

Seeing Geeta silent, Pari said, 'Binniji, don't be upset; there are other ways of helping Sita. You can give her a big dowry and so help her to get a good husband.' Pari's voice was gentle. Then she added softly, 'Binniji, a girl who has to live in the village must be sturdy. She cannot be pampered. Her limbs must be strong to pull water from the well, to plough the fields, collect the cow dung. As it is, Sita is lazy. You send her to school and she will begin to think she is a little lady.'

'The girl already loves to play with the boys in the streets. Once she has no one to keep her in check, she will be up to all kinds of mischief. Who will be responsible? Not me. I have enough trouble with her as it is, she already thinks I am nobody,' said Champa with a sense of grievance.

Just as Geeta was about to get up, the sound of the horn from the .gate was heard. The maids fled in various directions. The arrival of the master of the haveli was always a sign for the maids to stop talking and get on with their work. The cook took the lentils off the fire and put a big pot of water to boil for the master's bath. There was instant activity in the courtyard.

Geeta straightened her sari and pulled it over her face as Gokulji entered the kitchen verandah.

'Hukkum, Kanwar Sa will be ready for his food in half an hour,' he said to Geeta with deference.

Pari got up. Her limbs seemed no longer stiff. She moved lightly and swiftly taking out the special savouries and pickles from the cupboard.

'Binniji, you rest a little. As long as I have strength you do not have to worry,' Pari said gently, going about her work.

Geeta had been waiting for an excuse to leave the kitchen. She felt tired and her head ached. This was the first time that she had come up against Pari. The encounter had left her drained of energy. She wanted to be left alone but she knew she would have to wait until her father-in-law had eaten before going up to her own room.

She went and lay down in the downstairs living room. The room was cold and there was not the same kind of comfort as she had seen in the men's sitting room. There was also nothing beautiful in it. The painted scenes on the walls were crude.

Geeta stretched her legs out on the thick mattress and closed her eyes. She felt depressed and all of a sudden she felt a great desire to be back in her parents' home. In Bombay, her father was always ready to answer any of his children's questions no matter how busy he was. Then she thought of the day when she got married. How her mother had stood at the door fighting back the tears that clouded her eyes, but had managed to say to Ajay, 'Take good care of my child. She is very precious to us. Do not be impatient with her if you find her too outspoken.' Two big round tears dropped on Geeta's cheeks. The room seemed to suffocate her. She felt trapped in the haveli, with its tradition and its unchanging patterns. She thought of the big gilt-framed portraits in the men's apartments. Six generations of the family looking down on her; each face reflecting the confidence of his lineage.

Geeta said to herself, 'What if I cannot trace my ancestry beyond my grandfather? That is no reason why I should surrender.' She was filled with rebellion and her face stiffened. She was determined not to be crushed by the haveli.

The verandah outside was filled with the sound of women. Sarju, the midwife, had come especially to bring news about Gopal Singhji's health.

Dhapu came into the room, looked at Geeta's sad face and said gently, 'Binniji, do not be so upset.' She sat down on the edge of the mattress before continuing to talk. 'Are you really serious about sending Sita to school? Then I will tell you how to go about it. You should never have blurted out what was in your mind, especially to Parijiji. How often I have cautioned you! But never mind. It is still not too late to get your way.'

Geeta gave her a dry, uninterested smile.

'Binniji, your father-in-law is a big man with a big heart. Suggest it to him. He is afraid of no one. You are fortunate that Kanwarani Sa is not here. After what Lakshmi did, he will not take any risks with her child.'

'How do you think I can get permission from Kanwar Sa when I cannot talk to him?' said Geeta impatiently.

'In the past that has not prevented you from making known your wishes. Do you forget when you wanted to go to your parents' house and Kanwarani Sa refused because it was Diwali? Well then, think who conveyed your wishes to him,' said Dhapu, her eyes sparkling. 'Now listen carefuly. While Kanwar Sa is having his food, I will tell him you want to ask his advice. Then you tell me what is on your mind and I will convey it to him just like the last time. Kanwar Sa will take the right decision. Now smile, no more frowns,' said Dhapu with satisfaction as she and Geeta got up.

Dhapu straightened the sheet over the mattress, pulled the curtains aside and went out of the room with Geeta. Gokul had already announced to the cook that the master was ready to eat.

Bhagwat Singhji came into the women's courtyard. He wore a white starched shirt over loose white pants. His tall, erect body was wrapped in a grey shawl. Geeta stood behind the maids and with them bent low with folded hands and touched the ground in front of him. There was a natural simple elegance in the man that commanded respect. A wonderful calm seemed to radiate from his reserved personality. In his presence people were subdued. There was an aloof reticence in his bearing that did not permit frivolity.

He talked a while to the maids, enquiring about their children, and then went into the women's sitting room. While he talked Dhapu nudged Geeta; she understood that she should go into the adjoining room, and wait there.

Gokul put a small lacquered stool in front of him. Pari sat on the floor at a little distance from him, her sari drawn over her face. Gokul brought in the silver thali and placed it on the stool. Pari looked into the contents of each cup to make sure that the cook had put enough ghee in the vegetables.

'The food is not as good, Hukkum, as when Kanwarani Sa is here to supervise,' said Pari humbly.

'There is too much, Pari. I cannot possibly eat all this,' said Bhagwat Singhji, taking out a cup from the thali and putting it on another stool.

'This is not too much, Hukkum. Binniji has personally seen to the cooking; you must taste a little of everything,' said Pari, putting the cup back in the thali.

'How is Binniji?'

'She is well, Hukkum.'

Bhagwat Singhji ate while Pari talked. She told him about his brother-in-law's health and how things were in other havelis. She told him that the accountant of Jeewan Niwas had had a son. Bhagwat Singhji listened attentively. He depended on Pari to keep him informed about his obligations to other havelis.

'Pari, I hope Binniji does not feel lonely. This is a big house and it can be depressing at times especially for someone like her. This time both her mother-in-law and Ajay are away. I hope you are taking good care of her.' There was deep concern in his voice as he spoke. A great surge of affection flooded Geeta's being as she heard the words from behind the door. She longed to express her feelings of love and appreciation to her father-in-law, but then the old despair damped her emotions. She hated the etiquette that prevented a daughter-in-law from talking freely to her father-in-law. 'Even after seven years I am a stranger to those that are mine, and I will always remain a stranger,' she thought hopelessly.

'No, Pari, I cannot eat another roti. I can no longer digest all this rich food. You forget, I am getting old,' said Bhagwat Singhji with a smile.

Dhapu had come and sat with Geeta after she had helped Khyali in the kitchen. This was the moment to speak. Bhagwat Singhji was about to get up.

'Hukkum, Binniji wants to ask your advice,' said Dhapy in a supplicating voice, dragging herself nearer the half-open door.

Bhagwat Singhji pushed the stool away and waited for the maid to continue.

'Hukkum, Binniji wants to ask you whether Sita should go to school.'

Bhagwat Singhji looked at Pari who sat in front of him with a wooden expression on her face, as if she were not concerned. It was not for her to interfere when family members talked.

Then, after a minute of silence, he leaned forward and said, 'Education is a good thing. I know it is not the custom in Udaipur to send girls to school. People are afraid of marrying educated girls. But times are changing, Pari,' he said, looking at her intently. 'After all, it is better to be in school than play in the streets.' Then, as an afterthought he added, 'We must think this out carefully. It is an important decision to take. We must not do anything in haste,' Bhagwat Singhji said getting up, 'Sita is our responsibility.'

Geeta stood aside until her father-in-law left the courtyard. Her eyes were smarting with the unshed tears of love and gratitude. There was such goodness hidden behind his austere formality.

'What did I tell you?' Dhapu turned to her and triumphantly continued, 'I warned you the first day you came to the haveli, "Never get into an argument with the women in the haveli." We are all mean. The men are generous and understanding. They look beyond our little world. Come now and be happy. I left my ladoo half finished; seeing your sad face, I could not bear to eat it,' she said with a broad grin.

'Bai, but Bhabhi will be furious with me,' said Geeta in a small, timid voice.

'Why should she be furious? You have not stolen gold, have you? She will not be happy, that is for sure. She will immediately think of the extra expense, but don't let that worry you. That is her habit. One cannot change one's nature,' said Dhapu philosophically.

Geeta walked across the courtyard to go to her room not quite convinced with Dhapu's assurances. She also felt apprehensive about Pari and what she would think of her.

The courtyard was quiet. There was no chatter in the verandah. Sarju had left. It was only around Bhagwat Singhji's wife that the maids and their children all clustered.

Chapter III

THE ROOMS IN the haveli were difficult to keep warm. They were either too big and airy or too small, damp and dingy. Geeta had opened the tiny windows in her room to let in the fresh air and the rays of the morning sun. Her eyes fell on a beehive which hung from the corner of the roof. It had become heavier with honey since she last noticed it. The pigeons were cooing from the parapets of the haveli. Women in the street below ambled along with pitchers balanced on their heads. The hawkers arranged their wares in their carts, ready to start their rounds. Geeta stood watching the life below as she absent-mindedly combed her long black hair. The thought that her mother-in-law was not yet back revived her listless spirits. She had decided not to go down to the kitchen. Her presence made little difference as Pari took out the rations and the cook did as he pleased. Then, as she turned away from the window, she heard the defiant voice of Vijay from the next room. Her daughter always made a fuss before putting on her school uniform. The maids were right, she thought, about Sita going to school. It takes two maids to get Vijay ready in the morning. Who will get Sita ready in time?

'I should never have interfered in her life,' Geeta said to herself. 'Sita was happy playing in the courtyard with other children. She would have got married like the daughters of the other maids. Now I have disturbed her life and, above all, my own.'

Geeta was already filled with remorse for having acted impulsively. She recalled Pari's anxious face full of understanding and love as she had said, 'Do not interfere in Sita's life. She does not have a haveli behind her. We must guard her reputation.'

Pari was right, thought Geeta as she stared out of the window. Going to school may give Sita wrong ideas. She may think herself special and this the maids would not put up with. All these years it was they who had seen that Lakshmi's child was covered in the cold night. They had given their share of delicacies to her. They had consoled her when she cried. They had nursed her when she was ill. All this they did because they knew she was one of them. It was because of them that Sita had not known what it was to be without a mother. Whereas Geeta realized she had watched their love and concern with admiration, but like an observer, looking on but not involved in Sita's life. Going to school would change her, and the maids would resent that, and she could not replace their attention or love.

'What a terrible mistake I have made,' said Geeta to herself. The screams from the next room became louder, but Geeta absent-mindedly continued to twist the strands of her hair. She did not hear the door creak open.

'Binniji,' said Champa with deference, 'Pariji says it is time we left for Gopal Singhji's haveli.'

Geeta was instantly brought back to reality. In her daydreaming she had completely forgotten that she had to visit her mother-in-law. She hurriedly plaited her hair, while Champa took out a starched green sari from the cupboard and unfolded it for her.

'Bhabhi, when will Sita go to school?' asked Vijay bursting into the room. Her brother stood beside her smiling. Geeta did not answer her. She continued pleating her sari.

'Bhabhi!' shouted Vijay. 'When will Sita go to school?' When she got no answer, she stamped out of the room in anger.

Geeta found Pari in her usual corner in the kitchen verandah hugging her threadbare shawl around her shoulders. 'May you live in your husband's shadow for a hundred years,' she said when Geeta touched her feet. There was no rancour in her voice, no change of expression in her kind eyes as they looked over Geeta's clothes.

She got up slowly. Her hands trembled a little as she straightened a pleat or two of Geeta's green sari. Then she fondly drew the sari over her young mistress's face. 'Come, let us go now,' she said.

The car moved slowly, the street was narrow and filled with people. Gopal Singhji's haveli was at the far end of the walled city and to go there one had to take the main road that passed through the city bazaar. The busy scene diverted Geeta's thoughts from Sita. She could hear the lusty shouts of a peddler as he pushed his cart and rang a small bell.

'New brass or old. Come before it is too late.'

Heeralal pressed the horn but the man kept going in the middle of the road shouting, 'Bring your broken vessels, change them for new.' The car had to come to a crawl till the man turned into a side street.

At the corner of the gully, the balloon man yelled, 'Come, little ones, poor and rich, come one and all and make your choice. Balloons of all colours. For two annas only. Come. I will not wait forever.'

The streets were a tangle of bicycles, rickshaws, bullock carts, tongas and, of course, pedestrians, each threading his way through the congestion as if everyone else were an intruder.

Geeta's eyes fell on the village women carrying their baskets of vegetables on their heads and their faces uncovered. Tall and slender, their arms covered with lacquered bangles and their legs jingling with silver anklets, they tripped nimbly along, undeterred by the confusion and jostle of the road. Their heavy skirts swayed as they shouted, 'Eight annas a kilo, new onions, just eight annas a kilo. Sweet corn fresh from the field, four annas a kilo. Beans and cauliflower, six annas a kilo.'

In the distance Geeta could also see the pavement barbers shaving customers, cobblers hammering the leather soles of shoes, little boys soliciting passers-by to have their shoes polished.

The car passed the tonga stand where in the midst of puddles of urine the horses munched away of blades of green grass. A bullock cart forced Heeralal to change into a lower gear and stop. The cart-man prodded the ribs of his oxen with a short stick. He called them names, and pulled their tails, but the oxen moved out of the way in their own time.

In the cloth shops there were bright green, red and orange saris fluttering gently as they hung through rings from the ceiling. Men and women sitting on wooden stools outside the shops were bargaining with the shopkeepers.

As the car slowed down Geeta saw the eager faces of shoppers staring at the car, and she envied their freedom. They were free to choose saris from a hundred different shades and designs, but she could select only from the bundle that the accountant brought to the house. Geeta watched some children pushing their way through the crowd around the peanut vendor, and she yearned to join the happy boys and girls.

Heeralal had driven in the streets of Udaipur for thirty years and knew all the hazards of the gullies. He was accustomed to the little children who sat on the edge of the drains and eased themselves and then darted across the street. He was never surprised; and he never lost his patience with the vendors who ignored the horn of the car. He sat relaxed behind the wheel and recognized many of the pedestrians with a nod of his head.

As the car approached the clock tower in the centre of the city, Heeralal pointed to a shop and said it belonged to the haveli goldsmith. Geeta had seen jewellery made by him, but never seen his shop. Further down the street were the little stalls of the silversmiths and money changers. Pyramids of rupees, annas and four anna pieces were neatly arranged in front of them. These stalls were always crowded with visiting villagers coming into town. The village women wore red saris, printed saris and skirts, and the underfed half-naked children clung to their mothers.

The village men stared at the scales that weighed the silver bangles they wanted to buy. The women's faces beamed as they held the bracelets in their hands.

Geeta noticed how the eyes of these women sparkled with joy, whereas the women of the haveli always looked at their gold with greedy eyes. For them their jewels were something to hoard, to think about. They were never satisfied because there was always someone in another haveli who had more than they. Geeta envied the village women who walked proudly away from the shops with little bundles tucked under their arms and the newly purchased bracelets on their wrists.

The scenes in the bazaar were so fascinating that she

wished the drive would go on forever, that time could be suspended so that meeting her in-laws would be indefinitely postponed. Women behind thick walls had none of the exuberance of the women in the streets. They were like dressed-up dolls kept in a glass case for a marionette show.

The car turned abruptly into a narrow gully; the noise of the bazaar faded away. Heeralal changed gears again. There was just room for one car. Even the cyclists had to dismount. The pedestrians walked in single file almost touching the car. The open drains on either side of the street were full of stagnant yellow slush. The continuous row of connected houses behind the drains were in varying degrees of despair. Some had broken doors, others had large patches of peeled-off plaster on the walls. The unpaved road was littered with rubbish that women threw from their windows. Cows roamed carelessly, smelling the rubbish heaps and moved only when the car stopped in front of them.

Geeta was not aware that the traffic had diminished and the car had passed the private temple of Gopal Singhji's haveli. Her mind was still enthralled by the lovely street scenes and her own thoughts when the car came to a gentle halt.

'Binniji, be careful as you walk. Don't trip over the stones,' said Pari opening the door of the car.

The two maids walked on either side of Geeta. No one spoke. Women of the upper classes did not talk in the streets. The three women avoided the little heaps of cow dung that lined the gully. They went round the puddles of urine, holding their noses, to avoid inhaling its odour. The strong offensive smell followed them till they reached the huge carved wooden door of Gopal Singhji's haveli.

In the days of feudal glory, elephants carried their masters through the gate to dismount inside the vast open courtyard.

Now only stray cows and dogs hung around the solid walls. There was a musty smell of decaying hay that came from the cowsheds in the far corner of the courtyard outside. The women entered the haveli from a side gate to avoid walking round the haveli to the main entrance.

The old retainers of the haveli welcomed Geeta and the maids. Pari sat down on the verandah with them, panting a little. She had not the strength to climb the steps leading to the women's apartments.

Geeta entered the bare rectangular room which was full of women, but they talked in hushed voices, so unlike them.

'Gopal Singhji must be seriously ill,' thought Geeta, as she bent down to touch the feet of her mother-in-law who sat with her elder relatives. Geeta sat down next to her and in a whisper asked, 'Bhabhi, how is Mama Sa?'

'He is as well as he can be at his age. The astrologer says the next two days are bad for him. After that the stars combine favourably. We will see,' Bhagwat Singhji's wife said in a grave voice. Then she drew a deep breath and asked, 'How have things been in the haveli? I hope you saw how much ghee was taken out. Khyali cannot be trusted. He will give rotis to anyone who is around if no one is watching. These days no one can afford waste.'

'You are right, Kaki Sa, these days no one can be trusted,' repeated a woman on her other side, nodding her head in agreement. 'You know the other day a thali full of milk sweets just disappeared. But I dared not say a word to the servants. Their heads are swollen; they know we are dependent on them. The days when servants behaved as servants are over. They are so rude and insolent now,' the woman continued in a mournful voice.

Geeta lifted her head, relieved that nothing was seriously wrong with her uncle-in-law. She looked slyly through the muslin sari to see if anyone of her age were nearby. It was difficult to be sure who was who. With their heads bent and their faces covered, everyone looked alike. She wanted to be as far away as possible from her mother-in-law. Geeta knew that by now she must have heard about her confrontation with Pari and it was only a matter of time when she would talk to her. She did not want to be scolded in front of others.

Finally, Geeta recognized a few familiar faces through their thin rainbow-coloured veils and at the first opportunity she shuffled across to them.

'Why did you go and sit with all the elderly women?' said one of the girls, as Geeta joined them.

'What else could I do? My mother-in-law was there,' said Geeta in a low voice.

'At last you have understood our etiquette; remember how you used to jeer at us for not talking to you in the presence of the elders,' said the girl nudging Geeta.

'I wonder when we will be allowed to leave,' said another girl yawning. 'I have been here since early morning and now the children must be back from school. I came here thinking we would leave after half an hour but, as usual, my mother-in-law is enjoying herself talking, so I may as well forget the children.'

'Is Gopal Singhji Mama Sa really ill?' asked Geeta, intrigued that no one talked about his health, and yet it was because of him that they were all there.

'Sh . . . sh . . . you must not ask these awkward questions. Of course he is ill.' She leaned forward a little and smiled.

It did seem a little strange to Geeta to have everyone gather when the patient's condition was not serious. But no one seemed to mind leaving their houses so early in the day to sit chatting. The lady of the house moved among her guests accepting their solace with a sigh.

'When did you come? I did not see you come in. My eyes are getting worse every day.' Geeta heard the heavy monotonous voice of her aunt-in-law, Nandu Bua Sa, behind her. The young girls immediately lowered their heads coyly.

Nandu Bua Sa was Bhagwat Singhji's sister. She was thin and stern looking. Her face bore an expression of chronic disapproval. Her mouth was always caught in a pout and her lips twitched nervously. Her eyes constantly darted around from face to face trying to fathom their meaning. But, at heart, Geeta had learned that she was warm and loving. She had lost her husband only two years earlier. Before she became a widow she was known for her love of jewels and bright colours. Geeta had always felt a little under-dressed in her aunt-in-law's presence. She used to carry her jewels with pride and her satin skirts with an elegance that many half her age were unable to do. Even now her black sari was always starched and ironed.

'Binniji, when will I eat food cooked by your hands?' she said, lifting just a little of Geeta's sari to see her face. Geeta demurely lowered her head.

'Looking at you now child, who could say you were not one of us? You have become a real Rajasthani,' her aunt-in-law said fondly and with pride. 'But why have you become so dark? You were fairer when you came. What troubles you that you look like this? You are the only daughter-in-law and that too with a mother-in-law who is a jewel. What more can one ask for?'

'Yes, everything in the haveli is yours and God has also given you a son and by his grace you will have many more,' said another woman.

'Binniji, come closer,' said Nandu Bua Sa. Her voice dropped to a confidential whisper. 'Is it true that you are sending Sita to school?'

'Who is Binniji to make such decisions?' retorted Bhagwat Singhji's wife. She moved up closer as she said stiffly: 'My husband has been thinking for some time of sending the servants' children to school, even the girls. You know as well as I do that havelis can no longer give employment to the servants' children. Times have changed. It is our duty to prepare them for the future.' She talked rapidly as if to cover up something distasteful. She did not want anyone to think that Geeta had become bold enough to take decisions on her own without consulting her.

'You are right. Who can feed servants and their children today? In the old days the servants were satisfied with lentils and dry rotis, but today they want ghee on their rotis and sugar in their tea. They forget that havelis now have no money,' said a woman, nodding her head in agreement.

Geeta sat with her head bent low as she listened. She felt cold though the room was warm. All these old women shared a common past; they had all tasted—some more, some less—the grandeur of feudal glory. They worshipped the Maharanas of old and were forever living in the past. They never forgot that their prosperity, their havelis, their gold, were all due to their beloved Maharanas, and deeply regretted their eclipse. They had confidence born out of hundreds of years of unbroken tradition. They never faltered or hesitated. If ever in doubt, they consulted the astrologer. Life, with all its suffering, was never unbearable. They shared each other's joys and wept together in sorrow. They were strong and even ruthless when it came to upholding family customs and ties. Tradition was like a fortress protecting them from the outside world, giving them security and a sense of superiority.

Geeta felt an outsider, an onlooker. She could never share their past. But Geeta, over the years, had come to appreciate their tradition though she could not regret the passing of an era.

The room was becoming stuffy. The women were moving

restlessly. Geeta longed for some fresh air but she dared not get up as she was encircled by too many elderly in-laws.

'Binniji, come out on the terrace with me. I feel a little unwell,' said Manji Bua Sa, a cousin of Bhagwat Singhji. She was in her early sixties but her skin was smooth and unwrinkled. Each feature in her face was beautifully proportioned. Her chiselled nose was as finely shaped as her mouth. Her walk was stately as if she never had to bend to anyone's wishes. Though she gave the impression of being aloof, her innate tenderness drew people to her. At first Geeta had been impressed with her cousin-in-law's beauty and dignity only; but when she came to know her better, Geeta loved her for her compassionate understanding of other people's problems.

On the terrace the sun was pleasantly warm. Little sparrows twittered on the edge of the latticed wall and then flew away. Geeta felt revived by the cold air. She wanted to pull back the sari from her face and inhale the fresh, clean air, but she knew she could not in the presence of her cousin-in-law. Instead, she leaned against the wall, her sari fluttering over her face.

'I am glad you are bringing new ideas into the haveli,' said Manji with a directness that made Geeta feel at once at ease.

'I do not know, Bua Sa, whether it is right to disturb the life within the haveli.' Geeta replied without hesitation.

'Do not be afraid. It is time things changed. Once we, the old, are dead, the havelis will no longer survive. It is no good living on in the past; for the sake of our children, we must look to the future.'

'But I don't know whether that is so for the poor,' Geeta mused. 'Perhaps it is better to leave them alone to carry on as they have always done. They stand together in their poverty. Education could even be harmful if it separated them from one another.'

'Can education harm anyone, child?' asked Manji. 'Our sacred writings say that to educate the poor is the highest form of charity. If Sita can learn to read and write, she will never feel helpless.'

A slight shadow of regret fell on Manji's calm face. She brushed it off with a shake of her head and then said in a solemn matter-of-fact voice, 'Binniji, I have been a widow since the age of fourteen. I know what it is to be illiterate; the days and nights have been long for me. Do not look like that at me. No one is to blame for this. When I was a girl, we were not allowed out of the inner courtyard after the age of seven. There was no question of going to school. But times have changed and even the thick walls of the havelis are crumbling.' Geeta watched her face through her green muslin sari. 'Our men cannot continue to live off the land any more. They will leave the havelis, so their women must be prepared to face the world.'

As she spoke, her eyes became abnormally large. The years of suffering welled out simply and naturally. Her voice was clear. Her face wore no mask. It was a sad face, an unforgettable face, but a face so proud that it did not ask for pity.

'How did you pass these many years?' asked Geeta after a little while. She had always wanted to know more about her cousin-in-law's life.

'Yes, I almost a child widow, but remember not without a family. My in-laws were wonderful people. You should know that. We have the same ancestors.' She smiled. 'I lost my husband in the same year his brother lost his wife. So, I brought up his two children. They became mine. Of course, I have not known many of the pleasures of life,' she sighed. 'As a young girl I could not understand why I was forbidden to wear jewellery and coloured saris like the other women. A widow's presence on religious occasions was considered inauspicious. That hurt me most; I loved the gaiety that goes with our festivals. But later on I understood. No one was to blame for that, it was the custom in Udaipur. It was my fate to be a widow in this life. I had to learn to accept that. All of us have to pay for our past actions. Who knows what sins I must have committed to have lost my husband? Still, I have had compensations. My nephews love me like a mother. Binniji, I do not need to be pitied. A widow has her place too in our society; do not forget. These women, our relatives you see here, feel responsible for me.' A thin smile parted her lips. 'But the children are grown up now and they will leave one day. If I could read and write, I would not feel so lonely. Once they are gone, time will hang heavily on my hands. No, you must send Sita to school, even if it means a little inconvience to you,' she said with renewed force in her voice.

Geeta stood silent, too moved to say anything. She did not notice her mother-in-law come out on the terrace.

'Manji, I thought you had left when I did not see you,' said Bhagwat Singhji's wife casually.

'It was getting hot and stuffy inside so we came out here to have a little fresh air,' replied Manji, smiling.

'What have you both been talking about?' asked Geeta's mother-in-law, lifting a little of her sari from her face.

'Oh, nothing special. I was telling Binniji about my life.'

'I hope you told her that once a girl is married, her home is where her husband is, whatever happens,' said Bhagwat Singhji's wife. She never missed an occasion to bring home to Geeta that her first and in fact only duty was to serve her husband's family.

'There, your mother-in-law is right,' said Manji, tenderly looking at Geeta, who stood fidgeting uneasily.

'In order to become one with the family, one must first learn to listen to one's elders,' said Bhagwat Singhji's wife, stiffening up her body and looking a little forbidding. Then, after a moment of silence, she said, 'Just imagine sending Sita to school now, just when she is getting to be useful in the house. But Binniji thinks that I am old and foolish. Well, I may be that, but I do know that once a girl has gone to school she will never take a broom in her hand. I have my maids, Binniji. They will never leave me. But I was thinking of your comfort. You have a long life ahead of you. Sita would be a perfect maid for you. I would marry her to one of the servants' boys and both of them could serve you. But not if she goes to school.'

'Kaki Sa, you may be right but we should not be selfish if we can help the poor to improve their lot,' said Manji, firmly.

'But you will agree with me that Binniji should have asked my permission first before doing anything?' Bhagwat Singhji's wife insisted.

'There you are completely right, but we all make mistakes. You must forgive Binniji this time. She won't do it again,' said Manji with an indulgent smile.

Bhagwat Singhji's wife noticed that some of the women in the room had already started making their gestures of farewell. She would have liked to continue talking but she knew she had to be with her sister-in-law when the guests left. Geeta followed her mother-in-law and Manji inside.

Nandu, seeing the three women enter, left the women she was talking to and went over to Bhagwat Singhji's wife; she tapped her lightly on the shoulder, and took her aside.

'How did you manage to get your brother to divide the property so quickly and so fairly among the three sons?' she asked admiringly.

'I did nothing. It was all done according to the wishes of my brother. He did not want the name of his haveli to be tarnished after his death. You know how many of the havelis have disgraced themselves with property disputes.

He wanted everything clear and on paper while he was still alive,' replied Bhagwat Singhji's wife, trying to sound convincing.

Nandu did not wish to contradict her, although she knew that it had taken Bhagwat Singhji's wife three days to convince her brother that his son from his first wife must be treated equally with his other sons. She had also heard that strong words had been exchanged between the two sisters-in-law. Nandu would have liked to probe a little deeper, but women came up to Bhagwat Singhji's wife before leaving to urge her not to worry, that her brother would soon recover.

When distant relatives had gone and only Manji and Nandu were left, Bhagwat Singhji's wife got up and said with a great show of reluctance to her sister-in-law, 'I hate to leave you alone, but if I don't go today, then I can't for the next three days for they are not auspicious. But don't worry. I will come again. Keep the butter lamp burning in front of the goddess. I have already told the accountant to give the priest a hundred rupees to propitiate the planet Jupiter.' Bhagwat Singhji's sister-in-law lowered her head in gratitude and silently bent down to touch her sister-in-law's feet.

Chapter IV

BHAGWAT SINGHJI'S WIFE waited to get home before saying anything to Geeta. She had got all the details of what had transpired between Geeta and her father-in-law. Pari told her, as she changed her sari, how she had dared to contradict the young mistress, but then once Kanwar Sa got interested, she had kept quiet.

While Pari talked to the mistress in her room, Bhagwat Singhji's wife planned how to meet the situation. She knew no purpose would be served if she directly confronted her husband. She decided the best way to influence him was through the trusted family accountant.

Bhagwat Singhji's wife called him to the inner apartments and urged him to tell her husband that to send Sita to school was not right. A small, shrewd man, whose father and grandfathers had served the family, the accountant had already made up his mind to caution the master against such a step. When the mistress spoke to him, he readily agreed with her. He was not afraid to advise Bhagwat Singhji when it came to upholding the name of the haveli. But he waited to be summoned by Bhagwat Singhji rather than ask for an appointment.

Two days later, after the accountant had finished reading out the monthly accounts of the haveli, Bhagwat Singhji told him to look for an appropriate school for Sita. The accountant rubbed his hands nervously and then meekly said that such an act on the part of the master would be resented by the other servants. He pointed out that there were other servants who had served the haveli longer than Gangaramji, that Dhapu and Ganga had children too. Bhagwat Singhji listened attentively and then reminded him that all the servants had been given land by his father, that Dhapu's children had been given in marriage by the mistress and that her husband, in addition, had been given three acres of irrigated land by him. The accountant nodded his head but kept looking at the ground. This was his way of showing disagreement. It was a fact that Bhagwat Singhji had given generously to all his servants and provided long-term security for them. The reasoning of Bhagwat Singhji could not be disputed by the accountant, but he still was not completely convinced. But he knew his master well enough to realize that nothing he said would change his mind. He had decided to take a calculated risk in permitting Sita to go to school and he, therefore, had to follow his instructions.

For a week, he had gone from school to school in the city but there was always something that did not meet with his approval. At last he found a private school run by a charity organization that seemed right for Sita. The fees were a little high but he knew that his master would not hold that against it. He registered Sita's name and completed all the formalities. But the mistress still refused to let Sita join immediately. An auspicious day had to be found. The family astrologer was consulted and the day that Sita could go to school fell a week later.

The courtyard was filled with the sweet smell of incense that morning. Special prayers had to be offered to the image of the goddess of learning before Sita could start. An oil lamp flickered at her feet. The women of the haveli, the neighbours and their children came, touched the ground with their foreheads, and muttered a prayer before leaving to do their early morning chores.

Afterwards Champa watched the sky and only when she was convinced that letting Sita sleep longer would be imprudent, she shook the girl awake.

Sita got up without protest. She knew it was the day when she was to start school. From the day she had been registered in school, Sita had gone about the haveli like a lost child. The maids let her do as she pleased. The mistress gave her money for salted peanuts, but nothing brought a smile on her face. She even refused to play with Vikram, whom she loved to push around in his little green car. So when Champa woke her up, she followed Champa silently, as if she was in a dream, and sat down on the edge of the verandah near the tap.

Champa took a handful of cold water in her hand and splashed it on Sita's face. The sting of the icy water brought the child back to life.

She turned her wet face to the maid and in a little, timid voice asked, 'Bai, will the teachers beat me in school?'

'Of course not!' replied Champa firmly. 'Do you think teachers are paid a hundred rupees a month to beat girls? I could do that,' she said, swallowing the lump that rose in her throat. 'Come, wipe your face and I will oil and plait your hair. You cannot have your hair flying all over your face.' Champa's voice was full of tenderness.

Sita sat down meekly, her head bent low. Champa put oil in her hair, massaged a little, and then combed out the knots.

'What has happened to your voice, little squirrel?' said Champa, no longer able to bear the silence. 'Now that you will need your voice, you have lost it,' she said affectionately patting the girl on the back.

'Bai, who will give me my roti for lunch?' asked Sita timidly.

Champa covered her mouth with her hands to swallow the sob that she could no longer contain. Then when the little girl turned her face and looked at her for an answer, she said with a tinge of tender reproach, 'Do not think you can fool me with those big eyes of yours. Do you think I have forgotten your loud cries when the dal was salty or when the roti was slightly burnt? This is the first time in all your seven years that you have sat still and allowed me to comb your hair. Have you forgotten all the slaps I have had to give you, little mouse?'

But Sita sat cross-legged and continued to look at the maid, with imploring eyes brimming over with tears.

'I suppose you eat when the others eat. How should I know, child, what happens in school? I have never been to one.' A big tear fell on Sita's cheek. Champa wiped it off with her sari and said softly, 'Do not cry in front of the girls or they will know you are afraid and will bully you. From now on, you are on your own and you must be strong. Come, let me help you put on this old dress of Vijay Bai Sa.'

'Sita, oh Sita! Come and drink your tea,' shouted Ganga from the kitchen. 'The goddess alone knows when the poor girl will again get anything to eat,' muttered the maid as she stirred the luke warm tea with her finger.

Sita, small and defenceless, stood at the door of the

kitchen. Her teeth were clamped tight with fear, her eyes were moist with unshed tears.

'Sit down and drink the tea, and eat this roti. I have especially made it nice and crisp,' said Ganga, looking pityingly at the small body standing in front of her. 'Hurry, or you will be late.'

'Now remember not to fight with anyone like you do here. Those teachers cannot be trusted. You just do as they tell you and you will be all right.'

Sita stared at the cup in front of her as if she were afraid to touch it. Her face was smudged with dried tears. Ganga pulled her down gently and then broke a piece of roti and dipped it in the tea.

'Open your mouth,' she said lovingly. Sita opened her mouth and closed it to swallow as if she were a mechanical toy.

'Do not worry, child,' said Ganga stroking Sita's smooth oily hair. 'In a few hours you will be back home and then you can tell us all about the girls in school.'

'Bai, I cannot eat any more. I am not hungry,' said Sita gulping down the roti with a sip of tea.

'Finish the roti,' coaxed Ganga wiping her nose. 'On an empty stomach you won't be able to remember what the teacher says. Your stomach will growl and the girls will laugh. So eat, there is only half the roti left.'

Sita finished the roti, then wiped her mouth with the back of her hand and went and sat in her usual place behind the pillar in the verandah, her head buried in between her knees.

Dhapu came running down the stairs, her teeth chattering, and her sari closely wrapped round her body, and went into the warm kitchen.

'Where is our little schoolgirl?' she said cheerfully.

'Leave the poor child alone,' said the cook as he poured milk into a silver glass. 'Just look at her sitting there. She has not opened her mouth the whole morning. Even a man's heart would melt looking at her face. Does Binniji think just because we are servants she can do as she pleases with our children? Let her try and send a daughter of mine to school and see. Yes, you can do what you like with boys but to expose a girl to the world! Never!'

'Sh! Do not talk so loudly. As it is, Binniji is sorry she ever suggested school for Sita,' said Dhapu putting her fingers to her lips.

'She should be sorry. All this would never have happened if Gangaram were not spineless. It is easy to beat one's wife but to stand up to the mistress requires real guts. He works like a donkey and never looks at his only child.'

'What need has he to look at his child, when we are here? Do you think we neglect her?' said Dhapu in a sharp indignant voice.

'Look at that sorrowful bundle of flesh and then talk,' replied the cook with sarcasm.

'Sita, Sita, where are you? Are you ready for school?' shouted Vijay excitedly, from the top of the stairs.

She ran down the stairs and then across the courtyard and stood in front of the despondent girl. 'Do not worry, Sita. I will teach you the alphabet. It is not difficult. I will do your homework for you. Do not worry,' she said gently holding the girl's hand. 'Come with me while I drink my milk.'

Sita got up as if there were no strength in her to resist and followed Vijay into the kitchen yard.

'Dhapu, tell Sita not to be afraid,' said Vijay looking at her little friend's downcast eyes. 'Every day on the way back we will buy peanuts and toffees. Sita, don't be sad. We will have such fun together,' Vijay tried to encourage her, and got up.

'Wait, Vijay Bai Sa, don't be in such a hurry to go, you get lunch in school, what about Sita? Left to you the girl would starve to death,' said Ganga, giving Sita a wrapped-up packet. Then lifting Sita's chin she said, 'I have put a lot of sugar in between the rotis. Don't let anyone snatch them from you!'

Pari sat watching everything. She did not have the heart to console the wide-eyed Sita, but when she saw the two girls walk out of the courtyard she called out, 'Eh, Sita, haven't you seen that a lamp burns in the prayer room? First go and prostrate yourself before the goddess of learning.'

Sita turned back and Vijay followed her into the prayer room. Both the girls bent down on their knees and touched the ground with their foreheads and then hurriedly left the room.

The maids silently watched them go out of the courtyard. Gangaram stood in a corner with his eyes fixed on the ground. As soon as the car was out of the gate, Pari got up with a deep, long grunt. She limped across the yard to the kitchen and picked up the handbroom.

'What are you doing, Jiji?' said Dhapu, snatching the broom out of Pari's hand. 'Are we all dead that at your age you should sweep the floors and put us to shame!' Pari did not resist; she sat down again and gazed vacantly in front of her.

Though Pari had not looked to Sita's daily needs, the little girl was very dear to her. Sita was not a cuddly child nor pretty. Her dark, thin face was pinched, her eyes were big and her nose was long and crooked like her father's. She whined and cried for the least little thing, but her ways were endearing; she hung around Pari, especially when there was no one with her. When everyone slept in the afternoon, she sat and pressed Pari's legs and told her little stories she knew.

'The haveli seems empty without the little mouse,' said Pari at last. 'If no one else, the goddess will take care of her.' Then, drawing a deep breath she mumbled: 'We are only servants. Our destinies are tied with the mistress but, no matter what she does for us, we and our children will remain servants. No one but God can change one's destiny.' Her usually soft voice was harsh and dry.

'If only Gangaramji had not lost his temper, Lakshmi would still be here,' said Dhapu scrutinizing Gangaram with black, hostile eyes as he dumped firewood in the kitchen verandah.

Bhagwat Singhji's wife had heard all the sniffing and sighing from the puja room and she finished her prayers hurriedly, bowed her head reverently in front of the deity and then came out of the room.

As she neared the kitchen she walked more slowly and stared at Pari: 'What is all this crying about? Looking at you all, people would think we were murderers. Yes, servants will remain servants, no matter what you do for them. It is not in their nature to be grateful. Here I am spending money on the girl. I have fed her and clothed her all these years but today you women are behaving as if she had been sold for gold.'

Bhagwat Singhji's wife shook with anger as she spoke. 'Tell me now, if you don't want Sita to go to school, I will see that she does not. Keep her in your laps but don't complain about her.' She gave a cold, scornful look at the maids before she walked away proudly.

As soon as Bhagwat Singhji's wife turned her back, the maids looked up, stunned. No one spoke. In spite of the mistress gossiping with them and sharing her life with them, there was never a question of taking any liberty with her. Pari got up immediately and went towards the mistress's room. She knew the mistress was especially angry with her and this she could not bear.

Chapter V

THE STRONG WORDS of the mistress had a sobering effect on all the servants. Even the cook was silenced. But in the confusion everyone had forgotten that Bhagwat Singhji's widowed niece Kanta was coming that day to stay in the haveli for a brief vacation. It was only when loud persistent banging was heard on the side door later in the morning that they remembered and then the maids rushed around.

Bhagwat Singhji's wife got up hurriedly. She straightened the sari over her head and greeted Kanta as if she had been waiting for her the whole morning. The maids brought in the luggage, the cook quickly took down the silver plates and put the oil on the fire to fry savouries. Gangaram, seeing everyone was busy, slunk away to have a quiet smoke.

'How is your mother-in-law, Bai Sa?' asked Bhagwat Singhji's wife as soon as Kanta sat down in the sitting room.

'The same as ever, Hukkum; sometimes pleased with me, otherwise nagging as if I were the cause of all her troubles. She hardly talks to me, she spends most of her time going to the temple.'

'Then it is true that she is thinking of giving away her money to the temple?'

'She keeps threatening to do that from time to time. But where is the money to give? That is just her way of keeping me under her domination.'

'Don't talk like this. You know she has gold and that's money. Bai Sa, you can't afford to displease her. Remember sweet words cost nothing.'

The conversation was suddenly interrupted by Pari who came in agitated, She asked the mistress for the keys of the store. The cook was angry, Gokul impatient. There was not enough milk for Bhagwat Singhji's guests. Even after diluting the milk with water, there was not enough.

The two ladies got up hurriedly and went into the kitchen. One of the servant's children had already been sent to buy milk; another had gone to buy sweets. There was complete confusion; voices rose, and the servants exchanged accusing glances with each other. The master of the haveli was never to be kept waiting. His guests were always to be served in a manner appropriate to the haveli's reputation for hospitality. In the women's side anything could do; no one was too upset if the milk fell short or there were not enough refreshments to go around. The cook knew how to stretch things for the ladies, but it was dangerous to play tricks when it came to serving the men.

'If you servants had not sat and cried the whole morning, we would not be in such a confusion. We have never before been short of milk,' said the mistress haughtily.

The cook listened with a mischievous glint in his eyes, while he fried the savouries.

'Why was everyone crying?' asked Kanta with surprise, while arranging a tray for Gokul to take inside.

'Ask Dhapu. Her sari must still be wet with all the tears she has shed,' the mistress taunted.

Dhapu kept her head down and went on peeling the fruits.

Before the question could be repeated Gokul's twelve-year-old grandson stood panting in front of the door, holding an earthenware cup of milk in his hand.

Once the trays were taken inside there was quiet again in the kitchen.

'Bai Sa, eat something now,' said Bhagwat Singhji's wife placing a plate before Kanta.

'Not just yet, Hukkum. First I will go and see Geeta Binniji. Is she not feeling well? Why isn't she here?'

'If you had heard the servants this morning, anyone would be afraid to face them. No wonder she has not dared to come down. I am glad Ajay Bapu is coming back today. So much has happened during his absence. I hope he does not think we have been hard on his wife.'

Kanta found Geeta in her room reading a book. She closed the book and got up as soon as Kanta came in.

'Binniji, I am disturbing you. You go on reading and I will come back later. I will be here for a couple of days. There is no hurry,' Kanta grinned apologetically.

'No, no, Bai Sa, come and sit with me.' Geeta's voice was warm and welcoming. Though she had heard her mother-in-law's sharp words to the maids, she was still not easy in her mind. She yearned to talk to her husband about Sita. She could still be withdrawn from school.

Kanta eased herself down and made herself comfortable on the mattress. She took out her betel nut box from her blouse pocket and delicately put a pan in her mouth and chewed it with satisfaction and then looking at Geeta's drawn face, said with concern, 'Binniji, don't pay attention to the servants. They are all spoiled. They feel we exploit them, especially these days when people in factories earn a hundred to two hundred rupees for just eight hours of work a day.'

'Bai Sa, this time the servants are right,' Geeta answered sadly. 'They are all angry with me because Sita was miserable about going to school. After all, the girl has been brought up by the maids. They treat her like a daughter. Where else in the world would you find this kind of devotion?'

'There you are right,' she answered. 'My maid has really had a hard time with me, especially after I became a widow, but she refused to leave me and go to work in another haveli for more money. She said, "My mother put me in your care and I will die in your home." Binniji, when my husband was living, we were comfortable. I had servants, not as many as there are in this haveli but enough for our needs. But he died suddenly and then I had very little, and there were my two sons to bring up. My mother-in-law has always resisted spending money on us. Even to this day she feels that I have hidden wealth which I am hoarding until she dies.' Kanta spoke with little emotion, as if she didn't care.

Geeta looked at her placid face, intently trying to fathom what really went on in her mind. She had heard her cousin-in-law's story from others; but, like so many stories in the haveli, it was difficult to discern how much of it was enlarged by gossip. Geeta liked Kanta, who was always cheerful. She carried her stout body gracefully. With all her bulk she seemed always to be gliding rather than walking.

Geeta found nothing that intrigued or interested her in Kanta. She was open and simple. Her calculations were obvious and that made it easy to contact her. She was in her early thirties but widowhood had not sapped her vitality nor destroyed her self-confidence. She lacked the serenity and compassion of Manji. Kanta was not interested in other people's problems except at the level of gossip. She was too preoccupied with herself to take the suffering of others seriously. Her pleasantly smug manner almost successfully covered her arrogance. She talked incessantly of predestination but seemed to be waiting to avenge her fate in the success of her two sons.

'My mother-in-law has reason to feel as she does,' continued Kanta after swallowing the betel nut and tobacco leaf with relish. 'You know my husband died young, but that was no reason why I should have had no money. It was my fate. No one is to blame,' she stated in a matter-of-fact tone and sat silently for a while, thinking.

Geeta fidgeted with the end of her sari, waiting for Kanta to resume talking.

Then dreamily Kanta continued: 'Though I was married into a poor family my father had plenty of money. He never worked, as you know, just lived like a rich man's son. But my paternal grandfather was kind and shrewd. He knew that his son had got into bad habits that made my mother's life very hard. He worried about her and wanted to give her money so that she would have enough for her few needs after his death. But by now you know how difficult it is to do anything in secret in the havelis. Besides, he did not want to annoy his son and face family criticism. Then he fell ill. I was his favourite grandchild and I spent a lot of time with him. He was not happy about me as I had been married into a poor family though a very respectable one. One day, when no members of the family were in the haveli, he called me to his bedside and said, "Listen carefully, don't miss a word I say. I have not much longer to live. In our farm house outside Udaipur where your asthmatic uncle lives, in the store room where old brooms and buckets are kept, in the left side wall as you enter are hidden gold and silver. No one knows this. I had it all cemented in, many, many years ago when you were still a baby. It is always wise to live unpretentiously and think of the future. When I am dead, have the wall torn down. This money is for you and your mother. I know you cannot buy happiness with gold but it helps to make life a little less hard to live.'' After a few weeks he died.'

'Did you ever find the gold?' asked Geeta eagerly.

'Of course, it was all there. Slabs of yellow metal with gold and silver coins neatly built into the wall.' Then her voice trailed off; she took a deep breath and in a voice tinged with sadness added, 'Binniji, you only get what is your fate and never more. My mother was a wonderful woman, God-fearing and pious. What a pity she died before you were married. She was afraid when I told her what my grandfather had said. She knew no craft. She was simple and trusting. She told my father where the gold was but never what my grandfather had said. She did not want to say something that would cast doubt on my father's character. She was a true Hindu wife who worshipped her husband. Well, when my father died, all the money, everything, naturally went to my brother.'

She paused briefly and then continued in a monotonous voice, 'For a few years his wife was kind to my mother, but then she began to resent spending money on her. My mother never complained. When relatives asked her why she wore torn, patched skirts, she made excuses but never said a word against her daughter-in-law. If only my mother had been saved the sorrow of seeing me become a widow, her last years would have been bearable. My widowhood added to her grief. She died an unhappy woman.' She tried to smile to hide the storm of emotions that raged within her.

Geeta sat rigid, staring at her cousin-in-law through her suppressed indignation. She looked at the round and cheerful face, and she was filled with anger. She wanted to shout and shake her from her apathy; she wanted to tell her that it was criminal to accept everything as part of one's predestined fate and that she should fight to get her share of the money from her brother; she should stop wasting her life just being pleasant to everyone. But she did not speak; only her lips trembled with anger.

'I have been talking so much that I have lost count of the time. The children must be back. There is so much noise downstairs,' said Kanta wearily, and got up slowly.

'I, too, forgot today is only half-day school,' said Geeta standing up abruptly; all her uncertainties about Sita were forgotten listening to Kanta's story. She pushed her hair back and covered her head properly and then followed Kanta out of the room.

Sita and Vijay were on the kitchen verandah, turning the pages of an illustrated book.

'Look, Sita, this is A for apple,' shouted Vijay, her eyes sparkling. 'This is B for ball. I will teach you two letters every day. You must be a good girl and practise writing,' she said as her finger moved slowly deciphering the printed alphabet for Sita.

The maids fluttered around, their eyes brimming over with sympathy, ready to clasp Sita to their bosoms, but Sita's eyes were glued to the glossy pictures illustrating each letter of the alphabet. She did not even raise her head when Geeta stood before her.

'Bhabhi, look at all these books Sita got. They are even better than mine,' said Vijay excitedly.

'Sita, did the teachers beat you?' asked the mistress, looking at Ganga.

'No, Hukkum.'

'Did the girls snatch your rotis?' the mistress asked again, emphasizing each word.

'No, Hukkum. I like my school,' replied Sita, reluctantly lifting her eyes from the book.

The maids felt the sting of the mistress's words, and

dispersed, feeling guilty for the fuss they had made that morning.

The cook listened with amusement. He felt happiest when there was a mild storm brewing in the kitchen. He worked better and ordered the maids with impunity. Normally, he would have provoked the mistress some more but the dish he was preparing needed all his attention. Ajay Singh was returning home after ten days in Delhi and Bhagwat Singhji's wife had ordered an elaborate meal for him. The maids carried out Khyali's instructions silently.

Geeta quietly watched Khyali mix the different spices before he put them in the oil to fry. She was relieved to see Sita happy and engrossed in her book.

Kanta was already deep in conversation with Pari outside the verandah. It was not long before the sound of a familiar horn alerted everyone that the car bearing Ajay Singh had entered the gates of Jeewan Niwas.

Ajay Singh came to the inner courtyard after he had first paid his respects to his father. He touched his mother's feet, exchanged a few words with her and then went upstairs to his apartment to bathe.

Geeta stayed on in the kitchen helping to arrange the thalis. Ajay Singh and his parents, with Kanta, ate in the sitting room. The maids nudged and winked at each other watching Geeta with unsteady hands pour out the lentils, take out the steaming rice, spread the ghee on fire-hot rotis. They let her do the work waiting for her to spill something before they took over.

The cook muttered under his breath. He didn't find it at all amusing to have the young mistress in the kitchen; she got in his way. He liked to work fast.

After everyone had been served, Geeta had her food in the kitchen verandah and went up to her room. She was impatiently waiting but she knew that her husband would only come when his mother had finished telling him all about Sita.

'You have been through a real storm,' said Ajay coming into the room smiling. Geeta was taken unaware as she stood looking out of the window.

'So you have heard all about my great victory over Pari,' said Geeta lightly and turned from the window and sat on the bed. 'Dhapu with her cunning mind should really get the credit. But I was so mad with Pari that I went ahead regardless of the consequences.'

'You did the right thing; I am proud of you. It is time for new ideas to enter the haveli,' said Ajay Singh with conviction.

'It is so easy for you to say that, but it was I who had to face the anger of the maids, the relatives, and your mother. I can't tell you how I regretted having been so impetuous. If I could have, I would have run away from here; it was awful, especially without you,' said Geeta passionately. 'But now sit by me and tell me about Delhi. What did you do there?'

As soon as the word Delhi was mentioned Ajay Singh's face lost some of its colour and his eyes darkened. He ignored Geeta's question and after a moment of silence said, 'What you did was right; in your place I don't think I would have had the courage to take such a bold step, but don't worry. I am now back and will support you in every way possible. These old maids are little tyrants; don't be frightened by them. They don't realize that my mother's generation will die and with it the traditional way of life and purdah too. It is time you taught them something new.'

'The change won't come as quickly as you think,' Geeta said sadly. 'You don't know the women here; they are all rooted in ignorance and supersitition. For the slightest thing they run to Arjun the fortune teller, even though he was so wrong with Lakshmi. He is such a convincing crook to these ignorant women. Ninety-nine times out of a hundred he is wrong, but still it is to him they all go, clutching money in their hands. How can you educate such people? But let us not talk about the haveli. I have had enough now of the haveli. Tell me what you did in Delhi,' she insisted eagerly.

'I was kept very busy in the university. I hardly went out,' replied Ajay Singh.

Geeta studied him, her eyes open wide and waited for him to continue.

Ajay Singh got up slowly from the mattress, where he had sat nervously, and went and sat on the bed beside Geeta. Then in a halting voice he said, 'Geeta, I am going to disappoint you terribly. I have been made Head of the Department of Physics in the Udaipur university. I prefer to stay here than go to Delhi. There are many like me there while here I can be really useful.'

Geeta hid her face for a moment. Then she burst out defiantly, 'I knew something was wrong. Why were you afraid to tell me this before? Do you think I am so blind not to have guessed that you would never leave Udaipur? But don't look at me like that, I don't need your sympathy.'

Ajay looked at Geeta's proud flushed face and gently drew her close to him.

That night Geeta went to bed as if a heavy stone had been removed from her path. At last she knew that her hope of leaving Udaipur was a flimsy, unreal dream. Instead of feeling desperately trapped, there was a strange peace within her. A few words had put an end to her restlessness. She fell into a profound sleep as if she had not slept for months.

Chapter VI

THREE MONTHS HAD passed since Sita's first day at school. The maids' fear that Sita would be difficult proved wrong. She got up without having to be awakened; she gave the maids no trouble about getting ready. She washed her face, changed her clothes and even tried to plait her own hair. But in the last three months she had become more subdued; she never argued with the maids when they asked her to sweep or clean the utensils. She now never fought with the other servants' children and gave in to them even when she was in the right. In spite of this the servants' children liked her less and sniggered at her each time she put on an old frock of Vijay's. They grinned at her menacingly and behind her back called her the little mistress. But Sita ignored their taunts and did all she could to help in the haveli. Every evening she mixed the oil cakes with the fodder for the cows, something she had refused to do before. She never talked about her school. When asked, she hung her head embarrassed and nibbled at her fingernails.

The maids missed her whining and her former tantrums.

The truth was that Sita knew that the girls were all poor like her. They did not notice that her frock was too long, or that her sweater was faded and torn in places. The teachers were kind and did not chide her if she repeatedly made mistakes in learning the alphabet or if she did not do her homework. Still the best part of going to school for Sita was the drive to and from school with Vijay.

The girls in the school surrounded her when she got down from the car. She enjoyed telling them all about the toys that Vijay had and of all the other enticing things in her cupboard. The other girls listened to her with rapt attention.

On the way back from school Vijay always insisted on buying hot savouries. Sita was careful to wipe off the crumbs from her mouth before she entered the courtyard. Sita had learned in the three months that she was more privileged than the children of the other servants. She knew instinctively that this annoyed the other children. In fact, she did not feel any different from them but since joining school she had little time to spend with them.

The days passed rapidly for Sita and it was soon time for the school to close for the summer vacations.

The hot winds of summer had begun to sweep through the haveli, bringing with them dust and masses of dry leaves. The pavement stones burned the soles of bare feet. The verandah was no longer a place where the women gathered; they sat inside the large sitting room with the mistress till the afternoon sun cooled down. The flies covered the verandah, when everyone else felt sweaty and weary they seemed to have the energy to flit from one thing to another.

The routine of the haveli changed only in terms of the hours of rest and work. The whole household got up before dawn when the air was still cool and tried to finish the heavy work of cleaning and cooking before the sun became unbearable. The afternoons were quieter in summer than in winter. It was too hot to go out visiting.

The servants' children were the happiest as the days grew warmer and the winds more dusty and sharp. It was in the summer that the trees behind the haveli were laden with fruit. Every year the children from the streets as well from the neighbouring havelis came to plunder the mango trees and eat the raw fruit in the backyard of Jeewan Niwas. One day Sita sat under a shady tree sucking her lips after she had nibbled a raw mango. Vijay, with the other servants' children, threw stones at the branches of the tree to bring the unripe fruit down. Some other children were perched on the branches of a jamun tree, busy rifling the juicy purple plums.

'Look, Sita, what I have,' said Vijay triumphantly emptying her frock of little green mangoes.

'Vijay Bai Sa, when will school open again?' asked Sita as she sat down next to Vijay.

'Oh, I forgot that tomorrow is our last day in school. What fun, now we can come here early in the morning. Sita, we too will climb the jamun tree. Just see those boys eating all those jamuns. They let only the bad ones drop to the ground.'

'Vijay Bai Saheb, after how long will school open again?' asked Sita absent-mindedly.

'I don't know,' said Vijay carelessly. 'But not for a long, long time. I am so happy. I hate school.'

'Bai Saheb, you know I like my school,' said Sita in a small confidential voice.

'You stupid! You like school, do you? You are a real silly. You can't even read or write properly and you like school,' Vijay mocked. 'Stop talking nonsense. Get up and help me gather the mangoes.'

Sita's little dark thin mouth closed up immediately as if a

thorn had pricked her finger. But she did as she was told. She felt hurt at Vijay's remarks but did not answer her back. She picked up the mangoes without any joy.

The children were running to and fro gathering up the fallen fruit, when Gokul came down the stairs shouting and waving a stick.

'You little thieves! Who do you think you are to steal the fruits of the haveli? Come here, all of you and see what it feels to have your bones crack.'

The children fled in all directions carrying what they could and leaving the rest behind. They were afraid of Gokul; they knew he meant what he said. But he could not run after them and so they always got away with their loot and returned for the rest later.

Gokul walked slowly, his arthritic legs moving unsteadily, but he flourished his stick in the air and shouted, 'You rascals, this time I will let you go but if I see you here again, not a bone in your body will be left.'

Vijay and Sita huddled together trying to suppress their giggles. Then as Gokul's eyes fell on the two girls, he lowered his stick and deferentially folded his hands and said gently, 'Vijay Bai Saheb, don't eat raw mangoes. You will get a sore throat. Those rascals leave nothing to ripen. They carry everything to their mothers who grow fat on stolen fruit. One day worms will eat their insides. Then they will learn.'

Vijay burst out laughing and Sita tried hard to keep a serious face as Gokul climbed up the stairs with difficulty and went back into the house.

'Dhapujiji will be happy with all these mangoes. She makes lovely hot pickles,' said Sita, holding up the bottom edge of her frock and picking the green unripe mangoes from the ground.

'Be careful that my grandmother doesn't see you or then you will be the hot pickle,' said Vijay laughing.

'I know that, Bai Saheb. That's why you go up to the haveli and I will go round the backyard to the servants' quarters.'

'Come up soon. I want to show you the new toys my father got for Vikram,' said Vijay, running up the steps to the haveli. She had forgotten that she had hurt Sita with her harsh words.

'Where is Sita?' asked Bhagwat Singhji's wife, a few minutes later when she saw Vijay entering the verandah alone.

'Bara Bhabhi, she has gone to wash her face in the servants' quarters.'

'What has come over her today that she goes down there to wash leaving you alone with all those children?' said the mistress with annoyance.

'Bara Bhabhi, she was with me till this very minute. I told her to go,' said Vijay, trying desperately to sound convincing.

'Vijay Bai Sa, I was not born yesterday,' said Pari drawing Vijay to her side. 'Kanwarani Sa, you forget this is the mango season.'

The mistress smiled and looked fondly at her grand-daughter and said, 'Ah! Now I understand. I am old and stupid and it takes time for me to see things.'

Just as Bhagwat Singhji's wife had finished, Sita appeared in the courtyard. Vijay wrenched herself free from Pari's clasp and ran towards her.

'Vijay would do anything for that girl,' said the mistress with a sigh to Pari. 'I don't know what she sees in her.'

'Sita has been born under a lucky star, that's all,' replied Pari, looking at the two children sneaking quietly up the stairs. 'In spite of not knowing the love of a mother, thanks to your generosity, she has never felt the loss.'

'But, Pari, I often think of Lakshmi. Poor girl, she must be miserable without a home. She must miss her child.'

'She is in the city somewhere but no one knows exactly where,' said Pari with concern as she fanned the mistress.

'I suppose Binniji was right in sending Sita to school. The girl so far has no fancy ideas. She is obedient and does as she is told. Education has not done her any harm,' said the mistress.

Pari nodded her head and then, after a little thought, said meekly, 'Kanwarani Sa, if you have some extra old frocks of Vijay Bai Sa's, I would like to give one or two to my nieces.'

'I am glad you mentioned this, Pari. I have been thinking of the same thing. Vijay doesn't understand and gives away all her clothes to Sita. It is for Binniji to look around and see that there are other children in the haveli too. We can't forget Dhapu's children or Ganga's. After all, they have all been born here.'

'You are right, Kanwarani Sa,' said Pari with greater confidence.

'I have already noticed that the other children resent all the new clothes that Sita has. They feel left out and then they are mean and nasty to Sita. It is not her fault. Binniji should have realized this long ago. I can't keep an eye on everything,' the mistress said wearily.

'Kanwarani Sa, don't blame Binniji. She doesn't think of these little things. Her mind is on other things. Were it not for her Sita would never have been sent to school.'

'I suppose you are right. I should be grateful. An educated girl like her could so easily have been a total misfit here.

What could we have done, Pari, if she were insolent, or worse, indifferent? No, she has never raised her voice to me, and in her own way she is proud of the haveli,' Bhagwat Singhji's wife said slowly reflecting on each word she uttered. 'Pari, remind me to tell Binniji to give me all Vijay's clothes. Instead of finding fault with Binniji, I should have told her myself.'

Chapter VII

ON THE LAST day of school, the two girls were ready and in the kitchen earlier than usual. The cook was in good mood. He hummed while he stirred the milk on the blazing fire. Dhapu sat outside the kitchen fanning herself and Vikram, who sat happily in her lap.

'Khyali, here are two annas. Buy some vegetables,' said Gangaram, coming into the verandah. His little watery eyes were ablaze with anger, and his face was taut.

'What's come over you? The heat seems to have burned out your intelligence,' said the cook lightly, thinking that this was one of Gangaram's bad days.

'See these dry rotis. Even dogs won't sniff at them and you expect a child to eat them,' Gangaram replied stuttering with rage.

The cook took the milk off the fire and stood up ready for a fight.

'Mind what you say to me. There is nothing wrong with the rotis. They are just dry. You talk as if you had never seen dry rotis in all your life,' the cook mocked turning his back to Gangaram.

'No child can eat plain rotis every day. Take this money and buy vegetables,' replied Gangaram, his voice shaking with emotion. Sita heard her father's angry voice from the verandah and her heart began to beat a little faster. She closed her book and sat still till she heard Dhapu calling her.

'Come here, Sita,' said Dhapu as Sita entered the kitchen with Vijay. Hurriedly, Dhapu put Vikram down from her lap and took a step forward. 'Do you get plain rotis to take to school? Speak, don't stand there like a stone image. What does your father mean by accusing us of starving you?'

'Stop shouting. Look, even the crows have flown away hearing your shrieks,' said the cook raising his hands to keep Dhapu quiet.

'What's all this about Sita being starved?' said the mistress, walking across the courtyard.

'Nothing, Hukkum. I asked Khyali to buy some vegetables for me,' said Gangaram. 'Dhapu Bai has a habit of shouting for nothing.'

Before Gangaram could finish, the mistress picked up the rotis. She felt them and then confronted the cook and said, 'Khyali, is this what you give Sita to take to school? Not even a beggar could swallow these dry rotis. I know the haveli is not what it was, but Kanwar Sa is still not a pauper that you have to starve a child.'

'Don't ask us, Hukkum. Ask Sita. Let her speak. Look at her standing there silent, making us all look like murderers—the ungrateful wretch,' said Dhapu without trying to conceal her temper.

'Sita, come here. Tell me what you take to school,' the mistress asked in a gentle coaxing voice.

'Kanwarani Sa, I get rotis and vegetables, sometimes sugar also, but yesterday I ate the vegetables with the puree that the old lady gave me during lunch time. I was full, so I brought the rotis back home.'

'There you are, Gangaramji. Did you hear that? Now what do you have to say?' said Dhapu, still furious. Gangaram did not reply. He just walked away, his head slumped low on his chest.

'Khyali, I hope Sita is getting milk and not tea in the morning,' said the mistress.

'Of course, Hukkum. Once I have my orders, why shouldn't she? It doesn't cost me anything.' Vijay hearing loud voices from her room hurriedly put on her school dress and came down.

She enjoyed the scenes between her grandmother and the servants. Her face clouded as she saw Dhapu's severe face looking at her. 'Drink your milk, Bai Sa,' Dhapu said as if she didn't really care.

'And Sita, you too drink your milk,' added the cook sarcastically.

The two girls quickly emptied their glasses of milk and ran out of the kitchen verandah. The mistress went out to the storeroom, followed by Pari.

'Really, what a fuss,' said the cook. 'The whole house now seems to be revolving round Sita. One would think that our children were not human and didn't need milk too,' he added maliciously.

'What are you grumbling about, Khyali? Your children are not likely to starve. You have fields that are fertile. You are also a moneylender,' said Dhapu in a cutting voice. 'By the way, this month I won't be able to pay the interest on the two hundred rupees I borrowed.'

'I don't care. That only doubles the interest for next month,' the cook replied. 'Don't you cast envious eyes on my fields. If your husband didn't fight with everyone in sight including his relatives, your fields would also yield enough to feed you. Don't forget, Kanwar Sa gave us all equal land.'

'Stop insulting my husband. Did you give up an inch of your land when it came to your own brother's children claiming a little part of it? No, of course not. You held on to every inch but you want us to give up our land to strangers,' lashed out Dhapu in anger.

'Where do you women get all your gossip from? My brother's children have more land they can manage. Why should they want mine?' the cook answered with an air of superiority.

Someone was banging on the side door. Dhapu looked at him with disdain and walked out of the kitchen to investigate.

Manji Bai Sa and Kanta, with her two sons, came in quietly with a maid. Seeing this, Bhagwat Singhji's wife put down the thali of rice from which she had been picking out the little stones and stood up.

'Why do you strain your eyes, Kaki Sa,' said Kanta, picking up the thali as the women sat down on a mat in the verandah.

'You know me, Bai Sa, I can't sit still. I must do something,' Bhagwat Singhji's wife said lightly.

'Where is Binniji?' asked Manji.

'In her room,' said Bhagwat Singhji's wife. 'I don't know why she wastes her time on those children when there is so much to do in the house.'

'Mami Sa, is it true that Binniji has started a school in the haveli,' said Kanta, her betel-stained uneven teeth parted into a smile.

'I don't know what she has started but all morning there are little urchins running up to her room. Because of this, I keep the main door closed.'

'There are not only children. Let me tell you, Bai Sa,' said

Manji with a twinkle in her eye. 'I know two women from my gully who come. Soon you are going to have all the young maids here. They are all talking about the stories Binniji tells them and all the coloured pencils they are allowed to scribble with.'

'Don't blame me, tell Binniji I am not responsible for what goes on in her room,' Bhagwat Singhji's wife retorted.

'Don't worry, Bai Sa. No one will blame you. Lots and lots of women will bless you. After all, which one of our daughters or daughters-in-law has brought the gift of learning to the poor?' Manji said leaning forward.

'These are grand ideas, but Manji Bai Sa, when you have to sit and roll out the rotis next to the fire and your maid is upstairs listening to stories, then let me see what you say,' said Bhagwat Singhji's wife wistfully. 'I can already predict that these classes will bring a bad name to the haveli.'

Manji kept quiet. Bhagwat Singhji's wife had a point. If the classes became popular, they could cause a problem for the havelis, she reflected. All of a sudden a peal of laughter from upstairs seemed to confirm her worst fears. The three women looked up to Geeta's apartment. There was silence again but as a door opened, the whispers of song and laughter would escape and then be smothered as it closed again.

'Manji Bai Sa, have a slice of the melon. They come from Dhapu's village,' said Bhagwat Singhji's wife in order to change the topic of conversation.

Kanta and Manji each took a piece of the melon and passed the plate to Kanta's boys. After sipping the cool sherbet and tasting the juicy melon, Kanta said in a soft, confidential voice, 'Mami Sa, is it true that Ajay Bapu has been offered a big post in Delhi?'

'With all his degrees he can get any post in India,' Bhagwat Singhji's wife replied more softly than usual.

'Who can doubt that, but if he leaves Udaipur the haveli will be empty,' said Kanta with feigned melancholy.

'But Bai Sa, who ever told you that he was leaving Udaipur?' Bhagwat Singhji's wife said casually, raising her eyebrows. She did not want to share her anxiety on this question with anyone.

'My maid's sister, who works in the Vice-Chancellor's house, mentioned something like that,' said Kanta defensively.

Dhapu exchanged a quick glance with Pari. It was she who had overheard the conversation between Geeta and her husband that evening when he had returned from Delhi. She had not understood everything, only enough to know that they were both agitated and it was about Delhi that they spoke.

She had immediately told Pari and Pari had confided in the mistress. But when Kanta came out with the question Dhapu was surprised. Her little foxy eyes betrayed a trace of anxiety and she quickly withdrew to the quiet of the kitchen to try and solve the mystery of how Kanta knew.

To rescue Kanta from an awkward predicament, Manji inserted: 'I too heard rumours that Ajay Bapu may be leaving.'

'Women in the havelis have so much time on their hands that when there is nothing to talk about they fabricate gossip,' said Bhagwat Singhji's wife contemptuously. Then, seeing Geeta coming down the stairs, she said, 'Why don't you ask Binniji about Bapu Sa's plans, she should know.'

'There is nothing to ask. After all, as you said, women talk. Let them. Why should one take what they say seriously?' said Manji dismissing the question. She had guessed that Bhagwat Singhji's wife was not pleased and did not want to dwell on the subject.

Geeta sat down beside Kanta, after touching the feet of

the elders. She could tell from the awkward silence that they were discussing something they did not want to continue in her presence.

Kanta quietly swallowed the betel nut she was chewing and said, 'Binniji, I brought these two boys with me to ask your advice about what they should do, now that one has finished school and the other has graduated.'

'You must also tell me what to do with my nephew,' said Manji. 'These days every second boy is an engineer. No wonder they all sit at home filling in applications for jobs. Binniji, suggest some other fields so that the hundreds of rupees spent on their college education are not wasted.'

Geeta kept quiet. She still did not feel comfortable talking in front of her mother-in-law.

The heat made it impossible to sit in the verandah for long. The mild early morning breeze was now hot and full of dust.

'We must be on our way home before it gets too hot to walk,' said Manji, as she gestured to her maid to get ready to leave.

'Bai Sa, you can't leave now. There isn't anything special cooked today, but share with us what there is. You are no outsider,' said Bhagwat Singhji's wife, putting her hand affectionately on Manji. Before Manji could answer, Vijay burst into the courtyard screaming with joy.

'Bara Bhabhi, Bara Bhabhi, I am first in class.' The little girl's face flushed with perspiration trickling down on her cheeks as she flopped into her grandmother's lap.

'Coming first is all right, Vijay, but you must also learn to cook and sew. Don't become like your mother,' Bhagwat Singhji's wife teased. Then trying hard to conceal her pride, she turned to Dhapu and said, 'Don't forget to burn some chillies tonight. One never knows what evil spirits may be lurking around here.'

'Bara Bhabhi, did you know the old woman gave Sita ladoos and beautiful bangles today. She is going to give me a few of them,' Vijay said excitedly and wriggled out of her grandmother's clasp to join Sita who had just entered the room.

Before anyone had time to react, the curtain parted and Ganga came in muttering: 'No wonder Sita doesn't eat her rotis, Kanwarani Sa. Who would if they had ladoos and puris like these to eat?' Ganga sank down and carefully opened a little package wrapped in a newspaper.

The ladies sat up and looked at the little girl, who stood shyly in front of them playing with the red and green bangles on her wrists.

'This is the second time someone has given her ladoos and puris and now bangles as well,' Pari said in a thin, cracked voice as if she were talking to herself.

'It must be an ayah who works in the school. I know these women. They are clever. She thinks by pleasing Sita she can ask the haveli for a favour,' said Dhapu shrewdly.

'Sita, was she the same woman who gave you ladoos the last time?' asked the mistress, a little troubled.

'I think so, Hukkum, but I am not sure,' answered Sita respectfully.

'What does she look like?' asked Manji.

'An old woman came at lunch time. I don't know what she looks like. Her face was covered with a thick maroon sari. She just gave me the packet and these bangles and left,' said Sita in a halting voice. She had suddenly become afraid of all the cross-questioning.

'And what did she say to you,' asked Kanta.

'She didn't say anything. She just gave me these things and went away,' Sita replied impatiently and then quietly yawned. She couldn't understand why the ladies were interested in the old woman.

'She must be some unfortunate, unhappy woman who has lost a child and finds comfort in looking at children at play; who can tell what makes a heart ache?' said Manji with sympathy.

Pari shook her head. She was not satisfied with Manji's reasoning, but kept quiet. Then as the ladies started talking among themselves, she got up slowly and went out of the room. Sita, seeing Pari leave, slipped out with her. She was eager to share the ladoos and puris with her father.

The cook sat in the kitchen grumbling that no maid was at hand to help him. He had to cook an extra vegetable and try and stretch what was already cooked. Pari went into the kitchen and took down the thalis. She was preoccupied and didn't pay any attention to the mumbling of the cook.

'Parijiji, I am not a magician. I can't expand the food cooked for five people to feed an army. And on top of it, you women sit and gossip.'

'If I were twenty years younger you could accuse me of not helping you, but now I am too old,' said Pari bluntly.

The cook was taken aback by the old woman's brusque retort. He wondered what had upset her for Pari was the general peace-maker when everyone around was screaming. She hardly ever lost her temper.

'Parijiji, don't be cross with me. I wasn't thinking of you. It's all those fat, useless maids who talk from morning to evening that annoy me,' said the cook as if he were the most oppressed of the servants.

'Khyali, don't pay any attention to what I say. I am getting old and my nerves are on edge, that's all,' Pari replied listlessly.

'Something has upset you. I can tell, Jiji. Has the mistress been nasty? Remember, she too is getting old and becoming more and more cranky,' the cook said. Taking the thali Pari held in her hand, he started to polish it vigorously.

'Oh, no! It's not the mistress. She is always kind, but I don't like what is happening in the haveli,' the old maid said and shook her head solemnly.

'You mean the ladoos that Sita brings from school? Don't let that worry you. I will put someone on immediately to find out who this woman is. I should have done it sooner, but you know how busy I am kept here. I hardly get time to bathe.' Then as Ganga and Champa çame into the kitchen, he thrust his jaw out and said in a cold, sarcastic voice, 'So, at last you two have found time to look in here. You can go and oil your hair. I have no work for you. It's all done.'

'Don't be frivolous, Khyali. Kanwar Sa and Bapu Sa want to eat. They are in a hurry. Heeralal has already brought the car out,' Ganga said in a hushed voice.

'Do you think I have been sleeping all morning that you two come tripping in to wake me up? Go and tell Gokulji food is ready for Kanwar Sa.'

As soon as Gokul announced that the master was ready to eat, the ladies didn't even wait to finish their sentences. They hurriedly came into the kitchen and helped Khyali to prepare the silver thalis.

A few minutes passed before Bhagwat Singhji clad in a thin, white muslin shirt over loose white pants came into the courtyard, followed by his son. The maids got up quickly, pulled their saris over their faces and bent low and touched the ground in front of them. Geeta remained in the kitchen while Manji and Kanta, being daughters of the house, stepped out of the kitchen and greeted the men with folded hands.

Bhagwat Singhji talked to Manji and Kanta, while the two boys sat down to eat from the same thali as Ajay Singh.

Kanta never missed an opportunity to bring her problems to the attention of her uncle. As Bhagwat Singhji ate, in her usual ingratiating manner she sought his advice about the future education of her two sons.

Bhagwat Singhji patiently went over the possible colleges that the boys could enter. He tried to explain to Kanta the advantages of technical education and suggested that the boys go to colleges outside Udaipur.

Kanta was reluctant to see her sons leave Udaipur. Without saying so directly, she hinted in a dozen different ways that her uncle should use his influence to get them into colleges in the city itself.

Ajay Singh was visibly irritated by her persistence. He had advised the boys to take science in school but Kanta had dissuaded them, first on the excuse that she could not afford the laboratory fees, and then when that hurdle had been smoothed over by Bhagwat Singhji, she had pleaded that the boys did not have the physical stamina to do science.

Ajay Singh looked at Kanta with raised eyebrows that left her in no doubt of what he felt on the subject. But in the presence of his father, he exercised restraint and did not frankly tell her that all she was trying to do was to get his father to pay for her sons' education. Unlike his father, Ajay Singh was apt to be brusque with relations who camouflaged their demands and clung to old methods of getting their ends achieved. His mother had given up telling him to say things that pleased people. She knew that some of them thought he was indifferent and proud and contrasted him with the nobility of his father.

After Kanta had finished talking, Bhagwat Singhji asked Pari, 'How is Sita getting on in school?'

'She loves her school, Hukkum. Now that it has closed for the vacations, she keeps asking Vijay Bai Sa when it will open again,' Pari replied enthusiastically.

'I am glad you are satisfied, Pariji. I was really afraid of you when I decided to send Sita to school,' said Bhagwat Singhji with a smile.

'But Kaka Sa, have you heard of the school in the haveli?' said Manji, her big black eyes glittering with mischievous amusement.

'No, I know nothing, but that's not surprising. I am the last to know what happens in this part of the haveli,' Bhagwat Singhji replied lightly.

'Binniji is holding classes for illiterate women like me,' said Manji smiling.

'Bai Sa, who would ever call you illiterate? But tell me more about what Binniji is doing,' Bhagwat Singhji asked with unexpected interest.

Pari straightened her back and wiped her mouth with the end of her sari. Her face shone with a warm glow. She spoke with deep emotion, almost with reverence. 'Hukkum, for the last few weeks Binniji teaches the children from the neighbourhood. She spends hours and hours with these poor children. Who else would do this for them?' Her voice trailed off as she could not keep it steady.

'I am proud of Binniji. Tell her to let me know if she needs any help,' Bhagwat Singhji said in a low voice as he got up with unusual haste and left the room. He was moved by Pari's words and wanted to hide his feelings from the others.

Chapter VIII

THE CLASSES THAT Geeta had started came about by pure accident. One morning Ravi, a young boy, came into the haveli with the servants' children. While the other children helped the mistress with cleaning the grain Ravi sat and played on his little home-made clay-bottomed one-string violin. He kept stringing out tune after tune and the maids stopped talking, nodding indulgently at him.

Geeta knew all the other little children who came up but his was a new face. When she questioned Dhapu she learned that the child's elder brother had sent him to his uncle Gokul because their mother had died suddenly of high fever. The father had died a year earlier of cholera. The responsibility of feeding the six children had naturally fallen on the oldest brother. But the burden was too heavy for him, so Ravi had been sent to live with his uncle. The mistress had agreed to feed him, but Gokul was looking around to find some work for the boy.

After the grain had been cleared and put away, the

children ran down to the backyard to see if they could find some ripe mangoes, but Ravi sat on in the verandah.

'Have you ever been in a city before?' Geeta asked the thin, wide-eyed boy.

'No, Hukkum. This is the first time,' replied Ravi.

'What did you do in the village?' asked Geeta. She was touched by the boy's sad, vacant eyes.

'In the morning, I helped my mother to collect cow dung, milk the cows, and in the afternoon I took the cows out grazing. My mother was going to send me to school, but then she got fever and now she is dead,' said the boy acceptingly as if there was no point in challenging fate.

'If you want to learn, come to me in the morning,' said Geeta, not knowing what else to say to the boy who stared at her big diamond ring.

The next day after breakfast the boy stood outside Geeta's room and so from that day she started teaching him. After two days other boys and girls from the servants' quarters came up to Geeta's room with Ravi. The children sat quietly while Geeta first told them stories and then wrote out the alphabet and asked them to copy it. No one made a noise and after Geeta had finished with the lessons, instead of going home, they sat on practising the letters of the alphabet.

News of the classes spread like monsoon floods and the young maids from the havelis came and joined the children. At first they just listened to the stories; they did not dare to take a pencil in their hands for they were afraid the children would laugh at them. But gradually they started to print the letters and to their surprise found the alphabets were after all not so difficult to learn. Soon the maids began to recognize words, the meaning of which they understood.

Their success made them impatient to learn more and they urged Geeta to go faster. After the morning classes were over the women sat on and talked to Geeta. They told her about their lives, why it was important for them to abide by family customs, even if that meant getting into debt. Their only support came from relatives and if they did not keep up the traditions they were afraid they would lose the family's approval.

As the children and women learned to read and write Geeta got a deeper understanding of poverty. She at last understood that they too had need of fun and they too enjoyed gaiety. Before their expenditure on propitiating the gods or on marriage seemed to her irrational but now she saw that it brought joy into their lives. Geeta now looked forward to each morning. It was not just that the classes filled the empty hours but they also offered her a challenge. She had to think and plan so that her pupils' initial enthusiasm would not wilt. Though they were eager, they could quickly turn away if she failed to keep up their interest.

Geeta suddenly loved the large empty rooms of the haveli; they no longer looked unfriendly and haunted. The cobwebs that had become a part of their decor were now swept clean by the boys.

Gokul no longer went around the backyard trying to guard the fruit trees. There were no children to frighten and threaten with his stick. Vijay and Sita helped the children and the women when they were unable to form a new letter of the alphabet. They felt proud that they knew more than the others.

The mistress looked upon the classes with benign indulgence. She confided in Pari, 'Let Binniji amuse herself. Her enthusiasm won't last long; she will soon get tired of the women. Then let us see what she starts next.'

The maids of Jeewan Niwas at first laughed and joked about the haveli being turned into a school, but later they too found excuses to come up to the classes. Dhapu brought her sewing while Vikram slept. Ganga went upstairs taking the potatoes to be peeled with her. They sat listening to the stories that Geeta told her pupils.

Khyali grumbled constantly while he stirred the lentils; he was not used to working silently in the kitchen, and now that the maids were upstairs he had no one to listen to his gossip and no one he could tease.

The mistress continued to tolerate the classes because they gave Geeta a great deal of joy. Besides, she had nothing to complain about as her own maids did not neglect their work. Her life was not affected. The verandah was still full of chatter and gossip.

But the mistress's unconcern towards this novel activity in the haveli was short-lived. One afternoon a group of working women from the neighbourhood came to visit her. They had barely sat down, when they edged up to Bhagwat Singhji's wife and one after another started complaining.

'Kanwarani Sa, my niece's husband is already fed up. Before going to work he has to eat cold rotis left for him because his wife comes here to listen to stories; is that what a woman should do?'

Before she had finished another woman said, 'Hukkum, have you heard that the engagement of my brother's daughter has been broken off; who wants a girl who is already defiant? Now her poor mother weeps; she should have locked up the girl and starved her rather than allowed her to join these classes.'

Emboldened by what the others had said, another woman spoke up, 'If these girls are not careful, they will soon find their men deserting them, and then the haveli will have to give them shelter.'

The mistress listened in silence without betraying her disquiet. She sympathized with their complaints, but she was not going to say anything against her daughter-in-law to outsiders. Geeta did not know of these rumblings and got more and more absorbed in her new interest.

Bhagwat Singhji's wife had not told Geeta what the women had said to her. She had not taken them seriously. Anyway, she was sure that the classes would stop once her monsoon came.

Three months passed and the classes became more and more popular. On a particularly hot day, a thick sheet of dust covered the sky; the street peddlers were not out on their afternoon rounds and the ice-cream man had not set up his stall under the neem tree. Even the cows that roamed the street sat under the cool shade of trees. The courtyard was silent; the maids slept exhausted by the afternoon heat. All of a sudden a loud tugging and clanging of the latch chain on the side door jolted the maids awake. They quickly got up and arranged their saris while Dhapu hurriedly went to open the door. Nandu, Manji and Kanta came in; they waited for a second, wiping the perspiration off their foreheads, and without exchanging a word with Dhapu went straight to the sitting room, knowing that Bhagwat Singhji's wife would be there. Geeta, who was also resting there, was still drowsy when she bent down to touch their feet.

'Come in, Bai Sa, how nice to see you. I just this minute lay down, it's so hot. The rains must come soon or else there will be famine and cholera,' said Bhagwat Singhji's wife rather stiffly trying to cover up her unpreparedness to receive visitors.

'The rains will come; they always do; the question is how good will they be,' said Nandu in a severe tone of voice. The maids looked at each other nervously; they guessed something was wrong; they had not heard Nandu being so definite before.

Then as Dhapu and Ganga went out to prepare the

refreshments, Nandu set up erect, glared at Geeta for a second, and then turning to Bhagwat Singhji's wife said, 'Kaki Sa, we haven't come here today to sit and chat with you; I have something very serious to talk to you about.' The usual flowery introduction to every conversation was missing; instead, there was surprising sternness in her voice.

'Bai Sa, I know you are worried about the betrothal of your grandson. Don't blame me, I had already warned you the girl is dark and that her parents are poor. But I still maintain the girl is a jewel,' said Bhagwat Singhji's wife firmly.

'I did not come to discuss the girl for my grandson. I am in no hurry to fix his engagement. Today I have come to find out more about these classes that Binniji holds every morning,' said Nandu not bothering to disguise the harshness in her voice.

Geeta was just about to say something when she saw Champa gesturing to her not to speak.

'Oh, these classes are nothing, Bai Sa,' said Bhagwat Singhji's wife light-heartedly. 'Binniji likes to teach children; it's a blessing I can tell you; ask Gokul, he no longer has to keep guard over the mango trees; at least for a few hours in the morning there is peace for us all.'

'There may be peace in your haveli, Hukkum, but there is confusion in ours,' replied Nandu sharply. 'If you don't believe me ask Manji and Kanta Bai Sa; the young maids are not to be seen in the mornings at all. How much can my old maid do? Her daughters used to sweep the haveli; they washed the clothes, now they disappear for the whole morning. They come here and waste their time listening to stories that Binniji tells them.'

Manji and Kanta nodded their heads in agreement.

'Pariji, tell me, how would you feel if Ganga, Champa,

and the others disappeared, neglecting the household work?' continued Nandu aggressively.

Bhagwat Singhji's wife fidgeted nervously with the end of her sari; for the first time she felt tongue-tied.

Pari tried to lessen the tension by offering sherbet to the ladies that Dhapu had brought in. The little break gave Bhagwat Singhji's wife time to collect her thoughts. Her face was slightly flushed when she said placatingly but with a tinge of sarcasm, 'Manji Bai Sa, you are the one who said learning is a good thing; you were proud of Binniji when she started the classes. Have you forgotten?'

Manji, too, was in a challenging mood. She replied, 'Mami Sa, I still think knowledge is only next to the love of God, but not the way the lessons are being taught. The girls come to listen to Binniji's stories, not to learn. You know any pretext is good enough for them to shirk work. What Binniji did for Sita was different. She is in a proper school. She is young, for her it is good but for these girls it is just a wonderful excuse to get away from work. And this will harm them in the long run,' said Manji with a sad long-suffering smile.

'Kaki Sa, let me tell you also that all the havelis are criticizing you. They may not say anything to you, but behind your back they are saying that Jeewan Niwas always tried to maintain the dignity of your way of life—now this very haveli is undermining our authority and making rebels out of our servants. Because you are rich and have many servants and your son is well placed is no reason why you should disrupt the havelis of the less fortunate ones.' Nandu spoke with a passion that betrayed both malice and defiance.

Kanta sat contentedly chewing her betel. All this did not really concern her; she had only come to keep Nandu and

Manji company. Her maid was old and not likely to attend any classes.

Bhagwat Singhji's wife listened silently for a moment and then raising her head she said in a slow and measured voice, 'I am sorry that in my old age I should merit such criticism. Even when my husband became the Prime Minister of Udaipur and the Maharana honoured this haveli by conferring a title on him and gave me the right to put gold on my feet, no one considered me arrogant. But today, even my relatives are accusing me of undermining the traditional dignity of the havelis. My time is obviously over.' Her voice shook with emotion. It was clear to everyone that she fought back the tears which swelled in her eyes.

There was instant consternation among the ladies and the maids. They did not expect the proud mistress of Jeewan Niwas to break down in such a manner. Manji and Nandu immediately shuffled up to Bhagwat Singhji's wife.

Nandu touched her feet and, her voice had lost its harshness when she said, 'Forgive me, Kaki Sa. I did not mean to upset you. I just thought you would like to know what some women are saying. Don't let that worry you. We, who know you, can never make such accusations against Jeewan Niwas.'

Bhagwat Singhji's wife was not assuaged, but she kept still.

Meanwhile, Pari sat where she was, tears rolling down her shrunken cheeks.

'The classes won't last long,' said Dhapu quietly as she sat down to reassure Manji whose tear-filled eyes were half-closed. 'It isn't easy to read and write; Vijay Bai Sa has tried and failed to teach me even one letter of the alphabet. Do you think those stupid girls, who are already old enough to have children, can learn? This is all new so they come, but I can tell you, not for long; already a few have left.'

Dhapu's verdict on the classes seemed to be convincing; the ladies picked up a piece of juicy ice-cooled water melon which had been brought in by Ganga.

Geeta burned with rage as she sat with her face covered, her lips tightly pressed together as if they could not be trusted to relax. Her anger was making her body tremble. She wanted to lash out at Manji more than anyone else. She felt betrayed by her. How dare she say that these classes were an excuse for the women to shirk work? And what if they were, why should the young girls help in the haveli just because their mothers were servants of the haveli? Even Manji was like the rest, she thought bitterly.

Chapter IX

GEETA COULD NOT sleep that night after the visit of Nandu and Manji. Ajay slept soundly beside her; she did not wake him. Her thoughts were in a turmoil but she had no desire to share her anguish with her husband. She was afraid that this time he would not understand her feelings and would be upset. He would be furious with Manji and Nandu; he was not afraid to oppose them. But this was not what Geeta wanted. This time her inner ferment was different. She did not need anyone to fight on her behalf or give her moral support.

She got up early as usual, bathed and dressed, but still she felt listless, as if all energy had been drained out of her. She lay down on the mattress instead of going downstairs. Her thoughts went back, as they had throughout the night, to the afternoon visit. Never before had she heard her mother-in-law speak with such vehemence, weighing every word she uttered. She had, with aristocratic restraint, met the challenge of Nandu and silenced them both.

Geeta felt overwhelmed with gratitude and admiration

for her mother-in-law. But instead of feeling happy, she was deeply disturbed. She knew that nothing mattered more to Bhagwat's Singhji's wife than the dignity of Jeewan Niwas. She would do her utmost to maintain the untarnished reputation of the haveli. Nothing could have hurt her more than what Nandu had said. In those remarks there was a great deal of truth. The havelis were justifiably critical. Geeta was filled with remorse; she had again acted impetuously without clearly thinking of the consequences of her action. She had no right nor the desire to humiliate her mother-in-law or compromise the name of Jeewan Niwas. And yet this was precisely what she had done. The last thing she wanted to do was inflict pain on her ageing in-laws or discredit their name. From them she had received nothing but love and understanding. Geeta lay thinking, trying to rearrange her thoughts, to sort out her feelings. The desire to change the life in the haveli seemed to have subsided in her. Instead she said to herself, 'How dare anyone say a word against the haveli, these classes are not worth continuing. I will stop the girls from coming.' There was a new fervour in her, which she had not experienced before. She felt indignant as she remembered Nandu's words. For the first time she did not feel that she was the victim of blind prejudice or that she wanted to hit back. There was none of the desperation of being enclosed within windowless walls that she wanted to shatter.

'I don't want to leave Udaipur now. The haveli has made me a willing prisoner within its walls. How stupid I was not to see all that it holds. Where else in the world would I get this kind of love and concern? The children must grow up here. They must learn to love and respect this ancient house.'

Then as she heard Vikram gurgling with delight while Dhapu bathed him, she felt a new warmth flood her heart. Her thoughts raced through her mind as if she were being attacked by a swarm of bees; they stung her in every limb and their pain was acute but bearable. 'Where else in the world could children be enveloped in such affection? This kind of devotion is almost superhuman. The servants go hungry if the children haven't eaten, they go without sleep if a child has a slight headache. And yet for all this they get so little in return. But they are always cheerful as if they have their own secret source of happiness that no one can touch.' Geeta was so agitated within that she did not hear the quiet opening and closing of the door.

'Binniji, just look at the sky, it is as clear as Lake Pichola,' said Dhapu, coming into the room on tiptoes and looking out of the window. Then she came and sat down at the edge of the mattress on the floor and said wearily, 'The crops are already ruined. My poor husband, what can he do if the gods are against him? The priests say that this year is bad, that there won't be enough rain even to dampen the earth. Well, my hopes of paying back my debt to Khyali are over.'

'Bai, how much is your debt?' asked Geeta.

'Binniji, I am not worried about my debts to the haveli; it's only Khyali that keeps pestering me for the return of his two hundred rupees. The way he taunts me one would think he had made a gift of that money to me. One day I will tell him he is a blood-sucking moneylender, that's what he is. He charges two rupees interest on every hundred he lends out and still he has the cheek to grumble. But I can't afford to displease him, now. I will need to borrow from him again.'

'Don't, Bai, I will lend you the money,' said Geeta quickly.

'I couldn't let you do that, the other servants are in the same predicament as me. They would resent it; as it is, Kanwar Sa has lent my husband a thousand rupees free of interest. I can't ask you for more,' said Dhapu touching Geeta's feet as a mark of gratitude. Then she put her hand on her head, as if all of a sudden she had remembered something important to tell Geeta. Her eyebrows puckered and she said in a low confidential voice: 'Binniji, Sarju came the other day and said there was a gang of thieves from Jodhpur who don't break into houses but kidnap young girls. She thought the woman who gives ladoos to Sita may belong to this gang.'

It was just like Dhapu to change from a serious problem to repeat gossip. But this time Geeta was not annoyed by the abrupt change of subject. She sat up and smiled. She, too, had been curious about the woman who gave Sita ladoos. Why did she pick on Sita for her charity? Still the idea of a gang of kidnappers seemed a little exaggerated.

'Bai, you should be able to solve the mystery of the woman without Sarju's help. You are good at finding out other people's secrets,' said Geeta teasingly.

Dhapu immediately understood what her mistress was referring to and quickly said in self-defence, 'Binniji, I promise on my daughter's life that I didn't tell Kanta Bai Sa about Bapu Sa going to Delhi. I don't know how her maid heard of it.'

'But Bai, how did you know about Bapu Sa's plans?' persisted Geeta. She liked to catch Dhapu in her own net of intrigue.

'Oh,' replied Dhapu innocently, 'I happened to be on the terrace when you were scolding my poor Bapu Sa and so I just listened for a while, but I couldn't understand everything so I left; if you had not been speaking so fast I might have stayed longer.' Dhapu looked at her mistress with a mischievous glint in her eyes.

Geeta laughed out loud. This was not the first time that her conversations with her husband had been overheard. But now Geeta did not mind. Today she was more amused than annoyed by the surreptitious ways of the women to penetrate the privacy of others. She had worked out her own strategy against those who tried to find out more than she was willing to reveal. Before she could tell Dhapu that eavesdropping was wrong, the curtain parted and Bhagwat Singhji's wife came in followed by Pari.

'Binniji, how do you feel?' said the mistress as Geeta got up instantly and bent down to touch her feet. Bhagwat Singhji's wife sat down on the mattress and stared at Geeta as if she wanted to see her face better through the muslin sari that fell over her face.

Then, in a soft, loving voice she said, 'Binniji, don't let Nandu Bai Sa upset you. She is just worked up because her maids are disgruntled. She has always been a bit of a miser.'

'Bhabhi, it's all my fault, please forgive me. I should never have permitted the girls to join the classes; from tomorrow I will tell them not to come,' said Geeta with sincerity.

'You will not do that. Once your father-in-law gives his approval to something then I am not afraid of what the world says,' said Bhagwat Singhji's wife forcefully. Geeta just lowered her head. She did not know what to say in reply.

'But, Binniji, I did not come to talk to you about the classes. They must continue.' Then she paused a little; her face became solemn.

'Binniji, I know that Ajay Bapu has been offered a big post in Delhi. I didn't realize until Kanta Bai Sa mentioned it that people outside the haveli had also heard. Bapu Sa has not mentioned this even to his father. I know him, he would rather sacrifice his happiness than cause us a moment's pain. The men in the haveli are like that. Your father-in-law refused the Prime Ministership of Bikaner because he knew I would not be happy living outside Udaipur.'

Geeta tried to interrupt, but Bhagwat Singhji's wife silenced her with an impatient wave of her hand. 'Binniji, listen to me,' she continued gravely. 'I want to tell you that Bapu should not think of us this time. We are old and our work in the world is over. But you both are young and the future is open to you. Bapu should not let an opportunity like this pass. I am a mother. I want to see my children happy and fulfilled. You alone can make him see this, you must not let him give up something that will bring him respect and satisfaction. There are times when you must not think of the haveli.'

Geeta burst into tears. She put her head in Bhagwat Singhji's wife's lap and and sobbed like a child.

SECTION III

Chapter I

FIVE MORE YEARS had been added to the life of Jeewan Niwas. Its lime walls were darker; the wooden doors more patchy and the marble more yellow; the filigree around the scalloped balcony was broken in more places, destroying the continuity of the design. A portion of the haveli was shut. There weren't enough servants to do the dusting and sweeping, many of them had died and hadn't been replaced. Pari looked more shrunken; but still her mind was alert and her memory as vivid as ever. Gokul could no longer sweep or clean but he never let Bhagwat Singhji feel his incapacity. His sons did what he could not, though they were not servants of the haveli. Gangaram's leg wobbled more and his pock-marked face had an unhealthy leathery look. Dhapu had become a grandmother. Vikram was in school; Geeta had had another son to the delight of the family; Bhagwat Singhji's wife looked frail but she was as active as ever. She still continued to receive people with joy and never tired of talking. She had moments of worry for she realized that the haveli expenses could not be kept up in the same manner and was reconciled to the mouldy exterior of Jeewan Niwas. When she reflected on its condition, she thought of the days when, on Diwali, Jeewan Niwas was whitewashed and repaired by the personal order of the Rana.

In those days Jeewan Niwas stood out among the other havelis and every child in the gullies knew that it belonged to a minister of the State of Udaipur, a loyal and devoted servant of the Maharana. But even now, though there was an air of decay in its appearance, the old respect for the haveli had not lessened.

Ajay Singh had accepted the appointment in the Udaipur university. This had quietened the women from gossiping. They were a little surprised, for ever since Geeta had come as a bride they had taken bets among themselves that she would persuade her husband to leave Udaipur. They were sure that with all her apparent docility she hated being in purdah and would not for long stand the life in the haveli. Through the years they had come to admire Geeta's capacity to listen to their chatter, but still they knew that deep down she did not enjoy their company. They had detected that something gay and spontaneous had gone out of her life.

But Geeta no longer felt trapped in the haveli. She found that she too had changed. She had seen the value of kinship ties and wanted to preserve the ancestral dignity of the haveli. She still did not like the rigidity with which the women held on to old customs. But what irked her most was the ill-defined nature of her role in the family. She could not become one with the haveli women nor did she want to. The tension between her and them, though muted, remained. But it no longer preoccupied her thoughts nor did it trouble her. Her in-laws had given her enough freedom within the haveli to keep her occupied in the manner that satisfied her. The classes that she had started had given her great pleasure. Ravi, after being taught by her for three years, had been sent to school. She felt proud of him as he did well even in a class of older boys. Some of the young girls could now read and write; but there were others who found it impossible to master the alphabet. For them Geeta had started sewing classes and engaged a woman to teach them to cut and embroider. Bhagwat Singhji was interested in what Geeta was doing and encouraged her. He had given her two sewing machines and had instructed the accountant that all expenses for the classes would be paid from his personal account.

Geeta knew that some of the maids were forced to leave the classes, but even those havelis which tried to threaten or discipline their servants encouraged their own daughters and daughters-in-law to go and learn something useful from the classes.

In the last years the etiquette that completely separated her from her father-in-law had been relaxed. She was now allowed to sit in his presence when no outsiders were present and even talk to him directly. The years had ingrained in her a shyness that she found difficult to overcome. But the more she saw him the more she admired him. He saw more than the ordinary eye and felt more than the normal heart.

On a day in mid-winter, Bhagwat Singhji's wife, Geeta and Kanta sat in the sitting room, talking with other relatives who had come to pay them a visit.

'I don't know where everyone has disappeared today,' said Bhagwat Singhji's wife making a movement to get up.

'Hukkum, don't trouble yourself. We are fasting today, it's the eleventh day after the full moon,' said one of the elderly women putting a restraining hand on the mistress.

'Just as well you are fasting, because there isn't even one maid here today,' said the mistress with an exaggerated air of grievance.

'Kaki Sa, thanks to Binniji, would you believe it that my

maid's daughter is earning a hundred rupees as an ayah in a school?' the woman said. Her dark timid eyes rested affectionately on Geeta.

Kanta added, baring her tobacco-stained teeth, 'The other day my one-eyed maid who has never raised her voice in all her thirty years, lectured me about the benefits of education until the smell of burnt chillies choked her.'

Bhagwat Singhji's wife wiped the smile off her face. She did not want to remind Kanta of the day she had come with Manji and Nandu to plead their case to stop the classes. Instead she called out to one of the servants' children and said sternly, 'Go and tell Dhapu, Ganga, Champa, the whole lot of them, that they needn't come up. They can stay in their quarters and sleep. I don't need them. I can still work with my own hands.'

Before the little boy had left the courtyard, Pari, hearing the mistress's words, came limping in. 'Kanwarani Sa,' she said from the middle of the courtyard, 'the maids are with Gangaramji, he has visitors from his village; they have brought a proposal for Sita.' She spoke excitedly. The mistress forgot her anger and looked inquiringly at Pari.

'There are two proposals, Hukkum. Gokulji and Khyaliji are talking to the first party; they look well-to-do. They have four boys and three unmarried girls. They are looking for a wife for the eldest boy who is seventeen but has never been to school.'

'Pariji, you know Sita would never be happy living in the village; you women have spoilt her and now you want to throw her to the first boy that comes,' said the mistress raising her eyebrows. The other ladies nodded in agreement.

Before Pari could explain further, Dhapu followed by the other maids hurriedly came in panting and sat down on the cold floor at the edge of the carpet.

'Kanwarani Sa, our little Sita has not one but two

proposals,' Dhapu gasped. Then once she had got back her breath, she added: 'Here I thought we would have to bribe someone to marry her; instead people are coming to our doorsteps asking her hand in marriage. Her stars must be very strong for her face is certainly not her fortune.'

'Dhapu, don't you women rush into things. I want to know who these people are before I give my consent,' said the mistress hastily.

The elderly visitors muttered behind their veils. It was indeed an intriguing situation; they knew from experience the sleepless nights they had to spend trying to satisfy the demands of the parents of a suitor for their own daughters. It was not normal for boys' parents to ask for a girl directly. They thought to themselves there must be some deep reason behind this extraordinary situation.

As the women sat talking and speculating, they heard the horn of the car. Moments later Vijay came running into the sitting room, 'Bara Bhabhi, I was selected to be on the badminton team of the school,' she said her face glowing and confident.

Bhagwat Singhji's wife looked at her lovingly and then seeing her swallow something, she asked, 'What are you eating, my child?'

'Oh, Sita gave me one of the ladoos that the old woman gave her,' and she opened her fist to show the other half of the ladoo. 'It is delicious. I wish you would also get ladoos like this, Bara Bhabhi.'

The relatives knew that Bhagwat Singhji's wife liked to feed and fuss over her grandchildren when they came back from school and got up to leave. The mistress was glad to get rid of them; she had too much on her mind to continue chatting with them.

As soon as the side door was shut, the mistress went to the kitchen and sat down. Ganga and Dhapu followed her.

'Who could this kind woman be? I wish we had found out when Sita first brought ladoos home,' she said to them, taking her head in both hands.

'Hukkum, I inquired from the supervisor in the school. She said she is a widow who has no one in the world. They say she is a little out of her mind. She has no children and likes to watch the girls at play,' replied Dhapu blandly.

'Just imagine what she must think of this haveli. Our children accept puris and ladoos from a poor woman, and we don't even take the trouble to find out who she is or where she lives. How disgraceful. We can't let this go on,' said the mistress decisively.

No one had a solution and a heavy silence fell in the kitchen, which was broken by a shrill cry from the front courtyard of the haveli.

'Come out and see my little monkey, he can talk, he can sing, he can do a hundred things you never saw before,' chanted a man to the accompaniment of a little drum.

The children in the courtyard heard the familiar singsong with excitement. Dhapu shouted, as she saw Vijay shut her book, that he was a hoax and that his monkey was lame. Bhagwat Singhji's wife always wanting to indulge her grandchildren said, 'Let them see the monkey dance if they want to. He'll only ask for a rupee.'

As the children rushed out they bumped into the cook, who was absorbed in his thoughts, and didn't see them in the doorway.

'So, Khyali, what more have you found out about the marriage proposals for Sita?' said Bhagwat Singhji's wife nonchalantly as if she were deciding which sari to wear.

At first the cook seemed almost to ignore the question from the mistress. He stoked and blew to revive the kitchen fire; he rummaged in the vegetable basket, carefully selected some cucumbers and sweet corn and put them on a plate and took it out to the verandah and placed it before the ladies. Only then, as if he had enough time to sort out his ideas, did he lift his bushy brows, fold his arms ceremoniously, and say, 'Hukkum, there are two families; both are well-to-do, and surprisingly, both seem anxious to settle things with Gangaram.'

'What's so surprising about that?' said Pari, irritated with Khyali's unnecessary procrastination. 'They may be talking to Gangaram but they know the haveli is behind him.'

'Even if they are well-to-do and show an interest in Sita, we must be careful. After all Sita is a daughter of the house,' said the mistress, more loudly than she had intended.

'Hukkum, we have already politely told the first group which came in the morning to leave, saying we will think about it. After talking to them, Gokulji and I detected that they were only anxious to know how much dowry the haveli will give Sita,' said the cook. Then standing erect and with an air of exaggerated self-importance he went on, 'Hukkum, the second party which came later seems very suitable. The father is the headman of the village. They never talked of money or boasted like the first group. The boy is in the tenth class. If you permit, I will call the women so you can see for yourself what kind of people they are.'

The mistress nodded and the cook pushed the thali of cut vegetables to the side and got up. Dhapu and Ganga quietly went out of the kitchen with him.

In the background could be heard the sound of the monkey-man's drum beating faster and the excited voices of the children.

A group of women entered the courtyard all at once accompanied by Dhapu and Ganga. Some were thin, others were young and plump but all the faces were heavily veiled.

Their silver bracelets jingled as they bent down and touched the feet of the mistress, then shyly sat down on the floor.

'Kanwarani Sa, this is Shivram's mother; these are two of his aunts; one is his mother's sister and the other his father's sister,' said Dhapu. Three young girls that were with the women looked around the courtyard with bewildered eyes while Dhapu made the introductions.

'How much land does Shivram's father own?' asked the mistress, coming to the point directly without any fuss.

There was a moment's silence and then with folded hands the eldest of the women spoke. 'With your blessings he has five acres, a well, two bullocks and a brick house.'

The mistress trying not to sound pleased asked in a business-like manner, 'Is Shivram going to continue in school or not?'

'Shivram is in the tenth class; he has never failed so far; the rest is God's will,' replied the woman modestly.

'How soon do you want the marriage?' asked the mistress; her voice was softer than before.

'Hukkum, Shivram's grandfather is bed-ridden and I am getting old too; what more can I say?'

Bhagwat Singhji's wife having got the essential information about the family had nothing more to say. She got up with her usual composure, delicately brushed her skirt with her hand and then with Kanta and Geeta left the courtyard. She knew they would not talk freely in her presence.

As soon as Bhagwat Singhji's wife had left, the maids broke into a loud chatter. The older women lifted their saris from their faces, they talked freely about their village and Sita. Pari coaxed them to have the savouries that had been brought. The women shook their heads politely, saying that they were full, but the maids persisted; they knew that village women were proud and would not eat and drink unless they were properly persuaded.

'Bara Bhabhi, Bara Bhabhi,' shouted Vijay as she and Sita came running into the courtyard. 'The man wants money! The monkey can do a hundred tricks! We have asked him to come again.' She looked around to find her grandmother.

'Bai Sa, the man is a crook,' said Dhapu holding Vijay fondly in her arms.

'No he isn't, you should see his monkey dance before you talk. He is not lame either,' replied Vijay angrily.

'Bai Sa, you go inside, I will pay him,' Pari said putting her hand in her blouse pocket.

'No, give me the money,' insisted Vijay, stamping her feet impatiently.

'Bai Sa, what will you do when Sita gets married?' Dhapu teased as Vijay stood scowling at Pari.

Sita quickly ran out of the courtyard, a bundle of giggles, and Vijay ran after her.

'These two children are inseparable,' said Pari to the prospective in-laws, her eyes full of adoration. The women's eyes lighted up when they saw how Sita was treated by the granddaughter of the haveli.

Before leaving they went to Bhagwat Singhji's wife to thank her for her graciousness and beseeched her to give Sita to them for Shivram. Knowing that no reply is given directly, they touched her feet and left. Pari accompanied them out as they left by the side door of the courtyard. As soon as the sound of the women's anklets faded Bhagwat Singhji's wife left Geeta in the sitting room and went to the kitchen. An air heavy with the aroma of spices drifted out of the kitchen.

'A boy who is in the tenth class will never work in the fields,' said the mistress as she sat down in the verandah. She added, 'Khyali, naturally they wouldn't discuss the dowry with me, but how much will they expect?'

'Do you think, Hukkum, they would dare haggle with us over money?' the cook said. He grinned ingratiatingly, as if he had arranged everything.

'That's all very well, but don't be too sure. Remember Sita is not beautiful and the havelis are not what they were,' the mistress said a little anxiously.

'I told them we would feed the bridegroom's party but not more than fifty people,' said the cook decisively, as if he were the man to dictate the terms.

'Don't believe what Khyali says, Kanwarani Sa,' butted in Dhapu giving the cook a scornful look. 'Even when my daughter got married there were seventy to eighty people in the bridegroom's party and they town people. These are village folks. They can't afford to displease their caste community; we will have to feed at least two hundred.'

'Two hundred?' repeated the mistress with consternation. 'We will do our best of course, but Dhapu, don't forget the times have changed. When your daughter was married, Kanwar Saheb was a minister,' said the mistress in a sad voice.

'Kanwar Sa will never change no matter what he is. He will always remain generous where his servants are concerned,' replied Dhapu, proudly.

'Hukkum, don't worry about the expenses. Why do you think that a family with land, bullocks and a brick house have come knocking at our doors?' said the cook, as if he were the only one to understand the real motive behind the proposal. 'They want a girl who can read and write. Shivram is the first boy in their village to have gone beyond the primary school. They want to find a girl in their caste who has gone to school. I can tell from what they said to me that they will accept anything you give them. They will make none of the customary demands.'

Geeta came out of the sitting room. She had on purpose remained inside once the village women came. She had vaguely heard the questions and answers and wanted to know more. Bhagwat Singhji's wife looked at Geeta fondly and said humbly, 'Binniji, you will be blessed. It is all your doing. I am glad you did not listen to us ignorant women. We could never have arranged a match like this for Sita.' Geeta looked away embarrassed.

Pari seemed deep in thought as she came back into the courtyard after seeing the women up to the haveli gate. She sat down on the edge of the verandah and said with unusual force, 'These are really good, simple people; they are not like most villagers who say one thing and mean another. They are really not after a big dowry. But Binniji, they insist only on one condition.' Then she stopped as if what she were going to say was very important and that Geeta should understand that. 'They don't want Sita to continue going to school.'

'But that's absurd. Why shouldn't she continue, while she is still with us?' said Geeta impetuously.

Then, ignoring Geeta, Pari turned to Bhagwat Singhji's wife and said bluntly, 'The aunt took me aside and begged that Sita stop going to school as soon as she is engaged to be married. As it is, the village elders criticize them for educating the boy instead of putting him to work in the fields. It's enough for them to have a girl who can read and write. But a prospective daughter-in-law who is attending school would never be accepted by the elders and even the family would think she was lacking in modesty.'

'Kanwarani Sa, don't let this boy slip out of our hands. We won't find another like him,' said the cook avoiding looking at Geeta and addressing his remarks to the mistress.

'I don't understand what difference it makes to the village elders if Sita continues with her studies,' Geeta snapped. 'They can do what they like with her once she is their daughter-in-law but not before. Don't those stupid people realize that once she has passed the tenth class she could earn a hundred rupees?'

'Binniji, you should know by now that it would be an intolerable disgrace to have a daughter-in-law earning a wage. Money is not the only thing that matters to the poor, it is keeping to family customs that matters most,' Pari replied, in a gentle, coaxing voice as if she were talking to a child.

'Bhabhi, let Sita continue in school. It's good for her future,' Geeta pleaded, looking at her mother-in-law as if she was the only person who would understand the importance of education.

But Bhagwat Singhji's wife kept silent, her face sad. She knew this time Geeta would not succeed in persuading even her father-in-law. Then in a heavy sorrowful voice Bhagwat Singhji's wife, looking steadily into the dark anxious eyes of Geeta, said, 'Binniji, you have made Sita's life. We have all been proved wrong. But now we must accept their condition. Marriage is the only security for women. It is you who have made it possible for her to be married into a family with land, with a well, a brick house and bullocks. Don't insist further.'

Chapter II

THE NEWS THAT Sita was going to be engaged spread within hours of Bhagwat Singhji giving his approval. Jeewan Niwas was visited by a stream of inquisitive women. They came in groups at all times of the day and asked a hundred and one questions. Who arranged the match and how? What was the dowry? How did the haveli explain Lakshmi's disappearance? The women listened to the discreet answers from the maids, but when no one was looking they exchanged incredulous glances with one another. It was too good to believe that for a dark, thin girl with a mother whose whereabouts were not known, a family with land, a well, a pair of bullocks and a brick house would come begging.

The women left unconvinced, muttering among themselves. In fact, some said that the boy was blind in one eye; others that the family was heavily in debt and that the haveli had agreed to pay off the debt. They said the mistress was obliged to do this for Sita; after all, it was a servant of the haveli that had ruined her mother's life.

Meanwhile, the haveli got busy thinking about Sita's engagement. There were not many days left before the saris and jewellery would have to be sent for the engagement ceremony.

Bhagwat Singhji's wife and Pari sat in a low-ceilinged room about ten by twelve feet. Ganga opened the big tin trunks that were lined along the wall and took out the old clothes that were buried in camphor.

'These four old saris when dyed will look as if they were new,' said Bhagwat Singhji's wife, putting them aside. 'Pari, how many saris in all do we need?'

'For the present at least six new sets of clothes for the women; four sets for the men and two for Sita. Then we must start thinking of her trousseau.'

'Kanwarani Sa, this girl deserves nothing; just look at her,' said Dhapu dragging Sita by the hand in front of the open door of the room. 'She has been sitting under the banyan tree sobbing.'

'Leave her alone, Dhapu,' said the mistress gently. 'Why are you crying, Sita? Has Vijay again been mean to you?'

'Hukkum, let me go to school,' stuttered the girl between sobs.

'Who has said no to you, but today is Sunday, child; there is no school. So why do you cry?'

In order to distract Sita, Bhagwat Singhji's wife took out a four anna piece from her blouse pocket and gave it to Sita and said, 'Now wipe your face and go get the salted peanuts you like so much.'

'Only a mother-in-law will put her right,' said Dhapu acidly. 'She has got used to an easy life; that is why she likes school. Who wouldn't? It's better to be opening and shutting books than sweeping and cleaning.'

The mistress heaved a vast sigh of relief as Sita wiped her nose with the back of her hand and left.

'Dhapu, where is Binniji, is she still upset about Sita?' inquired the mistress anxiously.

'I don't know, Hukkum; but today Binniji sent the women away and said that she was not well and would not take the classes,' said Dhapu almost in a whisper.

'I am glad she did that. These classes have given her nothing but headaches. Pari, did you notice the other day, how Nandu Bai Sa and the rest avoided talking to Binniji?' said the mistress in a troubled voice.

'Whatever anyone may say, Binniji has changed the lives of these girls, Hukkum; most of them now can read and write; they can get work, they don't have to depend on the havelis,' said Pari.

'Yes, that may be so, Pari, but our life is with the women in the havelis; we can't afford to displease our own community beyond a point. I have noticed a change in them even towards me,' said Bhagwat Singhji's wife with an air of self-righteousness.

Pari lowered her heavy wrinkled eyelids and took out her snuff box, inhaling a pinch. She added after a little reflection, 'What are these ladies from big havelis complaining about now? Their own daughters and daughters-in-law come and sit for hours with Binniji. It's only the poor that they prevent from coming,' said Pari with bitterness. 'Do you know, Hukkum, that Kanta Bai Sa's sister-in-law has threatened her maid that if her daughter comes here once more she will take all her jewellery away? Many women are really afraid. Soon, no one who is poor will be able to come to the classes.' Pari spoke with unusual force, her sunken cheeks flushed with anger. She had forgotten her initial objection to the classes. Besides, her deep loyalty to the haveli always came to the surface when anyone was critical of her mistress.

Bhagwat Singhji's wife knew better than to contradict

Pari when she was defending the haveli. But the mistress had also noticed that fewer maids from the havelis were coming to the classes. She had not asked Geeta about it as she thought it would only ignite her simmering anger.

While the mistress and Pari were silently putting away the clothes, they could hear that there was excitement in the kitchen. Even across the courtyard the cook's voice, deliberately raised, sounded authoritative. 'The astrologer has given only three days as auspicious. The boy's family want the first, which falls at the beginning of next month. This gives you women only three weeks to get everything ready. As for Gangaram, he sits and smoked his bidi. He has not even arranged for the four hundred rupees, the minimum he will need for the engagement. The haveli cannot give him everything. He thinks money is like dry leaves on a tree that fall when you shake the branches. But he is not the only one who thinks I have money buried in the ground; they keep borrowing but never bother to pay me back,' the cook added, unable to conceal his pride in the fact that he was the only servant who had money to lend.

Dhapu looked at the cook with icy contempt; she knew the last dig referred to her.

'Don't shout so loudly, don't you know that Kanwar Sa has visitors?' said Gangaram coming into the courtyard. His gait was unsteady and his walk slow, but his voice was strong.

The cook did not finish the sentence he had started. Instead he looked menacingly at Gangaram and said, 'Just remember that there are three weeks left for you to make all the arrangements. Get some money from somewhere.'

The mistress came into the kitchen. But Pari sat on where she was; she felt tired and weak.

'Dhapu, go up and take this hot glass of milk for Binniji. I know she is depressed, but this time not even her father-in-law can help her,' said Bhagwat Singhji's wife, handing the silver tumbler to the maid.

Geeta was lying on the mattress idly turning the pages of a magazine. Sita sat curled up in a corner and cracked open the peanuts she had bought for herself.

'Binnijji, drink this; Kanwarani Sa is worried about you,' said Dhapu sitting down on the floor.

'Leave me alone,' said Geeta sharply.

'Binniji, you can kill me but I won't leave until you have drunk the milk,' said Dhapu as she raised the glass to Geeta's mouth.

Geeta took it and gulped down the milk and handed the glass back to Dhapu, but still she showed no signs of leaving. Instead, she said to Sita, 'Go and play with Vijay Bai Sa. She has been looking for you everywhere.' Sita for once obeyed. She gathered up the remaining peanuts in her hands and left, leaving the door ajar.

Seeing Dhapu's droopy face, Geeta said, 'Now what are you grumpy about? You should be happy; soon there will be enough commotion in the haveli to keep you satisfied for the next six months.' Geeta drew up her knees and rested her chin on them. Her thin nostrils were distended; her face tense, but after all these years she had learned to keep her emotions under control.

'Do you think I care what happens to that wretched girl?' said Dhapu. 'Ever since she was born she has caused nothing but trouble.' Her face seemed darker than usual.

'No, of course you don't care, now that you have succeeded in crippling her future.' Geeta could not contain herself. 'What is the idea of stopping Sita from continuing with school when she is going to remain in the haveli for another two years even after she is married?'

Dhapu did not react. She caught hold of Geeta's feet and

edged near the mattress. 'Forget Sita, Hukkum. Kanwarani Sa has already told Sita that she can go to school tomorrow. But, Binniji, I have something more important to tell you.'

'Now what have you discovered?'

Dhapu drew in her breath and said in a whisper, 'I heard Khyali telling Gokulji that perhaps the woman who gives Sita ladoos is Lakshmi.'

Geeta moved forward in astonishment. She pushed back the wisps of hair that fell over her face and said eagerly, 'When did you hear this?'

'Two days ago, but I waited until I could get it confirmed. It was only late last night that I could get a word alone with the cook. He was furious that I had overheard him talk. He said it was a secret and he didn't want women interfering; above all he warned me not to mention a word to the mistress.'

As Dhapu took a deep breath, Geeta stood up and defiantly said, 'Who is the cook to determine who should know and who should not? Tell me where Lakshmi is and I will myself go and get her.'

Dhapu looked at Geeta with frightened eyes and her voice shook as she pleaded. 'No, no, Binniji, don't do anything in a hurry; Lakshmi is not going to come back whatever you do, and if you try and see her, I can tell you, she will shut the door in your face.'

'But why?'

'Khyali has found out that she is now staying in the house of a tongawalla, whose wife is in the village. Before, she had worked for a tailor, so you see what she has become. But now her mother's heart aches to see her child.'

'That is why I say, let us bring her back; she won't then have to work for all these people.'

'Binniji, you don't understand; the cook has already made

inquiries through a friend. Lakshmi is happy and doesn't want to change her life.'

'I don't trust any of you; I want to find out myself,' said Geeta ignoring the heavy tears falling down Dhapu's cheeks.

There was silence; neither of them spoke. But when Dhapu had mastered her emotions she turned gravely to Geeta and said in a controlled voice: 'Binniji, don't do anything just now. If you do, Sita's life will be ruined forever. She will never find a boy, let alone a boy who will one day become a teacher. I beg you, let her get married and then you can do what you like.'

Geeta sat down as abruptly as she had got up. She knew there was no question of her going out in search of Lakshmi. She felt defeated and yet this time she understood Dhapu's reasoning and accepted it.

Chapter III

AS SOON AS the first rays of the sun came up, Sita quietly slipped from under her quilt, rolled up her bed and stacked it in the corner of the room. She left Vijay and her two little brothers sleeping, and came down to the courtyard. She quickly washed her face and put on her best frock. Then she combed and plaited her hair with the special red nylon ribbon and went into the kitchen verandah. The cook was already in the kitchen blowing hard into the fire to get it going. He looked at Sita and gave her an affectionate pat on the head. She took a roti, and a tepid glass of milk, and quickly munching the roti, gulped down the milk. Then she went to the outside verandah and sat down on the cold marble floor. She saw some village women swiftly walking past with balanced bundles of firewood and vegetables on their heads to the accompaniment of clanging anklets and jingling bangles. Men, pedalling to work, hunched over bicycles, rang their bells to warn the women to make way. But Sita paid little attention to the street's coming awake. She was preoccupied with the things she had made to give away as presents in school. 'I will give the crochet bag to the woman who gives me ladoos. But what if she never comes again?' She dismissed that possibility, drew a deep breath and reflected again: 'The bead fan I will give to Renu—my real friend. The embroidered handkerchief I will give to my class teacher.' She was so occupied with her own thoughts that she didn't hear the courtyard door open and Pari emerge limping.

'So you are sitting here dreaming while poor Vijay Bai Sa is frantically looking for you in every room. Come inside; Kanwarani Sa wants to see if the anklets are the right size for you.'

Sita got up obediently but looked at the old maid with cold, menacing eyes for having disturbed her in her reverie. They bumped into Vijay at the entrance of the courtyard.

'Where have you been?' said Vijay, catching hold of Sita's hand and turning her around.

'Bai Sa, leave her alone for a minute,' said Pari. 'Bara Bhabhi wants to see her in her room.'

Vijay accompanied Sita and Pari to her grandmother and, impatient at the delay, snatched an anklet from Dhapu's hand and fastened it on Sita's foot. 'You see? They are all right,' said Vijay standing up. 'Pariji, you don't understand. I have my monthly test. I can't be late to school today.' Vijay took Sita's hand and pulled her along. 'Come on, you can take it off in the car.'

Pari stood quietly but watched the two little girls leave. 'Well, there she goes to school again; Vijay Bai Sa treats her like a sister; nobody can stop her,' she observed affectionately.

'Let her go today, Sita knows that she cannot continue for long,' said Bhagwat Singhji's wife getting up. She went to the kitchen; Pari followed her.

'How times have changed. If I had run around like this,

Bhabha Sa would have chained me to her bed,' said Pari with a slight tinge of regret.

'There you are again talking about the past; thank your god that you don't have much longer to live. What the girls will do in the future will be much worse than anything you see now,' said the cook with an air of great wisdom.

'You are right, Khyali,' said the mistress with a sigh and sat down in the warm kitchen. 'Pari, you forget how Bhabha Sa scolded me if I even looked out of the window with my face uncovered, once I was thirteen. Pari, neither of us have known what it was to be young and carefree but don't let us talk of the past; it makes me sad,' said Bhagwat Singhji's wife. Then as if to get out of her reminiscent mood she turned to the cook and continued in an even voice, 'Khyali, leave the cooking to Ganga and go to the silversmith. The anklets are all right but get four more bangles and two bracelets.'

Just as she was explaining the details of what kind of design she wanted, there was banging on the outside door. The mistress rose quickly and hurried across the courtyard and went into her room. She didn't want to be seen in her old sari and skirt by outsiders.

'Now who has come at this time of the day?' said Dhapu throwing the broom in a corner before she went to open the door. She took two steps backwards with surprise when she recognized the visitors were ladies from Daulat Singhji's haveli, the most prestigious haveli in the city. She immediately bent down and touched their feet.

Pari saw the ladies enter from the kitchen verandah and got up, and walked towards them. With folded hands she said, 'Welcome, Hukkum, to the haveli.' The women accepted her greetings as they followed Pari and Dhapu to the sitting room. The maids accompanying them sat in the verandah as the ladies went in.

There was an awkward silence as the women sat down. Even Pari seemed at a loss for the appropriate words to say.

Daulat Singhji's wife lifted the sari from her face as she sat down on the thin mattress and looking at Pari affectionately, she said, 'I am sorry to disturb you but you know how it is in the havelis, my time is not my own. I had a little time today and so we came unannounced. I hope Kanwarani Sa is not busy.' Before Pari could reply, Bhagwat Singhji's wife entered the room. The younger women got up instantly, bent down and touched her feet. Daulat Singhji's wife stood up too. The formality over, Bhagwat Singhji's wife said in a well-modulated voice, 'Please sit down, Hukkum. You should not have taken the trouble to come. It is for me to pay my respects to you, especially when you have trouble walking,' she said addressing her remarks to Daulat Singhji's wife.

'Pains and aches are part of old age, but if I took to my bed, who would look after the haveli?' replied the senior lady with an affected air of melancholy.

'You are right, Hukkum, so many people are dependent on you that you can't afford to be ill but still you must take care of yourself,' replied Bhagwat Singhji's wife a little distractedly. Then she looked at Dhapu who took the hint that she must get refreshments for the visitors.

'No don't trouble yourself; on Monday we eat only once a day,' said Daulat Singhji's wife as she saw Dhapu get up to leave the room.

'You have honoured us with your presence; how can you leave without having something?' said Bhagwat Singhji's wife beseechingly.

'We have eaten and drunk in this haveli as in no other, Hukkum. Who can ever forget the past splendour of Jeewan Niwas? The names of Kanwar Sa and his forefathers are written in the annals of Rajasthan.' The younger women nodded as the elder lady spoke in an extravagant manner.

Bhagwat Singhji's wife flushed deeply; she clasped and unclasped her hands nervously. She looked into the dark brown eyes behind the gold rimmed spectacles to fathom the meaning behind the flow of words.

Daulat Singhji's father had had a grudge against Sangram Singhji, which he had passed on to his son. They, as a family, had done their utmost to poison the reputation of Jeewan Niwas to the Maharana, but when they failed they had tried other means to undermine the standing of Sangram Singhji. It was well known among the havelis that nothing gave Daulat Singhji's family more pleasure than the misfortunes of Jeewan Niwas. On every occasion they were the first to come and condole with the family especially when Sangram Singhji had problems with the palace.

But in spite of all this, Sangram Singhji and then Bhagwat Singhji were never amiss in showing them the highest courtesy due as one of the oldest families in Udaipur. This attitude only further infuriated them. Daulat Singhji could never forget that once the ministers of Udaipur were chosen from his family. This honour had been taken away from them and given to Sangram Singhji's father and remained with his family until the Rana lost his powers and the State of Udaipur was dissolved. Daulat Singhji's family were still the richest family but they resented the prestige enjoyed by Jeewan Niwas in the last two generations.

'Where is Binniji?' asked the wife of Daulat Singhji. 'Hukkum, you have been blessed with many things but your daughter-in-law is the haveli's greatest ornament.'

'You have always been generous in your praises for this haveli,' replied Bhagwat Singhji's wife with customary humility.

Just as she had finished her sentence, Geeta came in and silently bent down and touched the feet of the veiled ladies.

'May you always wear red and may your sons carry on the illustrious name of this haveli,' said Daulat Singhji's wife putting her hand on Geeta's hand.

Outside in the courtyard the chatter was getting louder. The maids of the two havelis were exchanging news. Dhapu and Ganga had cut the fruit and were impatiently waiting for the boy they had dispatched in haste to the bazaar to buy the milk sweets.

Bhagwat Singhji's wife was getting a little restless; she knew that her guests had come for some special reason and their polite small talk made her, for once, impatient and nervous. Daulat Singhji's wife was not one of her favourite women. She was arrogant and carried herself with a forbidding dignity. Her face was strong and determined. There was little gentleness in her expression; it seemed she never wanted others to forget that her family was the richest in Udaipur. Bhagwat Singhji's wife looked at the enamel necklace round her neck and recognized it as the gift of the Maharani to her on the occasion of the birth of her son. After a few more exchanges Bhagwat Singhji's wife was getting inattentive, she looked relieved when Ganga came in with the silver tray and plates.

'Hukkum, why did you take so much trouble?' said Daulat Singhji's wife looking over her gold rimmed glasses and surveying the tray.

Geeta got up to serve the guests.

Daulat Singhji's wife said with practised dignity, 'Hukkum, our children are growing up and we must think of their future before we are too old. While we are alive we must try everything to preserve our traditions and maintain the position which we have inherited from our forefathers.'

Then she shifted her weight from one leg to the other and continued, 'You know Vir Singh, my son, has just passed his B.A. with a first class. We are grateful to God, but you know my father-in-law is getting old; his last wish is to see his only grandson engaged before his eyes in a family of equal status.'

At last the purpose of the visit had become clear to Bhagwat Singhji's wife. Her eyes lost their nervousness; she tried to conceal her joy and satisfaction. But she kept silent; she wanted the proud Daulat Singhji's wife to spell out every word.

'Vijay Bai Sa is also growing up; she must be turning thirteen now,' Daulat Singhji's wife said. Then she hesitatingly cleared her throat, hoping that Bhagwat Singhji's wife would meet her halfway, but when she picked up a piece of the milk sweet and put it on her plate, Daulat Singhji's wife continued, her voice sweet and mellow: 'Bai Sa, I have come today to ask you to give us Vijay Bai Sa. One day I want to hand her the keys to the haveli safe; if I knew she were coming into our family, my happiness would be complete.'

'You honour us by this proposal, but Vijay is still a child even if she is nearly thirteen years old,' said Bhagwat Singhji's wife lightly. But she managed to keep her voice steady. She did not want Daulat Singhji's wife to think that a proposal from that family was automatically acceptable to her.

'I know Binniji is not like us, she won't approve of early marriages; but Vir Singh is going to England for higher studies. We only want to have his engagement ceremony before he leaves; marriage can wait and meanwhile Vijay Bai Sa can continue her education,' said Daulat Singhji's wife looking at Geeta who sat erect, her lips twitching with rage and her hands tightly clasped around her knees.

'Bai Sa, you are wise to settle Bapu Vir Singh's marriage before he leaves for a foreign land. I am told women there are very different from ours,' said Bhagwat Singhji's wife with an air of great wisdom.

'Hukkum, convey our desire to Kanwar Sa. I need not tell you that your child would be in want of nothing in our family. What more can I say?' said Daulat Singhji's wife with feigned modesty.

'Who can doubt the comforts that a daughter-in-law would enjoy in your haveli? Then to have a mother-in-law like you, what more could a mother want for her daughter?' replied Bhagwat Singhji's wife using equally exaggerated terms.

'Hukkum,' she said after insisting that Daulat Singhji's wife eat another piece of fruit, 'we must first see if the horoscopes match; I will send for the family priest as soon as possible.' She knew that astrologers provided the most polite way of declining a marriage proposal. No one ever felt slighted if a proposed marriage was not accepted because the stars foretold misfortune.

Pari and Dhapu offered the ladies sherbet with greater attention, their faces visibly happy. The ladies pleaded that they had eaten enough. Daulat Singhji's wife's face beamed with contentment as she got up slowly; her knee joints cracked and she winced a little. After an elaborate exchange of praises for each other's havelis, the ladies finally left. Bhagwat Singhji's wife and Geeta escorted them right up to the back door of the haveli.

As soon as Dhapu closed the door behind the ladies, she came running into the courtyard shouting: 'So at last the great Daulat Singhjis have come begging to us; who wouldn't for my lotus-faced Vijay Bai Sa?'

Ganga and Champa were going round and round hitting the back of a thali with their hands, laughing with joy.

Geeta walked slowly back into the courtyard; the corners of her mouth sagged as if she were about to cry.

'Binniji, you can't leave without giving us something,' the maids said surrounding her. But as they saw their mistress's flushed smouldering face, they quietly shrank away. Geeta followed her mother-in-law into the room.

'What do you think of the proposal?' said Bhagwat Singhji's wife lightly, as she sat down exhausted, and then as if it were pleasant to reminisce she continued, 'All these years they have resented your father-in-law's position in the State and his prestige in the community. However, they are not only wealthy but among the three or four families who have produced ministers and enjoyed a special place in the Maharana's court. Anyone would give their daughter to that haveli.' Half suspecting that these arguments would not appeal to Geeta, Bhagwat Singhji's wife added, 'What we want is a good boy for Vijay. Vir Singh is a clever boy and he will come back from England as educated as my son I am sure. Even your father-in-law won't reject the proposal out of hand.' Bhagwat Singhji's wife knew that was the only way to impress her daughter-in-law.

'Bhabhi, whatever happens, Vijay can't get engaged at this age,' blurted out Geeta. Bhagwat Singhji's wife looked up surprised. This was the first time that Geeta had spoken in a raised voice to her. Then as she saw Geeta's eyes darken and her pale face turn hard and stern she kept silent.

After the outburst, Geeta went up to her room and lay down on her bed. She saw the faces of the heavily bejewelled ladies on the morning and was once again filled with hate for all that Udaipur stood for. 'What a mistake I made to stay on here; I could have easily persuaded Ajay to leave. This had to come sooner or later. Now I am really trapped and cannot escape. But on this point I will never give in, whatever happens. If I have ruined my life, the children are not going to ruin theirs.' The violence of her thoughts sent shafts of pain through her head. Her lips were pursed together and her body was taut. The maids dared not go up. They knew that their chatter would only make Geeta more furious. This was a serious consideration and they knew that their young mistress would not stand nonsense from them.

Geeta lay on her bed engulfed in a cloud of emotion which she did not try to dispel. It was late in the afternoon when Ajay Singh came up to her room.

'So you are upset with all this talk of marriage?' he said sitting down on the bed.

Geeta sat up, her hair dishevelled and her eyes red, her voice trembling with anger. She said, 'I have put up with enough in your family, and I am not prepared to bend any more. I won't ever agree to this criminal act of deciding who Vijay will marry when she is still a child. I know exactly how these things work in this place. First they will only want an engagement and no sooner has that been done, they'll start talking about marriage. You are all a bunch of hypocrites. In order to get the girl you want you make any promise, agree to anything. Don't I know the smooth velvety language of the havelis. Well, Ajay, let me tell you that I don't care what family Vir Singh comes from or how much money he has buried in the ground. I will never agree to engage Vijay to a boy who is still in college. Who knows what he will be like when he is a man?'

'But why are you getting so worked up? Who has ever said that Vijay will be engaged? After all, if a proposal comes for our daughter, should we drown ourselves in disgrace? Now get up and answer me,' said Ajay Singh seriously.

His complacency infuriated Geeta even more. She said, her voice quivering and her eyes moist with tears, 'Don't think this time I am going to be taken in by your smooth soft words. I was a fool, I now realize, not to have insisted that you leave Udaipur. But don't think that I can be fooled again. I know nothing matters more than money and prestige to you all. I know your mother is happy that at last a rival haveli has been humbled by us to come begging for your daughter.'

'Geeta, before you jump to all these conclusions, just listen to me,' said Ajay Singh stretching his legs on the bed. 'Do you really think we would marry Vijay just for money? And have you ever seen my father do anything for the sake of money? He too could have mounds of gold had he not cherished principles of integrity and honesty above everything else, and now when it comes to his granddaughter's happiness, you think he will exchange her for gold.'

Geeta gulped down the words that were on her lips. She wasn't thinking of her father-in-law when she attacked her husband, but the women in the haveli.

'All right, then you tell me what you think of the proposal,' said Geeta sharply, trying to keep her voice down.

'I haven't even given it a thought,' said Ajay Singh carelessly. 'When you have a girl like Vijay, hundreds of proposals come, otherwise her parents send out a hundred proposals and wait and see which family accepts their daughter. How did your parents find a husband for you? Have you forgotten? I don't understand why you have made yourself sick over this visit. Now get up and stop wasting your energy on trivial things. Cooped up in the haveli, I think, you have lost your sense of humour. In the evening when no one can see you, I am going to take you out for a drive round Lake Pichola.' He gave a little pat on Geeta's shoulder and then pulled her to her feet.

'There you go again trying to appease me. No, I am not

going out alone with you; the whole of Udaipur will be talking the minute we are out of the gate. They are just waiting for a chance to attack me,' said Geeta defiantly.

'Why do you care what the others say about you? As long as I am with you, no one dare lift a finger against you,' said Ajay Singh resolutely.

Geeta got up; her husband's words had calmed her. His assurances to her were not mere words. He knew the strength she got from him was real. She straightened her hair with her hands and sat down on the easy chair.

'Now tell me, who told you I was upset? Was it your mother?' she asked finally breaking into a smile.

But before Ajay Singh could reply the door opened with a bang and Vijay burst in shouting. 'Bhabhi, Pari says Sita can't go to school again; that today was her last day. She is an awful bully. I hate her. Sita couldn't even give all the presents she had taken with her. The old woman with the ladoos, for whom Sita had especially made a bag, never came today. Please let Sita go to school tomorrow.'

'Vijay, you are a big girl now,' said Geeta gently, drawing Vijay to her side, 'You know Pari is doing this in Sita's interest, when she says she must not go to school any more. We must prepare for her engagement. If you love her, then don't make it more difficult for her. From now on she can join my classes and you can help her to go on with reading and writing.'

But Ajay Singh, thinking Geeta was giving in to Pari in her present temper with the haveli, interrupted and said, 'No, there is no reason to stop Sita from going to school. Pari is not the one to decide everything. Vijay, you go and tell her that Sita will go to school as long as Bhabhi thinks right.'

Geeta looked at her husband full in the face and said in a firm, determined voice: 'Pari is right. In three weeks Sita is to be engaged; the condition is that she gives up school. The boy is smart and we can help him to go on with his studies; he is already in the tenth and comes first in his class. We must not interfere. This means a life of happiness for Sita. But Sita cannot continue with school.'

Both Ajay Singh and Vijay kept silent.

Chapter IV

THE NEXT MORNING Geeta came down especially early and sat with the children while they drank their milk. She saw Sita's drawn face and was afraid that the child might burst out crying any minute. Her eyes were misty and she looked forlorn.

Sita stood silent behind the pillar while the other children ate.

Vijay too was sad. She didn't finish her milk nor her halva. Since her mother had taken her into her confidence, however, she didn't say anything. Then when she heard the horn of the car she said bravely, 'Sita, you stay with Bhabhi; don't be unhappy. I will buy you the pair of earrings you liked in the corner shop. It won't be long before I am back and then we will do something exciting.'

As soon as Vijay and her brothers were out of the courtyard, Geeta took hold of Sita by the hand and sat her down beside her. She told her that once her engagement ceremony was over she would give her lessons every day. She assured her that she would not permit the maids to give her household work; she had nothing to be afraid of, that her life would remain the same. After all, one could learn just as well at home as in school.

Sita smiled. She was pacified by what the young mistress said to her.

Geeta then got up and sat in the verandah. She called Ganga to bring the skirt and blouse that had to be tried on Sita. Sita willingly put them on. She neither cried nor made a fuss. She did as she was told. After Sita had tried on all the clothes Geeta took her by the hand and went upstairs to dress for a visit to Daulat Singhji's haveli. Pari looked on with wonder at the sudden change in Sita's mood. Ganga seeing her so docile was about to say something to provoke her, when she heard the loud coarse voice of the cook.

'What a day. I must have seen an unlucky face first thing in the morning.' Then, as he came into the kitchen and saw the mistress, he lowered his voice and said, 'Kanwarani Sa, Sita's future uncle-in-law is here.' He looked agitated.

'Khyali, the poor man must have come to borrow money from you. Everyone knows you are rich,' said the mistress with a little laugh.

'Hukkum, what he has to say is important,' replied the cook gravely. The mistress stopped measuring out the rice for the servants and waited for him to go on.

'Sita's grandfather-in-law is ill and the family wants the marriage in place of the engagement. They have already consulted the astrologers and found that the next full moon is the most auspicious day for the marriage scopes.' The cook having finished, sat down holding his head in the palms of his hands.

'The way you looked, Khyali, I thought the marriage was off,' said the mistress with a sigh of relief. 'I was afraid that someone had raked up the past and the family had changed its mind.'

'If they did that now, I would knock their teeth in. We have hidden nothing from them. They dare not insult the haveli at this stage,' said the cook, proudly pushing his shoulders back.

'Khyali, forget about knocking people's teeth out,' said the mistress with a smile. 'I suppose we must agree to having the engagement and marriage together. We would have got ready for the engagement in two weeks, but to be ready for a marriage is quite another thing. You know Gangaramji. He can't be depended upon for anything.'

'And Khyali,' added Pari, with a businesslike air, 'buy the sugar, get the wheat and oil, engage the cooks. Last minute arrangements cost more.' Then she paused a moment as if probing her memory and said thoughtfully, 'Send someone to the village to warn Dhapu's husband that he will have to come here in ten days. Gangaram without Lakshmi can't preside over the marriage ceremony. Dhapu and her husband will have to do that.'

The mistress nodded her head appreciatively. As Pari talked the mistress thought of the saris that were already dyed and ready. She remembered she had some old silver ornaments which she could have melted and made new for Sita. She was not unduly worried. She had got ready in less time than two weeks for some of her maids' and their children's marriages.

There was the jingling of anklets. Dhapu came into the kitchen looking worried; she said, 'Kanwarani Sa, have you forgotten today we have to go to Daulat Singhji's haveli? Their maids have come twice to remind us.'

The mistress got up wearily and went to change her clothes. All of a sudden, she felt apprehensive about going to Daulat Singhji's haveli. Were it not for Geeta's reaction to the marriage proposal, she would have looked forward to spending a morning in that haveli. In spite of being arrogant and reserved as she was with most other women, Daulat Singhji's wife had always been open and gracious with her. But today Bhagwat Singhji's wife was uneasy. She had not forgotten Geeta's sharp retort to her after Daulat Singhji's wife's visit. Bhagwat Singhji's wife was proud and sensitive and did not want to broach the subject again to Geeta. She did not even want to tell her that nothing is gained by openly showing one's feelings to others. She secretly hoped that Geeta would be civil to the ladies.

Geeta sat ready in her room waiting to be called downstairs. She felt a certain emptiness within as if she no longer had the strength to play a part. But still there was a strange calm within her that comes from being sure of oneself. She was not afraid of facing the domineering personality of Daulat Singhji's wife. Geeta knew this time she would never give in.

'Binniji, do you know Sita is not going to be only engaged but married in two weeks?' said Dhapu excitedly coming into the room.

'Just as well. This will save a lot of money. What difference does it make to Sita? She will continue to stay here anyway,' replied Geeta. 'Bai, when do we have to leave for the haveli?'

'We are already late and I haven't yet changed my sari, but it won't take me too long,' said Dhapu, going into the children's room. In a few seconds she was out dressed, looking very satisfied with herself.

'Bai, why all this gold? Are you going to attend a feast or what?' said Geeta, surprised to see Dhapu in her best red sari and her gold earrings and bangles.

'If Daulat Singhji's maids come here all dressed up, in all their finery, do you think I am going there in my faded sari? No, not me.'

Geeta smiled and then all of a sudden the confidence she

had had a few minutes before left her and she asked fearfully, 'Bai, will they discuss Vijay's marriage? What am I to say? How I wish I had high fever. I hate going to that huge haveli.'

'Binniji, why do you worry about things that don't concern you? As long as your parents-in-law are alive, you don't have any problems. Vijay Bai Sa is the eldest grandchild, the first daughter in the family after forty years. They'll never marry her unless they are absolutely sure of everything. Don't worry. Leave it to your elders to decide what is best for Vijay Bai Sa.'

'My daughter's marriage is my concern. I will never agree to Vijay's engagement like this, no matter what happens. Even if it were the son of Maharana of Udaipur, I wouldn't agree,' replied Geeta as if she had thrown all restraint aside.

Dhapu looked at her mistress with startled eyes. She had never heard her speak so firmly, clearly and decisively. She silently accompanied Geeta downstairs. There were moments when Dhapu did not know how to approach her mistress.

Bhagwat Singhji's wife was ready and sitting quietly in her room. She got up when she heard the sound of anklets and walked with Geeta slowly out to the car. Pari and Champa got in front with Heeralal. Dhapu sat with the ladies in the back seat. Sita managed to squeeze in next to Dhapu. She was delighted that she was going to the haveli that one day might belong to Vijay.

Geeta was so preoccupied with her thoughts that she did not notice the happy faces of the people, nor of the children who peeped into the car when it stopped to let a pack of donkeys move off the road. She did not even mind the obnoxious smell of the open drains as the car turned into a narrow gully. She only came to life when the car stopped in front of the mammoth gates of Daulat Singhji's haveli.

The maids were already waiting outside the courtyard gate to escort the ladies to the inner apartments.

Daulat Singhji's wife, who sat with a group of women, got up as soon as Bhagwat Singhji's wife entered the large, rectangular room. The walls and ceiling were distempered in pink. From the ceiling hung enormous blue chandeliers. The floor was thickly carpeted and the divans were covered with gold embroidered velvet.

Daulat Singhji's wife greeted her with folded hands while the younger women touched the feet of Bhagwat Singhji's wife.

'It is truly gracious of you to come, especially when you are so busy preparing for Sita's marriage,' said Daulat Singhji's wife effusively.

'Pariji is managing everything. I don't have to worry, and in any case, it will be a simple marriage,' replied Bhagwat Singhji's wife.

Geeta's impassive face became at once tense; she knew that talk of Sita's marriage would lead to Vijay's engagement. She sat rigid, her hands tightly clenched in her lap. She knew that the question would be posed to her and she was trying her best to take control of her emotions to be ready to answer.

Daulat Singhji's wife got up as the maids came in with trays full of refreshments; she personally served Bhagwat Singhji's wife and Geeta. The women talked while they ate. They exchanged news about other havelis and seemed to enjoy themselves recounting tales of the grand old days.

While the women were busy talking, Geeta looked slyly through her veil around the room. The walls were painted with beautiful murals of hunting scenes, the doors carved heavily and studded with brass knobs. The room was richly decorated, though overcrowded with an assortment of brass, china, swords and guns.

Just as Geeta fixed her eyes on an old stone sculpture that stood in the corner, Daulat Singhji's wife said, 'Binniji, what a blessing that Bapu Sa has decided to stay on in Udaipur.' Then looking at Bhagwat Singhji's wife, she said, 'Hukkum, I can't see you without your grandchildren around you. They are the joy of the haveli.'

'Yes, that is so,' she said. 'But very soon Binniji will have to take over the running of the haveli. Every day I feel weaker. My eyes are also giving me trouble,' said Bhagwat Singhji's wife, sounding a little pathetic. She was a great one at pretending when it suited her convenience.

'Don't say that, Hukkum. No one can take your place in the haveli. It is because of your graciousness that rich and poor alike flock to Jeewan Niwas,' said Daulat Singhji's wife with genuine appreciation.

The maids of Jeewan Niwas had finished eating. 'Pari came into the room and stood silently for a while. This was an indication for Bhagwat Singhji's wife to take leave of the ladies.

Bhagwat Singhji's wife gathered her skirt and said, politely, 'Hukkum, we have taken a lot of your time. We must go now.'

Geeta was surprised that no one had hinted about the engagement. It was on everybody's mind, but the haveli was proud and had its codes of restraint and behaviour. They had the confidence that they did not have to implore anyone for a girl for their son.

But as they were getting up Daulat Singhji's wife said, 'Just a minute, Hukkum. You can't leave without giving Vir Singh your blessings.'

While Daulat Singhji's wife was talking, one of the ladies got up and went out of the room. Geeta sat up as if someone had prodded her in the back. Her half-parted lips froze and a cold shiver went through her body. The dreaded moment had at last come. But she hadn't expected to be confronted by the boy. Before she could sort out her feelings the door in front of her opened.

Vir Singh came into the room full of women. His face was a little flushed, but otherwise he was quite composed. Geeta looked at him through her veil. He was tall with clear cut features, his complexion was light. His long limbs had still the awkwardness of youth. But there was a certain dignity in his demeanour. As he bent down in front of Bhagwat Singhji's wife, she said, 'God bless you. We are proud of your success. May you continue to excel in your studies.' Then, after a pause, she added, 'Bapu Sa, you are soon going away into a foreign land, but wherever you are, don't ever forget the traditions of your haveli.'

Before Vir Singh moved away, Bhagwat Singhji's wife, in the customary way, took out a five rupee note from her blouse and gave it to him. Vir Singh accepted it in both hands and stood aside, his head slightly bent in respect to his elders.

'Yes, remember this, Bapu, never give up what is ours. The old can only give you their blessings. The rest is in your hands,' Daulat Singhji's wife repeated.

After the formalities of taking leave were over, the ladies and maids of Jeewan Niwas quietly stepped out of the room accompanied by the women of Daulat Singhji's haveli.

Heeralal was battling with a group of little urchins who had gathered round the car. He threatened them with his clenched fists but they still crept up from behind and touched the car from all sides. As soon as he saw the ladies approaching, he opened the door of the car. The women got in and as Heeralal started the engine, the children scattered in all directions in fear that he would run them over in revenge.

Bhagwat Singhji's wife drew her sari lower than usual

over her face and sank back in the seat. She did not speak, nor did Pari. Dhapu, sensing the tension, kept quiet even though she was bursting with all the questions she wanted to ask. Sita too kept quiet as she sat crouched near the mistress's feet.

It was after midday by the time the ladies returned to Jeewan Niwas. The courtyard was full of servants' children. A marriage meant special excitement for them. They were sure of fun whenever a feast was being arranged. The cook sat in the verandah, telling the children all that he still had to do. He warned them that they too would have to help or else he would see that they were not given any ladoos.

Bhagwat Singhji's wife walked into the courtyard and without saying a word to the children or to the cook, went to her room. The cook looked on, puzzled. Usually after a visit to a haveli, the women returned full of gossip and sat down and talked to him before going in to change. He wondered what had gone so wrong that even the talkative Dhapu was silent.

Geeta went up to her room. Sita was the only one who was all smiles. She immediately joined the children and began telling them about the big haveli.

Once in her room Geeta took off her sari, her jewels. She was distracted; she was not prepared for such a morning. All her fears had proven false. Daulat Singhji's wife had conducted herself with dignity. There was no vulgar display of affectation. She was haughty and proud, of that there was no question. But still Geeta had not been offended. There was something arresting about her personality. She was not one to beg or implore anyone for anything.

After changing into lighter clothes, Geeta sat down on her bed. There were no signs of displeasure on her face as she thought of Vir Singh. He was tall and handsome and he had the reticence and shyness of a well bred young man. Geeta had had only a glimpse of him. She was now sorry that she had not looked at him more closely. But she was so tense when he came into the room that her eyes were glazed. She thought: he is going abroad; he is clever; he will do well. Then she tried to wipe out the memory of Vir Singh from her mind. 'I cannot agree to the engagement. It is too early. What if he does not turn out as well as he looks? My Vijay would languish in that vast haveli,' she said vehemently to herself.

Another part of her mind thought of her own marriage. Her mother had been on the lookout for good boys for her and her sisters as soon as they had entered their teens. She was always ready to see prospective husbands for her daughters, and at last had selected Ajay Singh. And the reason was that he came from a good family and was considered by others who knew him as a man of character.

Geeta remembered with a shock that she, too, had not known her husband before her marriage. She had been married by her parents with the hope that their judgement of Ajay was right.

Her thoughts disturbed her. She didn't want to dwell on the subject any more. She was confused. She got up from her bed, took a book from the shelf and began to read.

Chapter V

SARJU, THE MIDWIFE, came to stay in the haveli three days before Sita's marriage. Her presence was essential. She had to perform the purification rituals before the actual ceremony. Sita had to be bathed in various aromatic herbs, her hair washed with various kinds of sweet smelling shampoos, then oiled. On her body perfumed paste was rubbed so that the skin would be soft and radiant. Sarju had performed these ceremonies for thirty years and knew exactly what to do. She was careful in the ingredients she used even though it was only Sita who was to be married. She knew that the mistress would compensate her generously for her work. While Sarju went on with her grinding and pounding the other maids, in between their work, talked to her. The mistress sat with Pari, in her verandah. The bundle of old saris made to look like new had just been brought in by one of Gokul's grandsons. Pari opened it and put the bright coloured saris beautifully starched before the mistress, who looked pleased. No one could tell that once the saris were stained and faded. They looked as if they had been bought from one of the most expensive shops in the bazaar.

Vijay, for the last week, had got ready early and sat with her grandmother till she had to leave for school. She was interested in the new clothes and jewellery that were being made ready for Sita.

'Bara Bhabhi, when I get married will you also give me so many saris?' asked Vijay. Her striking dark brown eyes with long curled eyelashes unwinkingly gazed at the heap of saris.

'My darling child,' exclaimed Bhagwat Singhji's wife, 'if I live to see you married, I will give you the choicest of silks and brocades. There will be such rejoicing in the haveli that no child of Udaipur will ever forget your wedding.' Then she looked at Vijay, her eyes full of adoration, and added in a low, sad voice, 'But child, I am getting old. Who knows whether I will see you married.' There was a catch in her voice. She stopped and turned her face away to hide her tears.

'And, Hukkum, I will dance and sing for days and nights. No one, not even Parijiji will be able to stop me. And, Hukkum, once my Vijay Bai Sa leaves the haveli, I will leave too. I will go and stay with her,' said Sita, her eyes sparkling with excitement.

Vijay got up embarrassed. She shouted to Vikram to hurry up with his milk.

'Sita, go to school with Bai Sa. In all this confusion I completely forgot to send word to your teachers. What must they be thinking of us? Go quickly, change. Invite your friends and teachers and don't forget to ask your principal. Pariji, even you didn't remind me. I hope they will forgive us calling them at the last minute,' said the mistress with sudden misgiving.

Sita quickly went into the little storeroom where she kept her clothes. She put on her best frock, smoothed her hair on top, then stood on the stone grinder and reached on the shelf for the crochet bag, which she had made for the old woman but had not given it because the day she had gone to school, the woman had not come. Sita hoped that she might see her today and give it to her.

'Bara Bhabhi, today we will be back early from school,' said Vijay as she held Sita's hand and walked out of the courtyard. Bhagwat Singhji's wife smiled; there was a faraway look in her eyes when she spoke.

'Pariji, if only Binniji wasn't so prejudiced against the havelis, today we would be preparing for Vijay's engagement. What an engagement that would be. But it is not my fate to see even my granddaughter engaged,' sighed the mistress.

Pari nodded sadly.

'Hukkum, if Vijay Bai Sa is destined to go to Daulat Singhji's haveli, she will. Not even Binniji can prevent that,' said Sarju with conviction.

'Come, let us not waste any more time talking about something which is in God's hands,' said Bhagwat Singhji's wife philosophically. 'Show me the new saris we have brought for Sita. Gangaramji must not feel that because Sita hasn't a mother, we have neglected her trousseau.'

Pari winced a little. She resented the mistress's remarks, but didn't say anything. She continued to arrange the saris in different piles. She did not want to remind the mistress that she, too, was anxious and had not slept for ten days so that everything was done properly and inexpensively.

The maids had sat up late into the night stitching blouses and skirts for Sita. Their eyes were sore from tacking on the silver trimmings to the saris. All this they did to economize; they knew that Gangaram without Lakshmi could not manage.

Khyali was exhausted from his many trips to the

silversmith who was busy with the big orders; the small orders did not interest him. It was the marriage season and all the silversmiths were working overtime to make what profit they could. Khyali needed all his skill of persuasion to get Sita's anklets and bracelets in time. Everything was in short supply. The prices had gone up. The children had to go miles to buy hooks and buttons at the cheapest possible price. The mistress, Pari felt, had no need to remind the servants of Gangaram's predicament. Before making her remark she should have known that the servants too had feelings that could be bruised. Even Sarju was surprised and wondered if there was a deeper meaning to what the mistress had said, but in the presence of Bhagwat Singhji's wife she could not question Pari.

Sarju carefully sorted out the different saris, according to their quality, and the trimmings on them. The best ones she gave to Pari to put aside for Sita and her immediate in-laws. The second best were for distant relatives. Once the saris were tied up in bundles, the mistress got up. The rest of the trousseau was in her room. It, too, needed sorting. Bhagwat Singhji's wife, though prepared to spend on Sita's trousseau, did not want to be too lavish. At the same time she did not want even Pari to guess what was going on in her mind.

Only Gangaram seemed to go about doing his work as usual. But his eyes had lost their dreamy look. They were heavy with black shadows around them, as if he hadn't slept for weeks. When he finished his cleaning and sweeping of the haveli, he would join Gokul for a quiet smoke. It was then he would share his worries. Even though the mistress was paying for the clothes and jewellery for Sita, the feeding of the guests was his responsibility. He had borrowed four hundred from the cook but he needed more money. Gokul advised him to ask the master, but he hesitated to do that. He knew he would not be refused but he did not want to seek further help from the haveli. He was grateful that the major share of the expenses were being paid by the master. At the same time, he did not want the bridegroom's party to feel that he had not entertained them in a befitting manner. He was prepared to borrow at even four rupees interest on every hundred, but not let the master know his worry.

Geeta was already in Bhagwat Singhji's wife's room. She waited there for Dhapu to give her Sita's ornaments to put in the safe. 'Binniji, I want a pair of bracelets just like these, but in gold. But remember, I will accept nothing but pure gold for Vijay Bai Sa's marriage,' said Dhapu, her eyes dancing with joy.

'Bai, by the time Vijay gets married you will be an old woman, toothless and wrinkled. Gold will no longer suit you,' Geeta replied with a mischievous glint in her eyes.

'Wrinkled or not, I will wear my gold bracelets so Binniji—' she didn't finish her sentence. Instead, she put a finger on her mouth to warn Geeta that the mistress was coming.

Bhagwat Singhji's wife came in with Sarju and sat down on a mat Dhapu spread for her. Sarju immediately got down to work. She untied the bundle of skirts. Then she picked up the red embroidered skirt and said, 'Hukkum, in this skirt Sita will get married.' Then with a deep sigh she added, 'I am still haunted by the day when she was born. I often get up in the night, especially on a rainy night and hear her mother's accusing voice, "Who do you think I am that you neglect me like this?" If only I had known that her stars were against her, that she would never know the joys and sorrows of motherhood, I would never have scolded her. But, Hukkum, I will never forgive myself for being harsh to Lakshmi. Poor girl. What a price she has paid for her stupid pride.'

'Yes, she has paid heavily for something which was not

even her fault. But, Sarju, don't blame yourself. She was destined not to see her daughter married. Otherwise, why should she have run away in the dead of night? She knew I would never have pointed a finger at her,' the mistress said in a hoarse voice full of remorse and regret.

The mention of Lakshmi cast an immediate gloom on everyone. There wasn't a person who hadn't thought of Lakshmi in the last weeks. But no one had the heart to talk of her openly. Dhapu was especially careful. Since she knew that Lakshmi was in the city, she, in particular, had never mentioned her name. Once or twice when the mistress had broached the subject, Dhapu had quickly found an excuse and left. For the first time in her life, she had kept a secret without whispering it to others, after extracting an oath of secrecy from them. Hearing the mistress and Sarju talk, Dhapu looked at Geeta with troubled eyes.

There was silence in the room. No one wanted to talk. Sarju, having selected the wedding skirt, turned her attention to the jewellery. Pari counted the close relatives on the knuckles of her fingers. The mistress looked on as the maids sorted out the women's clothes from those of the men.

'Hukkum, I must go to the bazaar immediately,' announced the cook from the courtyard. He breathed hard for a moment, then dropped his hands helplessly to his sides and added, 'That cloth merchant whom I have known for years has cheated me.' He held the white cloth in his hands for the mistress to see. 'Just look at these turbans. They are not worth two rupees each and I paid for the best quality cloth. He thought I wouldn't check but he doesn't know me. I am a hundred times more cunning than he is.'

'Khyali you are right. We can't give these to the bridegroom's party,' said the mistress fingering the cloth carefully. 'Go and change them in the afternoon, but not now. The children will be back early today,' said Bhagwat Singhji's wife wearily. She sat down and leaned against the stone pillar. The memory of Lakshmi had shattered her calm and enthusiasm. She pushed aside the bundles of saris and got up and went to the kitchen verandah. There she knew she could always find something to occupy herself. She opened the cupboard in the wall and took out a tin of wafers to see if they were getting mouldy.

Ganga and Champa came into the courtyard with the washing. They sang while they hung the saris and skirts out to dry. Dhapu was pounding the turmeric pods into powder for the ceremonial bath before the marriage. Geeta came and sat down next to her, leaving her mother-in-law in the kitchen. Bhagwat Singhji's wife's silence made her fidgety; she was not accustomed to seeing her sit quietly.

It was midday when the familiar sound of the horn was heard again. The mistress's face immediately lit up; her voice got back its strength and she told the cook to put the halva on the fire.

'Bara Bhabhi, we had such fun in school today,' cried Vijay as she burst into the courtyard. 'Bara Bhabhi, we did not work at all. The whole morning we rehearsed the play we are giving at the end of term.' Sita came behind Vikram and flopped down on the kitchen verandah.

Seeing Sita, Vijay said excitedly, 'Bara Bhabhi, all Sita's friends are coming. They have brought presents for her. Even her teachers are going to give her gifts. Bara Bhabhi, they were just waiting to be invited.' Vijay tossed her hair back from her face and then as if she had forgotten to report the most important event of the morning, said, 'Sita, where is the package the ayah gave you?'

'Oh, I carried your books and so forgot the bundle in the car,' replied Sita casually.

'Then go and get it; I am curious if you are not.

Remember your promise that I can take what I like from your presents,' said Vijay.

Sita nodded her head and then got up reluctantly and ran out of the courtyard. In a second she was back, holding the package in her hands.

'That is what the ayah gave me,' she said, as she put the wrapped up bundle in front of the mistress. There was consternation on every face, but no one dared to speak.

'I hope there are some ladoos in it. I love them,' said Vijay as she undid the knot.

'Was the old woman there?' asked the mistress in a hushed, frightened voice.

'No, Hukkum, the ayah said she came three or four times till she told her I would not be coming to school again because I was getting married. Then three days ago she came again and left this bundle. Had I not gone today, the ayah was going to bring it herself. I wish I had seen the old woman. I wanted so much to give her the crochet bag I made for her,' said Sita a little sadly.

'Did you ask the ayah where the old woman lived?' asked the mistress in a low, urgent voice.

'No, Hukkum, I didn't but the ayah said that the last time the woman came she sat and cried. I am so glad that I wasn't there to see her! As it is, the girls in the school teased me about her. Each time she came they would surround her; make faces at her, try and lift the sari off her face, then she flung her arms around like a mad woman. This frightened the girls and they would scatter, calling her names and throwing things at her. Hukkum, I am glad I wasn't there to see her. I don't know why she cried because even I was afraid of her when she lost her temper. She wasn't a bit afraid of the girls.'

'Oh look, Sita,' said Vijay, who had opened the package. 'Look, there is a beautiful sari for you. This time there are no ladoos. What a pity. Oh, here is a red skirt, too,' said Vijay, lifting a tinsel embroidered skirt in her hand.

Suddenly Pari put her head in between her knees; Sarju turned her back; and from Bhagwat Singhji's wife a sob escaped.

Sita looked around in utter amazement. She could not understand what had happened. She was frightened and bewildered.

Geeta took the open package from Vijay and put her hand in it to see if there was anything else. She picked up two silver toe rings, a small box filled with red kumkum powder and then a pair of silver anklets.

Before she could put them on the floor, Bhagwat Singhji's wife said, in a husky but steady voice, 'Come here, child. Sit near me. Listen. These are the auspicious symbols of marriage. They come from your mother,' Bhagwat Singhji's wife said in a solemn voice. Then her eyes closed and her face wrinkled up in pain.

'My mother? That old woman my mother?' stuttered Sita unbelievingly.

'Yes, child, that good woman who gave you ladoos is no one else but your mother,' replied Bhagwat Singhji's wife, opening her eyes and looking with infinite tenderness at Sita. 'I should have known that from the day you got ladoos. But I didn't think; I was misled. I thought Lakshmi was not in Udaipur.'

Sita looked at the mistress with wide open eyes as if she did not quite understand what the mistress had said. Then suddenly she put her head in Bhagwat Singhji's wife's lap and burst out crying. 'That was my mother?'

Vijay quickly put her hand on the little girl's head and repeated helplessly, 'Sita, don't cry. Please don't cry. Sita, listen, I will give you anything you want, but please don't cry.'

Chapter VI

PARI AND DHAPU were apprehensive about Sita after seeing her cry piteously, once she knew that the old woman was her mother. They were prepared to cajole her, soothe her, explain to her, anything to help her to forget her mother. But Sita went about the haveli as usual. Her greatest regret was that she hadn't given the crochet bag to the woman. To her she remained the woman who gave her ladoos. She could not believe that the woman was her mother. She had not known a mother's love and did not miss it. Her world remained secure. Nothing had changed in it to disturb her peace of mind. Pari, Dhapu, Ganga and Champa were all there. It was from them she had received love and to them she continued to look for love.

It was the day of Sita's marriage.

The drummers were playing in the servants' quarters, the women singing. The servants' children were running in and out of the haveli courtyard. Manji, Nandu and Kanta were talking to the mistress. Other relatives were scrutinizing the trousseau. Geeta talked to Sita's teachers. The haveli ladies had come from the morning. Though it was only a servant's child getting married, it was still a family occasion. For two days, the maids of Jeewan Niwas had danced and sung late into the evening. The courtyard was full of activity. But the mistress had watched the simple festivities with a sad heart. She could not forget Lakshmi, especially now that she was certain that she was somewhere in the city. Bhagwat Singhji's wife wept quietly, hiding her tears even from Pari. She knew that on the day of a marriage tears were inauspicious, and she was relieved to see that Sita, after her first outburst, was cheerful as before.

She drew comfort from her decision that once the marriage celebrations were over she would go personally and get Lakshmi back. But she kept her thoughts to herself; she did not want to cast a shadow on the day of Sita's marriage.

Sita sat in the mistress's room, bewilderd and resigned after her bath. Her hair had been massaged with scented oil and plaited. Her hands were bright red with henna. The mistress had insisted that she wear the skirt and sari that Lakshmi had sent, though they were not as good as the ones the haveli had made for her.

As the auspicious hour drew near Vijay helped Sita to put on her bridal clothes. She fastened the bracelets on Sita's wrists, slipped the bangles on her hands, tightened the screws of her anklets.

Once she was ready, Sarju carefully covered Sita's head and pulled the sari over her face. Her head bent, Sita walked slowly to where the mistress sat watching. Manji and Nandu looked at the little bride and quietly wiped the tears off their cheeks. Then as Sita bent down to touch their feet, they put a five rupee note in her hands and blessed her. Bhagwat Singhji's wife coughed to hide her feelings. She could not speak. Instead, she put her hands on the bride's head. That conveyed more than words.

Vijay looked on perplexed. The change in Sita was so complete that she hardly recognized her as the same girl who, a week ago, pushed Vikram in his car around the courtyard and shrieked with joy as the maids, frightened she might run over their feet, got out of her way.

The servants' quarters were lit with a row of coloured lights. The light became brighter as the evening became darker. The astrologers had set the time just after sunset for the arrival of the bridegroom. In the front yard of the servants' quarters a square was marked by four uprooted banana saplings that held the canopy under which the sacred fire would be lit. It was gaily decorated with flowers, balloons and paper streamers. The priests were already there, making sure that they had all the auspicious ingredients to perform the marriage rites.

The time for the bridegroom to arrive was drawing near. Dhapu had changed into a bright pink sari and skirt. She was wearing all her jewellery. Her anklets jingled as she brought in a silver thali in which there were a little lamp, a coconut, five silver rupees, red kumkum powder, a lump of gur, and a spray of incense sticks. The faint sound of a band came from a distance. The women were alerted that the marriage procession with the bridegroom was on its way. The children ran out of the courtyard and stood outside, on the verandah.

Gangaram, in a green and red striped turban with a clean white kurta and pyjama, stood with Gokul, Khyali and Dhapu's husband at the gate to receive the guests. Then, as the sound of the four piece band became louder, Dhapu lit the butter lamp and the incense sticks. She drew her sari over her face. The singers broke out in a loud chorus. They sang of the separation of a daughter from her mother, the pain of parting, the travails of motherhood. The ladies got up. No one spoke. The memories the song evoked silenced them.

The group of women, still singing, walked to the entrance of the courtyard. Ganga and Champa, with the other maids of the haveli, formed a semi-circle around the bride and Dhapu. As the sound of the band grew louder, they moved forward escorting the bride out to the steps of the verandah to meet the bridegroom. Dhapu's hand gently directed Sita whose head was bent low. She walked cautiously. She could hardly see. The tinsel in the sari blinded her. She was not confused, she was not thinking, she did as she was told.

The women continued singing in a plaintive voice as Sita stood still with Dhapu and Ganga on either side of her, evoking the blessings of the gods on the bride, beseeching the goddess to protect her from evil, reminding the deity that she was about to leave her parents' home and enter a new family. They asked the goddess to give her strength and wisdom, never to falter, never to hesitate in serving her husband and his parents.

The bridal horse with the bridegroom sitting on the silver edged saddle came to a halt in front of the haveli gate. He stood docile while the crackers went off near his hooves; he knew that the sound was harmless; he had carried many bridegrooms on his back and seemed to neigh only from boredom. The band started playing a marching tune, the children screamed with joy as they came near the bejewelled horse, they threw flowers and confetti on the bridegroom. He remained seated, waiting to get instructions. He held the reins tightly in his hands as the children stood on tiptoes trying to see him. After clearing the children from his way Gangaram stepped forward and embraced Shiv Ram's father and his brothers and their relatives. Gokul and Khyali with great ceremony welcomed the elders and invited them into the yard. After the welcome formalities were over, the bridegroom was helped to dismount. Shiv Ram's face was not clearly visible; strings of silver thread and flowers fell from a band tied around his yellow turban. He walked between his father and uncle in his light pink achkan, that did not exactly fit him, to the verandah steps, where Dhapu and Sita stood ready to perform the first ritual. He was of medium height; there was an awkward grace in his walk; from in between the hanging strings over his face one could see his eyes with a searching look of a young boy as he stood before Dhapu and Sita.

The women sang while Dhapu encircled the bridegroom's head three times with the lighted butter lamp. Then she put flowers at his feet and a red kumkum mark on his forehead and five silver rupees in his hand. After Dhapu had put the symbols of prosperity and happiness on the bridegroom, she withdrew a little and handed a garland of flowers to Sita. Sita's hands trembled as she, without lifting her head, put it around Shiv Ram's neck. While the bridegroom was being propitiated, Bhagwat Singhji and his son came out and briefly talked to Shiv Ram's father and his relatives. This gesture was enough for the village people to feel proud and to know that the haveli supported the marriage. The faces of Shiv Ram's relatives showed they were satisfied; they nodded their heads to confirm that Shiv Ram's father had chosen wisely. The exchange of garlands over, Dhapu and her husband led Sita to the marriage altar. The priests had already started chanting the vedic hymns. Sita sat on the left of Shiv Ram and next to her, on a wooden stool, were Dhapu and her husband. They acted as the temporary parents of Sita. Gangaram alone could not give away his daughter.

The marriage ceremony started. The sweet smell of incense filled the air. The voices of the priests rose, though not above the noise of the children laughing and people talking. The sacred fire was lit and the priests poured melted butter into it while they chanted the sacred verses three thousand years old. As soon as Bhagwat Singhji's wife saw from the balcony the priest tie Sita's hands to those of Shiv Ram, her tears fell freely on her cheeks. Pari stayed with the ladies of the haveli on the balcony overlooking the servants' yard. As a widow she had no place where prayers were sanctifying a union of two people. Tears trickled down her hollow cheeks. She did not have the strength to wipe them off.

'Don't cry, Bai Sa,' said Manji, putting a comforting hand on Bhagwat Singhji's wife's shoulders. 'This is a day all mothers pray for. What more could you have done for Sita? You brought her up and have now put her in charge of her husband. You have fulfilled all the obligations of a mother. The rest lies in God's hands.'

Geeta's eyes were blurred as Sita followed Shiv Ram around the sacred fire. This was the seventh and the final round. From now on they would be considered as man and wife. Vijay clung to her mother sobbing. She didn't know why she was crying, but the tears seemed to flow out of her heart into her eyes and down her face.

Chapter VII

THE MORNING AFTER Sita's marriage, the mistress got up when it was still dark. She crept out of her husband's room and went to her apartment. The courtyard was quiet. The only sound that came was the regular, heavy breathing of the maids who slept in the verandah. Instead of waking up one of them as was her habit when she couldn't sleep, she quietly went into her room. As dawn gradually began to dispel the darkness, the cocks crowed and the birds twittered. The maids got up rubbing their eyes still heavy with sleep, rolled up their beddings and stacked them away. It was in semi-darkness that they went down to the servants' quarters to wash and get ready for the day ahead.

Ganga was the first to come into the courtyard. She had to get the things ready for the mistress's bath before she woke up. Ganga went to the kitchen, took the cup of curds, mixed it with gram flour, took the bottle of camphor oil from the shelf for the massage and went to the room to spread the mat for the mistress to lie down on. As she opened the door, she was surprised to see the mistress standing by the window looking out on the yard below. Bhagwat Singhji's wife's smile reassured Ganga that it was not she who was late but that the mistress was early. Ganga massaged her with the oil first; then rubbed it off with the gram paste.

Bhagwat Singhji's wife, having bathed and got ready, went to the kitchen. She looked at Khyali who, with swift, strong strokes, churned the curds into butter. The morning activity had started; Dhapu put the milk to warm for the children and on the other fire placed the pot of water to boil for the master's tea. There was the usual morning bustle, but there was not the same cheer on the faces of the maids. After a celebration big or small, there was an air of emptiness in the courtyard. The maids and their children went around as if they were exhausted and needed rest. They were also sad. Sita had gone to her husband's village for two days. She had to worship their family deity and pay respects to her mother-in-law before she could return to the haveli. The maids missed her. This was the first time since her birth that she wasn't lurking around the kitchen verandah and asking them for a roti and pickles.

The only person who seemed to have no worries left was Gangaram. Instead of resting as the mistress had told him he worked as usual. He had lost his harassed look. Even though he hadn't slept the whole night, his eyes were bright and his legs seemed to have got new strength, they wobbled less. The money he had borrowed at an exorbitant rate of interest did not bother him. He was pleased that the bridegroom's party left with praises for his hospitality; he was glad that for once he had not listened to Gokul or Khyali to give only one sweet instead of two. He was proud that he had been lavish. The villagers were impressed; no one in this community had been so generously entertained. It had cost more than he could afford, but he was still happy. The village people felt honoured. Gangaram had heard that they were surprised to get dhotis and turbans of the finest grade cloth. Shiv Ram's father had chosen Sita because she was in school. He was poor and in debt. In fact, his community had advised against the marriage because there was no talk of a dowry. When Sita wore gold bangles, earrings and a ring, they were sure it was borrowed just for the marriage ceremony. But when she kept the jewellery on as she left the haveli, they were impressed. Shiv Ram's father only expected to get silver jewellery for the bride. Gold was beyond his hopes.

Gangaram thought of the last few days and was filled with joy. He came into the kitchen with an unusually big load of firewood and dumped it in the kitchen verandah with unusual force. The mistress lifted her face as she heard the thud. She was so preoccupied with her thoughts that she did not notice that instead of two spoons of sugar Khyali had put three in each cup of tea for the servants.

'Khyaliji, tell me, where is Lakshmi?'

He did not answer as if he had not heard the question. He kept stirring the tea. Then quietly he said, 'Kanwarani Sa, she is living in the tailor's house in the gully at the other end of the city near the old railway station.'

'When did you know she was the woman who visited the school?'

'Three weeks ago, the day I went to the bazaar to change Sita's silver anklets. There I met Hari the panwala. You remember, Hukkum, it was in his house she first rented a room when she ran away from the haveli. He is a bad character but he knows what's going on in the city. He told me that he had often seen Lakshmi at the temple. He couldn't believe that she had all of a sudden become religious; so he observed her. Hukkum, he saw her buy the ladoos and puris and this further intrigued him. He knew Lakshmi couldn't afford to buy the special ladoos, so he decided that they must be for a special friend.' Khyali took a deep breath and then continued, 'Hukkum, Hari one day followed Lakshmi and saw her enter Sita's school. His evil mind immediately concluded she was going to see his friend, the watchman of the school.'

The mistress gave a deep sigh and looked sadly at the cook. She didn't speak. The cook half rose, took a log of wood from the corner and put it in the fireplace. The wood crackled before going up in a steady flame. Bhagwat Singhji's wife turned her gaze to the fire and then asked the cook, 'Khyali, why didn't you tell me? I am sure Lakshmi waited at the school for us to come and get her. Poor girl!'

'Hukkum, I did not tell you purposely. For once even Dhapu kept her mouth shut. You see, Hukkum, I was afraid you would try and get Lakshmi to come back. This would have caused a scandal. Once again, everyone would have been curious. A hundred questions would have been asked. What was she doing all these years? How had she lived; with whom? It was one thing for Shiv Ram's people to have accepted the fact of Lakshmi's disappearance from the haveli, but quite another for them to know that she lived in the house of a panwala, then a tailor and that too in Udaipur. Kanwarani Sa, now I can tell you, till the last minute—even after the bride and bridegroom were under the marriage canopy—I was afraid, you know. Marriages break even after the couple have taken the first round of the sacred fire. Hukkum, I don't have to tell you that for Shiv Ram's father to have known that Lakshmi was in town would have meant the break of the marriage. He could not have stood the humiliation in front of his relatives.'

The mistress nodded her head in acceptance. She felt a strange peace within; Khyali at last had made her understand that for Sita's happiness it was better that Lakshmi did not return to the haveli.

Pari sat in the verandah opposite, with neighbours. The sun was still pleasant, though the summer winds had started blowing. This was the time when the grain for the year was bought, cleaned and stored, though the cleaning and winnowing of the wheat and maize was usually done in the afternoon. Pari decided to open the sacks in the morning that day. She gave the women the winnowing basket. They talked while they separated the husks from the kernels. The mistress came and joined them. She felt at ease after a long time. She listened absent-mindedly to what the women said. They told her how pleased Shiv Ram's people were with the marriage. They had gone back full of praises for the haveli. Even those who had first opposed the marriage were silenced by what they saw and received. But Bhagwat Singhji's wife was not interested any more in Sita's marriage celebrations. Her thoughts were of Daulat Singhji's haveli. Nandu had told her that proposals were pouring in from all parts of Rajasthan for Vir Singh. Parents were offering big dowries. A well known family from Jaipur had even brought their girl with them.

Nandu had heard she was fair, tall with chiselled features and large, almond shaped eyes. Nandu had been told that Daulat Singhji's wife liked the girl and had given her horoscope to be examined. Even Manji, whose opinion Bhagwat Singhji's wife valued above everyone else's, had said that Daulat Singhji's family would not wait indefinitely for an answer. As it was, their pride had been hurt because they had not received immediate approval of their son by Bhagwat Singhji. Manji, who did not judge people by their wealth alone, had said Vir Singh was the only suitable boy in all the havelis for Vijay. He was extremely intelligent, but, at the same time, modest. She had urged Bhagwat Singhji's wife not to let Vijay's age come in the way of her engagement. In fact, all the relatives were surprised that the engagement date had not been announced. They could not understand the delay. It was a risk that no other haveli would take.

Bhagwat Singhji's wife knew that what Nandu and Manji had said was true. She did not want to tell them that she could not assert her authority as a mother-in-law. She did not want her relatives to know that Geeta was not like their daughters-in-law, obedient and willing to accept what the elders thought right. She was too proud to concede that as a mother-in-law she only had limited power over Geeta. Even Bhagwat Singhji had told her she was not to mention the subject of Vijay's engagement to Geeta. He would talk to her himself. But now, three weeks had elapsed and he had not mentioned the subject to Geeta. She knew that a proud family like Daulat Singhji's would not wait much longer for an answer. But she kept her anxiety to herself.

Bhagwat Singhji's wife was so absorbed in her thoughts, she did not notice Geeta touch her feet and sit down next to her. Dhapu joined the women cleaning the grain. She was still in an elated mood. She was delighted with the gold earrings that the mistress had given her for Sita's marriage. She knew she would get something special for taking Lakshmi's place at the marriage, but she never expected to get gold earrings, a new sari and skirt.

The cook looked anxiously at the women talking, but he could not join them. He had still to knead the dough. He was about to call Dhapu to help him, when Gokul came hurriedly into the courtyard and said nervously, 'Khyali, Daulat Singh and his brother have come. Get the refreshments ready. Don't look at me like that. Hurry! Yes, it is Daulat Singhji himself who has come.'

As soon as Bhagwat Singhji's wife heard Daulat Singhji's name, she got up. The maids put the thalis down and Geeta, too, hurried to the kitchen.

Bhagwat Singhji's wife took out a bottle of special sherbet. Khyali put oil on the fire. Pari opened the cupboard and took out the halva and other special savouries that were meant only for Bhagwat Singhji and his son. The women worked in silence, trying to keep their hands steady. In the midst of all the preparations, Dhapu slipped out of the kitchen. Geeta looked at her and smiled. She guessed what she was plotting to do. As soon as Gokul and Gangaram took the trays out of the kitchen, Khyali sat down and put his hands on his knees and told the mistress that the big merchants in the bazaar had already started going to Daulat Singhji's haveli. They took with them the finest Benares silks and brocades. The goldsmiths were trying to bribe the accountant to place the jewellery order with them. The halwais were sending their fanciest sweets and savouries to the haveli as samples. Everyone in the bazaar talked of the forthcoming engagement when the two biggest havelis of Udaipur were about to be joined by marriage.

The mistress only half listened to the cook. She was silently praying that what the merchants were hoping would come to be. This was also her deepest wish.

'Kanwarani Sa, Kanwarani Sa, the horoscopes tally,' said Dhapu in a hushed voice coming into the courtyard on tiptoes. 'I heard Daulat Singhji say that Vijay Bai Sa was born under a unique constellation of stars.' She was still holding on to her skirt so that the folds wouldn't rustle as she heard the two men talk from behind the half-opened door.

Chapter VIII

IT WAS LATE in the afternoon. The mistress, as usual, sat in the verandah surrounded by visitors and relatives. The wheat and maize were ready to be stored. They had been winnowed and cleaned by the women. Sita, who had returned from the village, was the centre of attraction. The minute she had entered the courtyard there wasn't a trace left in her of the shy coy bride of a few days ago. Her head uncovered and her hair flying all over her face, she ran around as if nothing had changed in her life. Vijay was delighted to have her back. The women tried to get her to sit down and tell them of her reception in the village. Was the house really made of brick? What had she received from her mother-in-law and grandmother-in-law when she touched their feet? But Sita was like a dove that had been released from captivity, prancing around the courtyard. Dhapu and Pari pestered her with questions; Ganga teased her; Champa reminded her she was married and couldn't go around just in a skirt and a blouse. But Sita paid no attention; she did as she liked. When the mistress asked her about her house in the village, she giggled and ran away. No one could get a word out of her about her two days in the village.

The verandah was humming with the chatter of the women; as usual they were full of juicy gossip. Their children sprawled all over the verandah as the little ones slept undisturbed by the flies that sat on their soft cheeks. The elder children were in the backyard with Vikram flying kites. Their screams could be heard from the verandah. The mistress looked happy. She did not mind the children dirtying the verandah nor was she disturbed with the confusion they caused. She liked company. But even in the midst of entertaining news no one ever forgot the master. As soon as the sun lost some of its warmth, Ganga got up and went to the kitchen to put the pot of water to boil for Bhagwat Singhji's tea. Khyali lay stretched out in the kitchen verandah snoring loudly. She did not want to wake him up. The maids recognized that he worked hard and deserved rest.

Geeta had come down to the kitchen to see that tea for her father-in-law was sent in time. The tray was ready to be taken out by Gokul. But when he came into the kitchen, instead of picking up the tray, he said in an anxious voice, 'Hukkum, Kanwar Sa doesn't want any tea today. He doesn't feel well. He has a pain in the stomach.' He left without giving any more details.

The mistress got up immediately; Geeta stood up and followed her out of the courtyard. Pari fumbled for the keys round her waist and went inside to open the medicine cupboard. The women silently picked up their sleeping children and left. Pari took out the herbs, the roots, the powders she knew were effective for a stomach pain. Khyali was on his feet. He sat down to grind the roots and boil the herbs.

Bhagwat Singhji lay on the couch, his eyes closed and his

face pale. A servant was rubbing oil on one foot and Gokul was doing the same on the other. As the mistress came in, the servants got up and Gokul coughed. Bhagwat Singhji sat up, his lips parted in a smile as Geeta bent down and touched the ground before him. Bhagwat Singhji's wife looked at her husband anxiously and then whispered to Gokul to ask Pari to hurry up.

The master of the haveli did not speak for a moment; he looked at Geeta's covered face with a deep and loving intensity. Then in a low, weak voice, as if it were difficult for him to talk, he said, 'Binniji, I have waited to talk to you. I wanted to be sure of my own feelings, before I spoke to you.' He paused, took a deep, long breath and then continued with a little more force. 'As you probably know Daulat Singhji and his brother came the other day; they again urged for Vijay's engagement to their son. -The horoscopes match perfectly. Our child has been born under the most auspicious constellation of stars. But I was not waiting to hear what the astrologers had to say before talking to you. Binniji, I have been agitated for the last few weeks. I have looked at the proposal from every angle. I am still not quite sure whether it is right to engage a girl as young as our Vijay. But a girl has to marry, if not today, then tomorrow.' Then he closed his eyes as if to reflect a little more before he spoke again. Geeta could see that his face, usually so calm and serene, was troubled. She desperately wanted to tell him he had no need to worry, that she loved and trusted his judgement, that he should get well. She wanted to ask him what she could do to relieve his stomach pain. But she could not bring herself to express her feelings.

'Your mother-in-law and I have talked over Vijay's engagement for hours. She is the Lakshmi, the goddess of prosperity of my household. She is very precious to us. But even so, she must leave us one day. No one can ensure anyone's future happiness. As parents, all we can do is to find the best family for our child. I like Vir Singh. He appears to be a boy of character. He isn't arrogant; money hasn't given him a false sense of his own importance. Binniji, you know how children are pampered in the havelis. I have seen so many good boys ruined because of that. But somehow Vir Singh has escaped.' Bhagwat Singhji's voice suddenly rose and he said with unusual vehemence, 'I have told Daulat Singhji that under no circumstances would I permit Vijay to be taken out of school. I am against early marriages. Girls must study; they cannot be kept ignorant.' As if the exertion were too much for him, he fell back on the couch and closed his eyes.

The mistress got up alarmed and went and stood beside him. Geeta was too frightened to move; she lifted the sari from her face and saw that the pallor on Bhagwat Singhji's face had deepened. He breathed with difficulty.

Pari came hurriedly into the room holding a cup in her hands. She looked at the master and then at the mistress and her sunken cheeks lost the little colour they had. She waited till Bhagwat Singhji opened his eyes and then she gave him the cup of herbal tea.

'Don't worry, Pari, I will be all right. I have a little pain in the stomach. It will pass, especially after I have drunk your mixture,' said Bhagwat Singhji, trying hard to sound cheerful as he handed the cup back to Gokul. He looked at his wife and then said in a soft voice, 'I will rest a little now.'

The women left the room as the master of the haveli sank back on his pillow and closed his eyes. The mistress went straight to the little prayer room and with folded hands before the little image of the goddess, took a vow that until her husband got well, she would not eat any cereal. She then sat down in front of the image and prayed.

The atmosphere in the courtyard had instantly changed. The kitchen fire was not lit. Khyali sat with his head buried between his knees. Dhapu cleaned the roots. Ganga soaked the herbs. Geeta lighted the earthenware lamp in front of the sacred tulsi plant.

Chapter IX

IT WAS THE third day since Bhagwat Singhji had had his first spasm of stomach pains. The herbal tea, the essence of roots, the pungent oil massages did not bring Bhagwat Singhji relief. In the past, these homemade medicines, the recipes of which had come down from generation to generation, had always been effective. But this time, not even the powder of crushed pearls and silver dust mixed with saffron given by the head priest of the temple had any effect. At last the mistress agreed that the doctors be called in.

Ajay Singh listened to the diagnosis with stunned disbelief.

'It can't be a heart attack, doctor,' he said in a dull voice, 'he has never before complained of pain in the chest.'

The doctor looked at him sympathetically and nodded his head sadly.

The news that Bhagwat Singhji was ill spread within minutes of the doctor leaving the room. Visitors started coming. Nandu and Manji came prepared to stay in the haveli. Kanta had already come. The courtyard was never empty. There were women at all times of the day enquiring after Bhagwat Singhji's health. Geeta received the guests, but her heart was heavy as she sat and answered questions. The mistress was no longer able to sit and talk to the women. She was too agitated to stay still in one place. She only waited for the men to leave her husband's room so that she could be with him. Ajay Singh's face had lost its youthful, carefree look. He moved among the men visitors silently and tried to hide his impatience with their words of comfort. He wanted to be with his father, but he knew he could not be abrupt with those who came to call at the haveli. He was conscious that the elders in the family were assessing him even as they comforted him. They were looking to see if he measured up to his father.

The courtyard had lost its lustre. Its walls did not echo the laughter of the maids, nor their songs.

In the sitting room Geeta sat and listened while the women talked, but her thoughts dwelt on what her father-in-law had said about Daulat Singhji's house. 'I like Vir Singh; he is a good boy and not spoiled. A girl sooner or later has to get married.' Geeta realized the wisdom of his words, but still she felt uneasy. But she was no longer sure of herself. She remembered the handsome young face of Vir Singh, and thought perhaps he was what he looked, straight and honourable. But then as if to dissuade herself she reasoned that Vir Singh like her husband would never go against his parents' wishes. 'His parents will want an early marriage. Vir Singh will not be consulted. He is young, he will listen. No, I can't have Vijay marry young, times have changed. She must study.' But some part of her unconscious mind was not convinced. She was troubled. She thought of her own marriage. Her parents had chosen the right man for her; she was happy; she had not gone on to higher studies. Geeta was glad that no one could see her face and guess the agitation and uncertainties of her private world.

It was early in the afternoon. The visitors had left. Nandu, Manji and Kanta had stretched out in the sitting room with the mistress. They were all tired of sitting the whole morning with the visitors. Geeta had gone up to her room for a little rest. The courtyard was quiet; the servants' children no longer came up to play. Vijay sat outside Bhagwat Singhji's room quietly learning how to crochet from Sita. She waited for him to wake up and then would go and sit with him. She was no longer interested in her books or running round with Sita. Vikram followed his father around as if he were afraid to leave him alone.

Pari, with the other maids, sat outside on the verandah talking in low voices. No visitors were expected as they usually came late in the afternoon. Dhapu pricked up her ears; she thought she heard a knock on the outside door. Then, when it came again, she quickly got up and went to open the door. Ganga went inside to wake up the ladies. Champa ran across the courtyard to the stairs that went to Geeta's room.

Daulat Singhji's wife and her relatives quietly entered the courtyard. Dhapu ushered the ladies in silently to the sitting room. After a few moments Manji and Nandu entered with Bhagwat Singhji's wife and with the usual formality greeted the ladies. Geeta slipped into the room and touched the feet of Daulat Singhji's wife and sat down beside her mother-in-law.

'I cannot believe that Kanwar Sa has had a heart attack,' said Daulat Singhji's wife with genuine concern. 'But don't worry, Hukkum, he will recover. There isn't a man in Udaipur who isn't praying for him. He has been a friend to the poor and an example to us in the havelis. Hukkum, you are not alone in your anxiety. We are all with you.'

Bhagwat Singhji's wife did not reply. She acknowledged the words of sympathy with anxious eyes. Words that had so easily come to her in the past stuck in her throat. Daulat Singhji's wife then turned and looked at Geeta. The diamonds in her ears and nostril flashed as she said with great tenderness, 'Binniji, look after your mother-in-law. She is already frail and now she has given up eating.' Her voice wavered as she said, 'Binniji, don't look so sad, your father-in-law will soon be well, and then the haveli will be full of laughter again.' With these words Daulat Singhji's wife and the ladies that accompanied her got up. Geeta, Manji and Nandu saw them to the door.

'Binniji, let's go up to the terrace. You need a little fresh air,' said Manji softly, putting her hands on Geeta's shoulders and walking up the stone stairs. The two women looked across the terrace. The air was refreshing, neither hot nor cold. The cows in the yard were munching the hay. The little calf nestled up to its mother's side as if frightened to stand alone. The stray dogs wandered aimlessly, their noses to the ground, trying to smell out the food from the rubbish heaps. Three small naked children played in the dust under the neem tree. A woman came out of her thatched hut, her body was emaciated, her skirt torn and her sari in shreds. With quick, long steps she went up to where the children were drawing circles in the dust. She caught hold of two of them, one in each hand, and dragged them behind her. The third got up and ran after them.

For a time Manji and Geeta silently watched the scene below. It was soothing to see life outside the haveli. Then Manji gathered her muslin sari round her and looked intently at Geeta's covered face. Her black eyes were full of warmth as she said, 'Binniji, I don't want to alarm you, but you must face reality. Your father-in-law has had a severe heart attack. We all pray he will recover, but think what joy it would give him if he could see his granddaughter engaged.'

'Bua Sa, how can anyone think of an engagement ceremony when he is seriously ill?' replied Geeta, taken aback by Manji's suggestion.

'Binniji, it is because he is so ill that I urge you to tell him that you agree to Vijay's engagement to Vir Singh.'

The sound of clanking anklets diverted Geeta's attention. Ganga had come up to tell them that more guests had arrived. Manji and Geeta went downstairs.

Bhagwat Singhji's wife had just come from the men's part of the haveli. Her face was drawn. She looked exhausted and worn out. When she saw Geeta, she said, 'Binniji, don't tire yourself out. Visitors will constantly be coming. Manji and Nandu Bai Sa can receive them. There is no need for you to sit with them all the time. My sister-in-law is also now here to help. You go up and rest. You are not used to staying up for such long periods. You must not fall ill.'

Chapter X

BHAGWAT SINGHJI LAY on his wooden bed propped up by pillows; his face was sunken and looked haggard. His hands lay limp on the silk coverlet. Gokul sat beside the bed, his ears alert to the slightest noise. He had slept in the master's room since the day he fell ill. No amount of persuasion or threats had any effect on him. He refused to leave the room except for his meals. His eyes dimmed with age and his legs unable to support him, he continued to keep guard over his beloved master whom he had served for over fifty years. He fanned Bhagwat Singhji and woke up several times in the night to see if he was covered. Gokul was not concerned that Ajay Singh was there all the time to administer to his father's needs or that other servants, younger and more agile than himself, were more useful.

The doctors had come and gone. There was nothing that they could do but prescribe new medicines and insist that Bhagwat Singhji take complete rest. Ajay Singh followed their advice with meticulous care. Manji, Nandu and Kanta looked at Bhagwat Singhji's fever-stricken eyes sadly. Geeta and her mother-in-law sat with their faces covered. It was not for them to show concern in front of others, even though they were close relatives.

'Manji Bai Sa, why don't you go home. I am not so ill that you and Nandu Bai should leave your homes and stay here. It will take time before I get up, but there is nothing to be anxious about,' said Bhagwat Singhji in a low, calm voice, trying to cover up his own fears about his state of health.

While Manji and Nandu talked, Geeta was lost in gloomy thought. She felt she had added ten years to her age. She saw herself no longer as the daughter-in-law of the house but its mistress. She felt a sudden shiver run through her body as she looked at her father-in-law's pale face drained of all its vitality. He won't recover, she said despairingly to herself. Everyone in the family had passed away quickly and silently, with no fuss, no complaints. She saw her husband sitting beside his father's bed. His chiselled features looked sharper. It seemed to Geeta that he had aged. Even as his father lay on his bed Ajay Singh was now in charge. He had taken over from him. He was no longer the Bapu Sa that everyone indulged, but from whom no one demanded conformity. Her mother-in-law now did nothing before consulting him. Geeta thought of the time before Bhagwat Singh fell ill, how her mother-in-law would say, 'Don't disturb him. He has work to do.' 'There is no need for him to pay a visit to another haveli, his father has already done so.' He was sheltered by the presence of his father, who abided by the traditions and customs of Udaipur, leaving Ajay Singh free to follow his interests.

Geeta glanced at her husband from behind her veil and felt sorry for him. He didn't know the customs of the family. How would he discharge his responsibility? He didn't even know the havelis. He had been allowed to be carefree. She would be of no help to him. She followed her mother-in-law's instructions without going into details. Who would help him? The relatives would criticize him. They would blame his indifference on her because she was an outsider who was never really interested in the customs of Udaipur. They would say the traditions of this ancient family would die for lack of someone worthy to carry them on. With these thoughts, she grew indignant and her face felt warmer. The blood seemed to race through her veins faster, but there was a sinking feeling in her heart.

Manji told Bhagwat Singhji about Daulat Singhji's wife's visit and how gracious she had been and how anxious about his health.

Bhagwat Singhji looked at Geeta and then at Manji. His eyes gleamed with pleasure as he said confidently, 'Let me get well and then we will give proper thought to my granddaughter's future.'

Chapter XI

BUT A FEW days passed and there was no improvement in Bhagwat Singhji's condition. In fact, he was getting weaker. The doctors came three and four times a day. There was no need to call them, they came of their own accord. Bhagwat Singhji was not only a patient to them, but someone they loved and revered. Ajay Singh kept his despair hidden from the gaze of others. He received the guests with dignity and composure. The visitors had become fewer. Only the close relatives remained in the haveli. The courtyard was dead. The servants moved silently and the maids spoke in whispers. They sat after the day's work was over, waiting to hear that the master was better. The butter lamp burnt continuously in front of the tulsi plant. The mistress was in the prayer room whenever she was not with her husband. No one asked her what to cook or showed her the rations for the servants. Geeta now had all the keys to the storeroom. Pari helped her, but even her heart was not in supervising the details. She followed the mistress around in a daze.

Bhagwat Singhji had awakened from his afternoon sleep.

The family was around him. His grandchildren sat on his bed. Vikram told him all about the airplane he had put together. Vijay showed him the scarf she had knitted for him, while he sipped a cup of tea. His eyes looked brighter and his face seemed less pale. He breathed more easily. Then, as she handed his cup to Gokul, he asked him to call Gangaram.

Gangaram came in, his head down, as if someone had beaten him over the head. He bowed low to the master but did not dare lift his eyes.

'Gangaram, I am told you are satisfied with how the marriage went off,' said Bhagwat Singhji with a smile. 'Of course, you servants never listen to advice. You go on following your old customs and get deeper into debt. Gokul tells me you have borrowed money at a very high rate of interest. This time I am going to forgive you for having been so foolish. I have told the accountant to pay all the debts that you incurred for Sita's marriage.' Having said this, he was forced to take a deep breath and his head fell back on the pillow. Gangaram did not move. He seemed rooted to the floor. He even forgot to fold his hands and bend down to touch the bed on which the master lay. It was Gokul who wobbled up to him and shook him by the shoulders to tell him he could now leave.

Geeta was struck with wonder. Her heart filled with pride and admiration for the man who was the father of her husband. All of a sudden, she realized what real greatness meant. He was like a towering tree under which the family sheltered. It was from him that everyone got their nourishment. Now that the tree had fallen, the saplings growing up at its base were exposed. The haveli might never again be as strong. Something already seemed to be shaking its foundations. Geeta clasped her hands convulsively. She did not know how to contain her feelings. Ajay Singh, seeing his mother's tears fall from under her sari, went and sat beside her. He tried to comfort her, assuring her that there was no need to worry. He said his father would get well as the doctors were pleased with his progress. But she looked at the bed hopelessly, tears streaming down her cheeks.

It was in the early hours of the night when Bhagwat Singhji finally closed his eyes on the haveli. He was not alone when he left Jeewan Niwas. His wife, who had stood by him for sixty years, was with him. His son and daughter-in-law stood beside his bed as the light quietly went out of his steadfast eyes. The servants who served him loyally were out in the verandah. Only Gokul lay stretched out on the floor beside the bed.

Ajay Singh pulled the white sheet over his father's face and touched his feet with his forehead. The master of the haveli had joined his ancestors.

Before the sun rose, Jeewan Niwas echoed to the wails of women who poured into the haveli from all sides. The courtyard was again full. Women in starched, clean saris, others in shreds, came and sat down together without any regard to their status. They sat and wailed the passing of the master of Jeewan Niwas.

Geeta was overcome with grief. Though she had a premonition of Bhagwat Singhji's death, she could not believe that the end had really come.

'Where is Bhabhi?' she cried as Manji put a comforting hand on her head and said consolingly, 'My child, she will be coming. She is changing.' Then, at last, the mistress of Jeewan Niwas came out of her room, her shrunken body draped in black, her hands bare, her neck empty, her feet naked without the anklets.

Geeta clasped her mother-in-law's frail little body in her arms and sobbed: 'Bhabhi, what have you done to yourself? I can't bear to see you in black. What has become of your bangles and necklace? Only a few minutes ago you were in a bright orange sari. Where have you thrown it?'

Bhagwat Singhji's wife took Geeta's face in her hands. In a voice that had lost all its strength, she said with infinite love, 'Binniji, the goddess has taken away my happiness. She has left me bereft. God bless you. May you always wear red. May gold always shine on your hands. Don't cry, my child. Your father-in-law lived honourably. He has gone, leaving you the mistress of this house. If you loved him, you will keep this haveli as a trust for your children. He did his duty by us all. Now it is your turn. Don't weep. If you don't show strength now, to whom shall I look for comfort? You are all I have. Everything else has gone.'

Geeta choked down her sobs and hid her despair in order to devote herself to comforting the noble and indomitable old mistress of Jeewan Niwas. Together they went to the verandah of the courtyard. The sound of the wailing women engulfed the whole haveli.

'Don't cry, Binniji,' said Manji, pressing Geeta's head to her breast. 'You are now the mistress of this haveli. You can't forget its traditions in your sorrow.'